TWO AGAINST ONE

Like a giant spring uncoiling, Clay launched himself at the outlaw on the right. The man had his hand on his revolver and went to jerk it even as Clay was in midair. Clay was quicker. With a swift thrust he buried his knife in the man's ribs. The outlaw stiffened and cried out and sought to use his spurs, but Clay, grabbing the man's shirt, gave a fierce pull.

Down they went. Clay alighted on his feet but the outlaw hit on his side and cried out a second time.

Clay spun. The other outlaw had reined toward them and was in the act of drawing a revolver. Clay could not possibly reach the man before the revolver went off, so he did the only thing he could; he threw the knife. . . .

Ralph Compton

Bluff City

A Ralph Compton Novel
by David Robbins

A SIGNET BOOK

SIGNET
Published by New American Library, a division of
Penguin Group (USA) Inc., 375 Hudson Street,
New York, New York 10014, USA
Penguin Group (Canada), 90 Eglinton Avenue East, Suite 700, Toronto,
Ontario M4P 2Y3, Canada (a division of Pearson Penguin Canada Inc.)
Penguin Books Ltd., 80 Strand, London WC2R 0RL, England
Penguin Ireland, 25 St. Stephen's Green, Dublin 2,
Ireland (a division of Penguin Books Ltd.)
Penguin Group (Australia), 250 Camberwell Road, Camberwell, Victoria 3124,
Australia (a division of Pearson Australia Group Pty. Ltd.)
Penguin Books India Pvt. Ltd., 11 Community Centre, Panchsheel Park,
New Delhi - 110 017, India
Penguin Group (NZ), 67 Apollo Drive, Rosedale, North Shore,
Auckland 1311, New Zealand (a division of Pearson New Zealand Ltd.)
Penguin Books (South Africa) (Pty.) Ltd., 24 Sturdee Avenue,
Rosebank, Johannesburg 2196, South Africa

Penguin Books Ltd., Registered Offices:
80 Strand, London WC2R 0RL, England

First published by Signet, an imprint of New American Library,
a division of Penguin Group (USA) Inc.

First Printing, June 2007
10 9 8 7 6 5 4 3 2 1

Copyright © The Estate of Ralph Compton, 2007
All rights reserved

Ⓟ REGISTERED TRADEMARK—MARCA REGISTRADA

Printed in the United States of America

THE IMMORTAL COWBOY

This is respectfully dedicated to the "American Cowboy." His was the saga sparked by the turmoil that followed the Civil War, and the passing of more than a century has by no means diminished the flame.

True, the old days and the old ways are but treasured memories, and the old trails have grown dim with the ravages of time, but the spirit of the cowboy lives on.

In my travels—to Texas, Oklahoma, Kansas, Nebraska, Colorado, Wyoming, New Mexico, and Arizona—I always find something that reminds me of the Old West. While I am walking these plains and mountains for the first time, there is this feeling that a part of me is eternal, that I have known these old trails before. I believe it is the undying spirit of the frontier calling, allowing me, through the mind's eye, to step back into time. What is the appeal of the Old West of the American frontier?

It has been epitomized by some as the dark and bloody period in American history. Its heroes—Crockett, Bowie, Hickok, Earp—have been reviled and criticized. Yet the Old West lives on, larger than life.

It has become a symbol of freedom, when there was always another mountain to climb and another river to cross; when a dispute between two men was settled not with expensive lawyers, but with fists, knives, or guns. Barbaric? Maybe. But some things never change. When the cowboy rode into the pages of American history, he left behind a legacy that lives within the hearts of us all.

—*Ralph Compton*

Chapter 1

The rider and his claybank were covered with dust. They came down the middle of Fremont Street, the man slouched in his saddle, the wide brim of his black hat pulled low. He appeared to be in his early twenties. His sun-bronzed face was fringed by a shoulder-length mane of raven hair. He wore buckskins, and knee-high moccasins instead of boots. He did not wear spurs.

Those who saw him noticed a pearl-handled Colt in a black leather holster on his right hip.

Only a few noticed something else. Only those near the rider when he raised his head to scan the street. They saw that he had piercing eyes the color of a mountain lake, and that he would be judged attractive by those of the female persuasion were it not for his disfigurement. At some point in the past his nose had been broken. Normally that was not a calamity. But in the rider's case his nose had not mended as it should. Instead of being straight and smooth, it bent sharply in the middle. At first glance it appeared he had a horizontal V in the center of his face. Below it grew a thick, bushy mustache.

The rider seemed self-conscious of his deformity,

for no sooner did he scan the street than he quickly lowered his head and pulled on his hat brim.

The owner of the feed and grain was sweeping the boardwalk in front of his store when the rider came to a stop at the hitch rail. "Welcome to Whistler's Flat, mister."

"Strange handle for a town," the rider commented as he stiffly dismounted. He did not look directly at the store owner.

"In case you haven't noticed," the townsman said good-naturedly, "flat is one thing Kansas has plenty of. As for the whistling, old Eb Wilcox, who founded the town, had a gap in his upper front teeth."

"So?" the rider said with little interest.

"So every time Eb breathed with his mouth open, he whistled." The store owner grinned. "The name doesn't seem so strange once you know the story." He paused. "I didn't catch *your* name."

"Probably because I didn't give it." The rider removed his hat and swatted at his buckskins, raising swirls of dust.

"Appears to me you and your clothes could use a cleaning," the store owner said. "The barber has a tub out back. For two bits he'll have your clothes washed and wrung out while you bathe."

"There's something I need more." The rider replaced his hat and walked past the feed and grain to the saloon. Hooking his right hand in his belt so it was close to his pearl-handled Colt, he shouldered inside. The murky interior gave him pause. He waited for his eyes to adjust, then strolled to the bar.

The Cocklebur was nearly deserted. It was early afternoon and, other than the bartender and the rider with the bent nose, five men were seated at a corner table playing poker.

"What's your poison, mister?" the bartender asked. He resembled a wad of bread dough poured into an apron.

"Bug juice."

"You particular about the brand?"

"So long as it burns going down and kicks like a mule, I'll be happy." The rider turned so his elbows rested on the bar. Coincidentally, he no longer had his back to the batwings or the corner table, where one of the five players was dealing cards.

"You're an easy gent to please," the bartender complimented him. "I wish all my customers were as agreeable."

The rider was given a glass but he chugged straight from the bottle, using his left hand although his revolver was on his right side. He took three long swigs that ended with him smacking his lips and smiling. "This red-eye of yours would grow hair on a rock."

The five poker players were examining their cards. They were a quiet bunch. They had not said a word since the rider came in.

Lowering his voice, the man with the bent nose asked, "Are they locals?"

"Never saw them before today," the bartender revealed. "Waltzed in here about an hour ago, set right down, and commenced to playing. They're not very friendly. But hell, why should they be when they don't know me from Adam?"

The rider took another long swallow while peering intently at the corner table from under his hat brim. "This town of yours have a law-dog?"

"We've got a marshal, but he's taking a prisoner over to the county seat," the bartender said. "Why? Do you need a tin star?"

"Just curious, is all," the rider said. Gripping the bottle by the neck with his left hand, he walked to a table at the opposite corner from the cardplayers and straddled a chair with his back to the wall. No sooner did he sit down than one of the players stood and came over to his table.

"I thought I recognized you."

The rider did not look up. "I recognized you, too."

Without being invited, the cardplayer pulled out a chair. He wasn't much more than an inch over five feet tall. Bushy eyebrows and glittering dark eyes lent him a sinister aspect. "It's been a while, Crooked Nose."

"Don't call me that," the rider said.

"Why the hell not? It's what everyone else calls you. The newspapers. The law. Crooked Nose Neville Baine. The scourge of the cow towns. Isn't that what they wrote about you after that shooting affray over to Salina?"

Baine set down the bottle. As he did, his other hand drifted under the table. "I won't tell you again."

"I don't see why you're so prickly," the cardplayer complained. "You have a bent nose. Me, I lost a toe once. I accidentally cut it off when I was chopping firewood. But you don't hear me gripe. At least we still have our fingers and hair, which is more than Beanpole Charlie could say after the Blackfeet were done with him."

"What I don't savvy is why you are being so

friendly, Stark. I have never been your favorite person and you have never been mine."

Jesse Stark's laugh was more like a growl. "Same old Baine. You always speak your piece and don't care who you offend. But I reckon you can afford to be uppity, as many hombres as you have bucked out in gore."

"Go away," Baine said.

"What is gnawing at you? I pay you a compliment and you bristle like a cactus. You should be friendlier. In case you have forgotten, we are a lot alike, you and me."

"You must be drunk."

"I haven't had a sip, believe it or not," Stark replied. "I have to stay sober. Me and the boys have something special planned." He glanced at the bartender, who was arranging bottles, then leaned across the table. "As for being alike, we both have a string of killings to our credit. Granted, your tally is higher, but it won't always be. I have plans. Big plans. Before I'm done, I'll be as famous as that other Jesse, Jesse James. Maybe more so."

"You misjudge me."

"Are you denying you have a string of shootings as long as my arm?" Stark snorted.

"I am not denying anything," Baine said. "But you are the one wanted by every lawman in Kansas and Missouri. Texas, too, I hear tell. I'm not wanted anywhere that I know of."

"You make it sound as if that makes you better than me," Jesse Stark said. "But when folks talk about gun-sharks, they mention you in the same breath as Ben Thompson, Jim Courtright and John Ringo."

"What's that brown coming out your ears?" Baine said.

Stark sat back and drummed his fingers on the table. "I was thinking of asking you to join us, but not now. Your trouble is that you always look down your nose at the rest of us. One day someone is going to shoot that ugly nose right off."

"Anyone who wants to try is welcome to."

"There you go again. You are one smug bastard." Stark spread his hands on the table. "But I didn't walk over here to sling affronts. Fact is, I want to be sociable and give you a friendly warning."

"How is that again?"

Just then a townsman in a bowler entered. Jesse Stark tensed and eyed the man suspiciously. When the townsman went to the bar and asked for a drink, Stark visibly relaxed. "A friendly warning," he repeated. "No one here has recognized you yet, other than me. Once they do, it wouldn't surprise me if they ask you to skedaddle, same as they did to you in Topeka." His grin was as cold as an icicle. "Out of the goodness of my heart I will spare you the inconvenience."

"Is there a point to this?"

"I told you. The boys and me have something planned. Once we light the fuse, hell will seem like a church picnic compared to Whistler's Flat. The people will be as riled as hornets. You might not want the attention."

Crooked Nose Baine did not say anything.

"Well? Don't I rate a thanks? Warning you is right neighborly of me, don't you think?"

"The bank," Baine guessed.

"Not hard to figure, was it? And a little fun, after."

"How soon before you light the fuse?" Crooked Nose Baine asked.

Stark took a badly scratched and battered pocket watch from a pocket and consulted the timepiece. "It is a little before two. We aim to start the festivities at six, just as the bank is fixing to close. We hear tell their marshal is out of town, but some of the good citizens are bound to come down with a dose of brave. They won't catch us, though. Not that close to dark. And if me and my men ride hell bent for leather all night, they never will." He chuckled. "I have it worked out in detail."

Crooked Nose Baine said, "All right. You have done your good deed for the year. Now scat. I do my drinking alone."

Stark pushed his chair back and rose. "I don't know why I bothered. I should have known better."

"You must be hankering to bed down with the sawdust."

The flinty edge in Baine's tone caused Jesse Stark to back up a step and to anxiously say, "Now just you hold on. I did you a favor. You can't blow out my wick here in the saloon."

"You mentioned Salina," Baine reminded him. "I put windows in the noggins of three polecats in a saloon there."

Without another word Jesse Stark returned to his friends. The other four leaned over the table to hear what he had to say, then all five glared at Baine. But only until Baine raised his head and returned their glares. Then they became interested in their cards again.

For the next half hour Crooked Nose Baine nursed

his bottle. A great sadness seemed to be upon him. Several more locals came in to wet their throats, but he did not notice them. They noticed him, however, especially after he stood and came around the table, kicking over a chair in his path. Crossing to the bar, he smacked down the empty bottle and growled, "Give me another, barkeep."

"Maybe you have had enough, sonny," the bartender suggested with a friendly smile.

"You are not my pa," Baine said. "I will decide when I am saturated." He pounded the bar. "Another bottle, and be quick about it." The bartender hurriedly complied, and Baine paid and crossed to the batwings. Pushing on out, he stopped in the shade of the overhang and tilted the bottle to his lips.

An elderly woman walking by tilted her nose in the air and sniffed.

Crooked Nose Baine finished chugging and grinned after her. He turned toward the window and his grin evaporated. He stared at his reflection; at the hideous mockery of a nose that once had been straight and smooth. Upending the bottle, he swallowed while continuing to stare. A low sound escaped him. Suddenly he stepped back and raised his arm as if to throw the bottle at the window. But then his arm dropped, his shoulders drooped and he walked from under the overhang into the hot glare of the sun.

Baine walked to the hitch rail in front of the feed and grain. He corked the whiskey bottle, opened a saddlebag and slid the bottle inside, neck up. He reached for the saddle horn to fork leather.

Squealing with glee, a small boy and girl came skipping down the street. The boy had a hoop and was pushing it with a forked stick. He passed the hoop to the girl, who also held a stick, and she laughed and kept the hoop rolling.

Baine watched them, the corners of his mouth curling upward. A puppy came from behind a rain barrel and playfully barked at the hoop. Farther down, the old woman who had sniffed at him saw the children and smiled.

A young man and woman strolled out of the millinery, hand in hand, the young woman wearing a new bonnet.

From the butcher shop stepped a middle-aged matron in a calico dress, with wrapped meat under one arm and a pink parasol under the other. She promptly opened the parasol and strode off in stiff-backed dignity.

"Damn," Baine said. Instead of mounting, he hooked his thumbs in his gun belt and crossed the street to the general store. A tiny bell tinkled as he opened the door. The interior was cool compared to outside and filled with tantalizing scents. Baine idly surveyed the many items for sale. A display of spruce gum caught his interest. So did an assortment of wine bottles. He was regarding a stack of canned goods when someone lightly coughed.

"May I be of service, sir?"

The proprietor was a bantam rooster whose clothes and apron were immaculate. His smile was genuine enough.

"Carry any Saratoga Chips?" Baine asked.

"Sure do. Follow me."

The section devoted to food rivaled general stores in much larger towns. There were the usual staples:

butter, cheese, eggs, coffee, tea and molasses. In the rear were vegetables and fruits. Baine was tempted by the beer and salted fish but did not give in to the craving.

"Here you are." The man held out the Saratoga Chips. "Just got in a shipment last week. Is there anything else I can do for you?"

Baine shook his head.

"Passing through, are you?"

"I thought I was."

"If you plan to stay the night, I can recommend a boardinghouse where the sheets are clean and the food is hot," the man offered.

"I am only staying until six," Crooked Nose Baine said.

Chapter 2

At ten minutes to six, Jesse Stark and his four partners in greed and mayhem ambled from the Cocklebur and strolled along Fremont Street. They joked and laughed, giving the impression they did not have a care in the world.

Whistler's Flat was about to roll up the boardwalk. The bank, the general store, the feed and grain, the millinery, the butcher; they all shut their doors at six. The owners and employees were busy getting ready to close.

It was also the hour when most of the town's womenfolk were busy making supper, and their children were helping or doing other chores.

Fremont Street was practically deserted.

The puppy came from behind the rain barrel and yipped at the five men filing by.

"Shut up, you mangy cur," Jesse Stark said, and delivered a well-placed kick that sent the pup yelping.

"That'll learn him," chortled the scruffiest of the outlaw fraternity. "Were it me, I'd have blown his brains all over creation."

"And have everyone in town fit to ride us out on a rail?" Stark said. "The idea is to *not* attract attention."

Another of the five stopped at a hitch rail they were passing. Five horses were tied to the rail. He unwrapped the reins. Then, folding his arms, he leaned against the rail and shammed an interest in the cloudless sky.

Only three of the remaining outlaws entered the bank. The fourth stopped in front of the large front window and fiddled with a spur.

Jesse Stark held the door for the other two. He scanned the street a final time before following them in. Only the teller and the bank president were present.

The teller was tallying the money in his drawer and asked without looking up, "What can I do for you?"

Stark unbuttoned his shirt and pulled out a folded flour sack. "You can start by filling this. Then we'll move to the safe."

The clerk glanced up in alarm. "I beg your pardon?"

"Are you hard of hearing?" Stark's Remington cleared the counter. The *click* of the hammer was ominously loud. "The bank is being robbed."

His Adam's apple bobbing, the teller blinked ten times in five seconds. "Robbed, you say? My word. You can't mean it."

"Does this hogleg look like I'm joshing? Start filling the sack, you goose-necked simpleton."

Instead of complying, the teller turned and bleated, "Mr. Randolph, sir. This gentleman says we are being robbed."

"What's that?" The white-haired bank president rose from his desk and came over. He had large jowls that quivered as he walked. "It must be a jest. No one would rob us. We don't have enough money to make it worthwhile."

Jesse Stark pointed the Remington at him. "Let me be the judge of that, you old goat. Now fill this, or else!" He wagged both his revolver and the flour sack to emphasize his demand.

"What do I do, Mr. Randolph?" the teller asked.

"Perhaps we should do as he wants, Horace," the bank president said. "These three strike me as rough characters."

"Quit jawing and fill!" Stark was growing red with anger. "I swear, the bank in Ellsworth wasn't half the bother this one is."

"We are a small bank," Randolph said.

"So you don't know how to be robbed?" Stark barked. "It's easy. You give us the money. Then you lie on the floor and don't let out a peep."

"All I am saying," Randolph said, "is that since we have never been robbed, we are not familiar with the etiquette involved."

"If it ain't chickens, it's feathers," Jesse Stark said, and shot the bank president in the head. The clerk squealed and turned to run, and Jesse shot him, too, square between the shoulder blades. "Goddamn stupid people! You tell them to fill a damn sack and they prattle on about eti—whatever it was." He stormed around the counter and into the teller's cage, bellowing, "One of you check the safe. The other keep an eye out. Folks will have heard the shots."

The man who ran to the safe yanked on the metal handle. "It's locked! Damn it, Jess. That itchy trigger finger of yours will leave us as broke as when we came in."

Hurriedly stuffing coins and banknotes into the sack, Stark responded, "Not quite. I've got pretty near sixty dollars here."

"Sixty? That's twelve dollars apiece! Hell, I lose that much at cards in an hour. You said we would each get a hundred."

Over at the door the other outlaw warned, "The butcher has come out of his shop and is looking this way. The same with the runt who runs the general store."

Stark opened another drawer, but all it contained were a ledger and pencils. Swearing viciously, he wheeled and kicked the bank president in the ribs. "Eti—whatever be damned!"

"Mills is bringing the horses," the man at the door reported. "No one is trying to stop him."

"They better not," Jesse Stark said.

"Maybe we should tree the town," suggested the man over by the safe. "With the marshal gone, it will be as easy as licking butter off a knife."

"These yokels might not scare," Stark noted, "and there's a heap more of them than there is of us."

"It's worth a try," the other argued. "We can take what we want. Make this worth our while."

"Breathing dirt isn't much to my liking," Stark said. He vaulted over the counter. "Come on. We're lighting a shuck."

They burst from the bank ready to sling lead, but the town was as quiet as when they entered. "See?" said the man in favor of treeing. "They're mice hiding in their holes. Whatever we want is ours."

"Your yearnings always did outstrip your common sense, Warner," Stark criticized. To the man bringing their mounts he bellowed, "Hurry it up, Mills! Those are horses, not turtles!"

Down the street the butcher cupped a hand to his mouth and yelled, "What's all the ruckus? Who are you men and what are you doing?"

"Minding our own business!" Jesse Stark shouted. "You should do the same." He moved to the middle of the street. He still had his Remington out, and he brandished it at a farmer who stepped from the feed and grain. The farmer scurried back in.

The butcher, his apron spattered with blood from the day's work, was advancing on them, a meat cleaver clenched in his right fist.

"Will you look at this," Warner marveled. "What does that idiot think he's doing?"

Stark pivoted and took deliberate aim. "That's close enough, meat-cutter! We're leaving and we don't want any trouble."

The butcher did not stop. "What have you done to Jack Randolph and Horace Stubbs?"

"They're lying on the bank floor with their hands and feet tied," Jesse lied. "But keep coming and that can change."

Reluctantly, the butcher halted. "Jack! Horace! If you're alive and can hear me, give a holler!"

"I gagged them, too," Stark said.

The butcher resumed his advance. "I reckon I will just see for myself. You better not have harmed them."

"I did the same to them as I am about to do to you," Jesse Stark said, and shot him in the chest.

The butcher was a big man. Years of handling heavy slabs of beef and wielding a big butcher knife had sculpted his arms and shoulders with muscle. The slug staggered him but he did not fall. Raising the cleaver, he charged the nearest outlaw, who happened to be the one bringing the horses.

"What the hell!" Mills was astride one horse and leading the rest. He let go of the reins to grab for his revolver, but he had only begun to draw when the razor edge of the cleaver sliced into his leg. Blood spurted in a scarlet geyser, and Mills screamed. By then he had his six-shooter out and, thrusting the muzzle against the butcher's forehead, he squeezed the trigger. In his excitement and pain, he forgot to thumb back the hammer. Nothing happened.

The butcher had gone berserk. Rather than finish off the mounted man, he charged the outlaw in front of the bank window. The outlaw quickly drew and fired, but in his haste he missed.

Jesse Stark swore and extended his Remington. "If you want something done right," he declared.

Abruptly, a shout from between two adjacent buildings caused the butcher to lurch toward the source. He was weakening and stumbled just as Stark fired. Lead bit into the wall and slivers went flying.

"Damn it, I missed."

The butcher sank from sight.

"Mount up!" Stark roared. "We're getting the hell out of here!"

Their horses, though, were milling nervously about in the middle of Fremont Street. The outlaw who had complained about the slim pickings dashed to get his animal, but the horse shied and pranced away.

"This is not going well," Jesse Stark said.

That was when Crooked Nose Baine stepped into

the street. He appeared out of the gap between the two buildings. The wide brim of his black hat was pulled low so the sun was not in his eyes. His right hand hung low at his side, nearly brushing the black leather holster and the pearl-handled Colt.

Jesse Stark could not hide his surprise. "What's this? Did you come to join us?" He had to raise his voice to be heard above Mills, who was shrieking like a gut-shot cat while trying to stanch the flow of blood from his leg, and above the racket raised by the milling horses.

"No," Baine said. One instant his hand was empty, the next it held his Colt. The Colt belched lead and smoke, and Mills's scream became a gurgle that ended with the thud of a body striking the ground.

Stupefied, Jesse Stark and the other outlaws gaped at the twitching form. Then the man who had been trying to catch his horse bawled, "You shot Mills!" and clawed for his hardware.

Crooked Nose Baine shot him through the heart.

Belatedly, Jesse Stark and the other two outlaws galvanized to life. All three squeezed off shots as fast as they could, but Baine was no longer there. He had ducked between the buildings.

"After him!" Stark roared. But he had only taken a couple of steps when a rifle boomed somewhere down the street, kicking up dust in front of him. The rifleman was on the roof of the feed and grain, taking aim. "Into the bank!" Stark commanded, back-pedaling.

Another rifle cracked before they reached the door.

"It's the damn townsmen!" one of the outlaws cried. "They're fighting back!"

The three of them made it into the bank and Stark slammed the front door after them. "Out the back!" he directed.

"We don't stand a prayer," the third outlaw lamented. "Not against a whole town and Crooked Nose, both!"

"We're not dead yet." Stark plunged into a narrow hall that brought them to the rear door. It was made of oak. He threw the bolt and put his shoulder to the door, but it would not budge. Stepping back, he fired two shots at the wood, close to the lock, then kicked with all his might. The door swung open.

"Now what?" the third outlaw asked as they hurtled outside. "Without our horses we're as good as caught."

"Don't you ever get tired of looking at the bright side of things?" Jesse Stark snapped. Wheeling, he raced along the rear of the buildings. "Ours aren't the only nags in town."

"What are you saying?" the second outlaw asked. "That we're going to help ourselves to others?"

"The stable is this way," Stark said.

"But stealing horses will get us hung!" the third outlaw objected.

"And robbing the bank won't?" Stark countered. To the thin air he said, "I have morons for partners."

They came to the end of the street. Ahead was the broad structure that offered salvation.

Stark ran for all he was worth, but he was not fleet of foot and the other two reached the rear of the stable ahead of him. From up the street came the heavy crash of rifles mixed with the lighter crack of pistols.

"Who the blazes are they shooting at?" the third outlaw wondered.

"Just so it ain't us."

The back door was ajar.

"I'll have a look-see," Stark whispered, and warily pushed it open so he could poke his head in. Half the stalls were filled. There was no sign of anyone.

"It's safe."

They found saddles and saddle blankets and bridles, and were ready to ride out in half the time it would ordinarily have taken them. One after the other they stepped into the stirrups.

Jesse Stark raised his reins and glanced at his companions. "Don't be shy about using your spurs. If you're hit, cling on for dear life."

"Going somewhere?"

The three outlaws twisted in their saddles and Stark blurted, "You again! What did you do, follow us from the bank? What in God's name are you up to?"

"You haven't guessed?" Crooked Nose Baine asked, and again his Colt blossomed in his hands. Two swift shots, and the men on either side of Jesse Stark pitched from their mounts.

Stark heeded his own advice and applied his spurs harder than he ever had in his entire life. As his sorrel streaked out the front, he swung onto the off side so he would be harder to hit.

Baine ran from the stable and raised his Colt. His trigger finger was tightening when a rifle thundered from a rooftop and hot lead ripped through his body from back to front. Baine staggered and nearly fell. Rallying, he shifted and had a clear shot at the townsman who had shot him. But Baine did not shoot. Instead he ran for his claybank. Other rifles opened up, and revolvers, too, until the street swarmed with leaden hornets.

Somehow Crooked Nose Baine made it to the claybank. Somehow he gained the saddle and brought the claybank to a gallop. He could not sit up, though, and his buckskins were soaked with blood. Gritting his teeth, he slumped over the saddle horn, riding for his life as more lead fanned the air around him.

Chapter 3

Jesse Stark was madder than he had ever been, and that took some doing. The horse he had stolen was racing pell-mell across the prairie. To the west the sun hovered on the horizon, and night could not fall soon enough to suit him.

Jesse voiced every swear word he knew, two or three times. He cursed Whistler's Flat. He cursed the bank. He cursed the banker. He cursed the teller. He cursed his partners. He cursed the butcher and the baker, but not the candlestick maker. But the one he cursed the most, the one he could not stop cursing, was Crooked Nose Neville Baine. He cursed Baine's mother. He cursed Baine's father. He cursed Baine's brothers and sisters, if Baine had any. He cursed Crooked Nose Baine as he had never cursed anyone, and after he ran out of breath and recovered, he cursed Baine some more.

The cursing ended with a declaration. "If it's the last thing I ever do," Jesse Stark vowed, "I will see that son of a bitch six feet under."

For all his swearing, Jesse did not forget to glance back now and then to see if anyone was after him. He had gone half a mile when he stiffened. "Dust!" he declared, and in a panic tried to make the sorrel go faster when it was already at its limit.

After a bit Stark stopped whipping the reins and using his spurs. He shifted in the saddle and stared hard at the dust, and as was his habit when he was alone, he talked to himself. "That's mighty peculiar. There's not nearly as much dust as there should be."

The minutes stretched into an hour.

Stark would gallop for a while, then walk the horse so it could rest, then gallop again. At the end of the hour the dust was still there.

"Whoever it is, I can't shake them."

A gully offered a solution. Riding into it, Stark dismounted and palmed his Remington. "I would rather have a rifle but mine is back in town," he bitterly said to the horse.

Stark climbed to the top of the gully and flattened. "I don't savvy why there isn't more dust."

The dust drew nearer, and Jesse swore again. Not in anger but in surprise. "It's just one rider!" he exclaimed. Grinning in vicious anticipation, he cocked the Remington. "Whoever it is, he must have a hankering to die. I reckon I will oblige him."

The rider came nearer, and Stark's eyes widened. "Can it be?" In his amazement he forgot himself and rose to his knees. When the horse was close enough that there could be no doubt, he stood and hollered, "Whoa, there!"

The claybank stopped not twenty feet away. It was lathered with sweat and breathing heavily. The rider half hung over the pommel, his arms and legs as limp as wet rags. His buckskin shirt was stained scarlet.

Jesse Stark voiced a nervous laugh. He cautiously

advanced, his Remington trained on the rider. When the man did not rise up and blaze away, Stark exclaimed, "It *is* really him, and he is really hurt!" Stark laughed as he poked the limp figure with the Remington. "Baine, can you hear me?"

Crooked Nose Baine did not answer.

Stark gripped a wrist and tugged, but the body did not slide off. He found out why. Baine's belt had snagged on the saddle horn. That was the only thing keeping him in the saddle.

"Well, I'll be," Stark said. Unhooking the belt, he tugged anew, and grinned when Baine thudded to earth.

"Why, Neville. You are bleeding like a stuck pig," Stark addressed the still figure. He nudged it with his boot, then hooked his heel under an arm and rolled the body onto its back. Baine's hat came off.

"Damn," Stark said. "It's too bad you're dead. I would surely have loved to buck you out in gore."

Shoving the Remington into his holster, Stark knelt. "Might as well go through your pockets. Never can tell but you might have something worthwhile." But he soon discovered the buckskin shirt had only one pocket, the pants none, and when he stuck his hand in the shirt pocket, his palm flat against Baine's chest, the pocket was empty. He was about to take his hand out when he gave a start.

Stark's mouth fell in astonishment. Careful of the blood, he pressed his ear to Baine's chest and listened. Sadistic glee lit his face. Straightening, he let out a whoop. He pressed the Remington to Baine's temple and held it there for all of ten seconds.

"What am I doing?"

Stark lowered the Remington and let down the hammer. "I want him to suffer first." He rose and turned toward the gully, but promptly stopped. "Wait. I don't have any water."

The claybank moved slightly. Stark glanced at it, and whooped again. A bound brought him to the saddle. Eagerly, he helped himself to Baine's canteen and shook it so the water sloshed. It was half full.

Stark hunkered, opened the canteen and proceeded to trickle water onto Baine's eyes and cheeks. At first it had no effect. Then Baine's eyelids fluttered, and he stirred and groaned but went limp again.

"Don't you die on me, you son of a bitch."

Stark pried Baine's mouth open. He touched the canteen to Baine's lips, allowing water to dribble out.

Baine sputtered and coughed and groaned louder.

Bending down, Stark eagerly asked, "Can you hear me?"

"Who?" Crooked Nose Baine croaked. He did not open his eyes. His breathing was labored.

"Take a gander and find out," Stark said, tossing the canteen aside. "I want you to see what is coming."

Baine's eyelids fluttered anew and this time stayed open. "Stark? Is that you or am I delirious?"

"It's me, all right. The one you always treat like dirt. The one whose friends you turned into maggot bait back there in that two-bit town."

A feeble spark of vitality brought a hint of recognition. "How? Where? The last I remember, I was shot."

"More than once, it appears. As for the how, let's just say the Almighty must have taken pity on me. The where is easy. West of Whistler's Flat a ways."

"How did I get here? I don't remember much."

"That's a pity," Stark said. He examined the buckskin shirt. "The slug went clear through. You've got a hole in you about as big as an apple. I wouldn't give a plugged nickel for your chances."

Baine's eyes had closed again.

"None of that," Stark said. "I need you to lend an ear." He stuck two fingers into a bullet hole and squeezed.

A gasp escaped Crooked Nose Baine and he opened his eyes. "What are you doing? That hurts like hell."

"It is supposed to." Stark removed his fingers. They dripped blood and gore, and he wiped them on Baine's shirt. "Stay awake or I'll do it again."

"I don't understand."

"Then let me educate you. It's as sweet as sugar, and it's mine to take, and before I am through you will beg me to put you out of your agony."

With visible effort Baine said, "You want to have revenge? Is that what this is all about?"

"Mister, I have yearned for this ever since Abilene. You remember Abilene, don't you? A dance hall girl called me a lousy dancer because I tromped on her foot and broke a toe. I was drunk, and I slapped her some, and you came up and laid the barrel of your pistol across my head. Remember now?"

"She was a friend of mine," Baine said weakly. "You about beat her into the floor."

"That didn't give you call to pistol-whip me," Stark said, emotion darkening his features. "The high-and-mighty Neville Baine." He snickered and poked Baine, hard. "Since that night I have nursed a hate for you. Some might call that pointless, but I have always been a good hater. I found out all I could about you, in case I ran into you again. Can you guess what I found out?"

"Let me die in peace."

"I want you to hear this. I want you to know I know." Balling his fist, Stark mashed his knuckles into the wound, causing Crooked Nose Baine to grit his teeth and arch his back. When Stark stopped, Baine sank back, beads of sweat sprinkling his brow. "Do I have your attention? Good. Because the truth is, Baine, you are a fraud. Oh, you're hell on wheels with a six-shooter. No denying that. But you're not the badman everyone makes you out to be. You're not snake-mean, like they say. Fact is, you're a kitten."

"And you're loco."

"Am I? Then explain something. Explain why it is that in all the shooting affrays you were in, every single one, it was always the other hombre who went for his shooting iron first. That gunfight in Salina? Those three leather slappers you sent to hell were beating on some farm boy. That time in Wichita? Those mule skinners were forcing themselves on a woman. In Abilene when you pistol-whipped me, it was a woman again."

Crooked Nose Baine was silent.

"And now, here in Whistler's Flat, you did the same thing. You were helping those folks, weren't you? When you saw the butcher get shot, you jumped in to stop us. I'm right, aren't I?"

Baine started to close his eyes.

"Don't you dare!" Stark growled, and jabbed the wound. "You'll hear the rest of what I've got to say whether you want to or not."

"Have your fun," Baine said.

"You are a fraud, mister. A fake. You with your big rep. Hell with the hide off, they say. Dabbles in gore like no one else. Bad medicine. The curly wolf of curly wolves." Jesse Stark snorted. "All of it hogwash. You are no more fearsome than that puppy I saw back in town. Oh, you act tough, but that's to fool folks. To scare off the peckerwoods who want to add a notch to their handle."

"Are you done?"

"I reckon so. No comment?"

"Think what you want, but you don't know the half of it. Now go away and let me die, damn you."

Stark drew his Remington and held it where the stricken man could see. "I figure you have some life left in you. Not much, but enough that you can do a lot of suffering before you breathe your last."

Baine scowled. "I expected as much from the likes of you."

"There's one thing I want to know before we get to it."

"Go to hell."

"You will be there ahead of me. But tell me why, first."

"Why what?"

"Don't play dumb. Why do you do what you do? Why go around sticking your nose into trouble? You're not a law-dog. You're sure as hell not a preacher. So why go around helping folks at the risk of a window in your skull?"

"There are some things," Baine said slowly, "best kept to ourselves. I've never told anyone why I do what I do. I sure as hell am not going to tell a no-account, cultus, four-card flush like you."

Stark's face twitched in a spasm of rising rage. "There's nothing counterfeit about me, as you're about to find out."

"Men like you are vermin, Stark. You prey on people who never did anyone a lick of harm. You kill and you steal and you enjoy it."

"Is there a point to this? Or are you trying to goad me into putting a bullet in your brainpan?"

"My point," Baine said, "is that scum like you make a misery of life for everyone else. Your kind should be exterminated."

Smirking, Stark said, "Your exterminating days are over. You had your chance at me in Whistler's Flat. If you had been a shade quicker I'd be lying in the stable with my pards."

"It's not my first regret," Baine said.

Rising, Stark straddled him and hefted the Remington. "I once beat a man to death. It took him an hour to die."

"There is one thing." Baine's voice was growing weak and he had to whisper.

Jesse bent lower. "What?"

"This," Baine said.

A gob of spit spattered on Stark's cheek. Instinctively, he recoiled, then cursed and wiped a sleeve across his face. "You have sand. I will give you that. Which is good. It means you will take a while to die. A good long while if I do it right."

The first blow brought a sharp cry. But not the second blow, or any after that. Jesse Stark stood over Neville Baine and pistol-whipped him, chortling with glee the whole while, blow after blow after blow. Most were across the face, but Stark also whipped the barrel across Baine's neck and shoulders and chest. Again and again and again, so many times that Stark lost count. So many times that Baine's face and shoulders were a welter of blood-seeping slashes and swellings. So many times that Baine's limp form became limper still.

The only reason Jesse Stark stopped was to catch his breath. Flushed with pleasure, his chest heaving, he stepped back and admired his handiwork. "He looks dead, but I need to be sure." He started to reach for Baine's wrist.

At that moment the claybank whinnied. Almost simultaneously hooves rumbled in the distance.

Unfurling, Jesse Stark spun. A roiling cloud of dust partially obscured a dozen or more riders. He sprang to the claybank, swung on, and flicked the reins, but the exhausted animal only managed several slow, weary steps.

"Damn it!" Stark fumed. "You are plumb wore out!" He resorted to his spurs, brutally raking the claybank as hard as he could while reining into the gully. At the bottom he vaulted down, quickly mounted the sorrel, and trotted along the bottom of the gully for over a hundred yards, to where the slope flattened and merged with the plain. As he broke into the open shouts erupted.

The posse had spotted him and was racing to overtake him. Several rifles cracked in random cadence.

Hunched low, Stark gave the sorrel its head and the animal fairly flew. He did not widen his lead, but neither did the good citizens of Whistler's Flat gain. By now the sun was setting, and Stark rode straight into the sunset. It would annoy his pursuers, having to squint.

In due course, though, twilight descended. The sorrel was tiring but Stark galloped on. Gradually the twilight gave way to the ink of night. The moment he had waited for had come.

Reining to the north, Stark went a hundred yards and drew rein. He sat perfectly still, his ears straining, and grinned when the posse went thundering on to the west. In a few minutes the racket they made faded and the prairie lay quiet under the canopy of stars.

"They'll never catch me now," Stark crowed, and patted the sorrel. "You did good. I reckon I'll keep you." He headed northwest at a slow walk, thinking out loud. "I've about worn out my welcome in Kansas. But where to go? What to do? Not that it matters much, so long as there are folks to rob and saloons to spend their money in." He laughed gaily and breathed deep of the crisp night air. "Yes, sir, horse. Life can be as sweet as sugar."

Chapter 4

There was the sun and the grass and the earth. There were buzzards circling high in the sky and flies buzzing noisily about the blood-caked form that had lured both like honey lured bears. Many of the flies had alighted but as yet none of the buzzards. Buzzards always liked to be sure.

In this instance the buzzards were right.

A groan came from the crumpled figure. A groan, and then a feeble twitching of fingers and hands. The trigger finger curled several times in reflex. The entire hand moved, but only an inch or so. The eyelids flickered, and opened. Blue eyes mirrored pain such as few ever experience.

Neville Baine sucked a breath deep into his lungs and tasted his own blood. He tried to sit but could not. His entire body was aflame with pain. Licking his swollen lips, he willed his arms to move and rose onto his elbows. He looked down at himself. Dried blood was everywhere—spattered over his shoulders and his chest, and caked like paint lower down. His buckskin shirt was a ruin. The upper half had been ripped and torn to ribbons. So had the skin and the flesh underneath.

Again Baine attempted to sit up, and this time he succeeded. His head swam, and when it stopped he gazed about him. He saw no one. For as far as the eye could see, he was the only living creature except for the flies and the buzzards.

Bracing his legs under him, Baine stood. He swayed but stayed on his feet. A nicker came from behind him. He shuffled to the rim of the gully and stared down in bewilderment at the claybank. Unwilling to trust his legs on the slope, he tried to call the horse to him, but all that came from his throat was a jumble of guttural sounds. Swallowing a few times, he tried again. "Here, boy. Come here."

The claybank stamped a hoof but stayed where it was.

Baine tried to whistle, but could not pucker his lips. He started down into the gully, slipped, and fell onto his back. Ordinarily the fall would not have bothered him. This one racked him with torment. His vision spun and he came close to blacking out. He lay there until the spinning stopped, then marshaled every iota of strength in his body and crawled back up to level ground where it was safe to stand.

Baine levered upright. As he rose he spied his black hat. Forgetting himself, he smiled. His mouth protested. His temples throbbed. Moving as if he were made of molasses, he picked up the hat and gingerly placed it on his head. The slight contact provoked waves of anguish that rippled clear down to his toes.

Suddenly Baine went rigid. He fumbled at his holster. A moan escaped him when he found it empty. He twisted to the right, then the left. A gleam caught his eye. He managed several swift strides without falling. Sinking to his knees, he clasped the pearl-handled Colt to his bosom. "Thank you, Lord," he said, and ran a hand along the barrel and over the cylinder.

Baine knelt there a while. Then, with reverent care, he eased the Colt into his holster and rose. He turned, and nearly collided with the claybank. "Don't sneak up on a person like that." Elated, he placed an arm over its neck.

Climbing on took twice as long as it should have. There was a delay when he spotted his canteen in the grass. It was only a third full and the water was warm and flat, but to him it was delicious. He allowed himself a sip, enough to wet his hurting lips and dry throat.

Baine tapped the claybank with his heels. He had nowhere special in mind to go. He was content with whichever direction the claybank picked, and the claybank headed southwest. So southwest it was.

Baine did not look down at himself. He did not want to know how bad off he was. He did not want to know if infection had set in. He pretended it was nothing, and in the pretending, found solace in the illusion that he might live through the day.

The sun was hot but hot was good. Hot was alive. Every minute, every second, had become precious. Baine savored them as a starving man savors every morsel of food.

The pain worsened. Baine had never hurt in so many places at one time. The bullet wounds hurt. The slash marks on his shoulders and chest hurt. But the worst was his face. It hurt so much he wanted to rip it off. Several times his hand rose toward it but lowered again.

Evening brought a cool breeze. Baine did not make camp. Midnight came and went and still he pressed on. He held the claybank to a walk so as not to overly tire it. Along about four in the morning it lifted its head and repeatedly sniffed. Its sensitive nose had brought them to paradise.

Trees framed a stream. Cottonwoods, mostly. Baine rode in among them and drew rein at the water's edge. The claybank immediately dipped its muzzle to drink.

Stiffly sliding down, Baine eased onto his belly, removed his hat, and submerged his entire face in the water. He held it under as long as he could. The relief it brought was exquisite. So much so that he submerged his face a second and a third time. Then, dripping wet, he touched his chin and both cheeks. Every spot he touched hurt. He ran his tongue over his lips, then over his teeth. Miraculously, none were broken or missing.

Exhaustion claimed him. Rolling onto his back, Baine closed his eyes. The sound of the claybank drinking motivated him to get up. It took forever to undo the cinch and strip off the saddle, saddle blanket and bridle. He had a picket pin in his saddlebags but he was too tired to bother.

Sleep claimed him almost instantly. Baine dreamed that he was a cowboy riding night herd. A rattlesnake spooked the cattle and he was caught up in the stampede. He tried to turn the cattle, but his horse was jostled and he was thrown to the ground. A seething wall of horns and hooves swept over him, trampling him into the dirt. He felt the stomp of every hoof. Hundreds of them.

Suddenly Baine was awake. The new day was under

way. He had slept for hours but he did not feel refreshed. He hurt all over, exactly as if he had been caught in that stampede. He willed himself to sit up.

The stream flowed past his boots. Barely wider than a buckboard, it had the distinction of doing what many streams did not; it flowed year-round. It did not dry up in the summer months.

The claybank was dozing.

Baine opened a saddlebag. He had a handful of jerky left and he ate half. He washed it down with water and sat back against his saddle. He had no intention of falling asleep again but that is exactly what he did.

The sun was high when Baine awoke. He felt warm, and not just from the sun. He pressed a palm to his forehead and confirmed his worst fear. He had a fever. He had no choice now. He must take off his shirt and examine the wounds. But deciding to do it was one thing; doing it was another. No sooner did he pull at the bottom of his shirt than he learned it was stuck to his body. The dry blood was to blame. There was only one thing to do.

Baine unstrapped his gun belt. His moccasins were always a challenge to remove, but never more so than now. He tugged on first one and then the other. He was spent when he eventually got them off. A short rest, and he was able to stand and walk along the bank. He found what he was looking for around a bend. A tree had fallen and partially blocked the stream, creating a pool. It was not more than a couple of feet deep, but it would do.

Wading out to the center, Blaine sat down. The water rose to his neck. He propped himself with one arm. Just like the night before, the relief the water brought was marvelous. He stayed in the pool until his buckskins were waterlogged and hung loose on his frame. Then he sat on the bank and peeled what was left of his shirt over his head. In doing so he accidentally bumped his nose. The pain it caused was the worst yet. Gritting his teeth, he tossed his head from side to side and made hissing noises until the pain subsided.

He had been shot three times. Miraculously, all three slugs had gone clean through. One was in his right shoulder but had missed the collarbone. Another was in the fleshy part of his calf and had taken some flesh, but not severed an artery. The worst was the stomach wound. The exit hole was ugly. Of frightening size, it had long since stopped bleeding.

Try though he might, he could not see the entry hole. He twisted his neck as far as he could. He bent his body into contortions a snake would envy—to no avail. At a guess he would say his vitals had been spared, but only time would really tell.

Baine decided to make camp by the pool. He brought the saddle and the rest, and laid out his blankets. It took hours. He had to rest between trips. There was grass for the claybank, and a rock to pound the picket pin in. He donned his spare buckskin shirt and munched on the last of his jerky while lying back on his saddle. A deep lassitude came over him and he drifted off.

The rest of that day and most of the next he spent sleeping. His battered body craved rest. It also craved nourishment. He had plenty of water, but food required that he rouse himself, slide his Winchester from the saddle scabbard, and prowl the cottonwoods in search of game. He flushed a doe and brought her down with a head shot. He butchered her where he shot her so as not to have the scent of her blood near his camp, where it might draw predators.

He kindled a fire and roasted a haunch. He had known he was hungry, but his need went beyond hunger. He was truly and extraordinarily famished. He ate more meat at one sitting than at any time in his entire life. The rest he cut into strips and dried over a crude frame of broken limbs. He now had enough jerked venison to last weeks.

The days became pleasant blurs. He slept most of them away. Two or three times each day he stripped and soaked in the pool. He had been there ten days before he felt anything like his old self. The wounds and lacerations were healing. He had more energy. He took to taking walks. Short walks initially, then longer and longer walks, until one day he covered several miles going and coming back.

Baine had seldom experienced such peace. Peace of mind, the peace of his healing body and a different peace deep in his being. He was content to stay there until winter set in.

Then the real world intruded.

It was late one evening. Baine had slept through the afternoon and was awakened by the distant yip of a coyote. As he lay enjoying the tranquillity and his restored sense of well-being, the acrid scent of wood smoke drifted to his nose.

His own fire was out.

Grabbing the Winchester, Baine rose and tested the breeze. The source of the smoke was west of him, somewhere along the stream. Whoever it was, he told himself, did not know he was there and would move on in the morning. The smart thing to do was let well enough alone. But it had been so long since he set eyes on another human being that he could not resist his own curiosity.

A shadow among shadows, Baine cat-footed through the undergrowth. He had been over every square yard of both sides of the stream on his many walks, and the encroaching night did not hinder him.

Baine slowed when he spotted dancing fingers of flame. Soon he spied horses and, dropping flat, he crawled until he heard voices. A tingle ran through him. The language was not English or Spanish. He worked his way closer and saw them: three warriors in buckskins much like his own. Cheyenne, he suspected. Since they did not wear paint, they were not on the warpath. A hunting party, he reckoned, looking for buffalo. If he did not bother them they would not bother him.

Baine watched them a while. They were talking and smiling and laughing, just as whites would do. Bows and quivers and lances lay near them, but no rifles or revolvers.

About to leave as silently as he had snuck up, Baine glanced at their horses. His blood froze in his veins. There were *four* horses, not three. Either the fourth was a packhorse—or the Cheyenne had a sentry.

Baine had to slip away, and slip away quickly. But before he could suit act to desire, the brush parted and a lithe shape sprang, the blade of a knife glinting in the light from the campfire. A piercing whoop rent the night.

Rolling onto his back, Baine brought up the Winchester. He already had a round in the chamber. He thumbed back the hammer and fired. The shot caught the warrior in midair and smashed him back.

The other three were on their feet, hastily scooping up weapons. One shouted, calling to the warrior Baine had shot. Uncertainty held them for a moment, allowing Baine to rise into a crouch. Running would be pointless. They would follow. They would find him.

All three warriors broke for cover.

Baine had fought Indians before. In the dark the advantage was to the Cheyenne. They would surround him and slay him. He must draw them out of the dark and into his gun's sights.

Baine ran toward their horses. The Cheyenne would think he was trying to run the animals off, and the last thing the Cheyenne wanted was to be on foot in the middle of the prairie.

A shriek and a rush of movement brought Baine around with the Winchester tucked at his side. He fired, worked the lever, fired again. The warrior crashed to earth mere feet away.

Crouching, Baine drew his Colt and set down the rifle. He was faster with the Colt. He waited, letting them come to him, and they did not disappoint. An arrow whizzed past his head, missing his ear by a whisker's width. The bowman made the mistake of being silhouetted against the fire. Baine slammed off two swift shots, and the warrior staggered into the firelight and fell.

So far luck had favored Baine. But the last warrior would not make the mistakes his friends had. Carefully groping with his other hand, Baine found a stick.

He tossed it high and wide to one side. From around a cottonwood glided the last warrior. He was peering at the spot where the stick had struck and not at Baine. Baine fanned the Colt, emptying it, and the deed was done.

Baine felt no sense of elation. He never did when he killed. He felt sorry about the Cheyenne. He should not have investigated the smoke.

The remains of a rabbit were skewered on a spit. A beaded parfleche caught his eye. Inside were a whetstone, extra feathers for arrows, an eagle's claw and a bear's tooth, and a small hand mirror neatly folded in a piece of cloth.

During his many immersions in the pool, Baine had never looked at his reflection. He could not stand the sight of his face, and he imagined it would be worse now, with the scars. But to his delight he had healed nicely. He had a small scar on his left eyebrow and another on his chin, but that was all. He started to put the mirror down, then snapped it up again.

"No!" Baine cried. Astonishment seized him, and he placed a hand to his face to confirm the testimony of his eyes. "It can't be!"

For over an hour Neville Baine stared into that mirror. For over an hour tears streaked his cheeks and his broad shoulders shook to quiet sobs. The only words he uttered in all that time were "Thank you."

Chapter 5

Bluff City was a product of the mining boom. A back-woodsman from Kentucky, looking for a spot to build a cabin, noticed a bright gleam high on a craggy bluff. He climbed up to find the source of the gleam and stumbled on a rich vein of silver. Word spread, more silver was discovered, and a new city sprouted on the broad tableland below the bluff.

The early founders were ambitious. Their first meeting was in one of many tents that lined the creek that flowed down from the bluff. They needed a name for their new town, and someone had a brainstorm.

Bluff City it became. But they did not stop there. The bluff laced with silver became Bluff Mountain. The creek became Bluff Creek.

The buildings that sprang up as the money-hungry poured in shared in the fondness for the name. There was the Bluff City General Store and the Bluff Creek Mortuary. The First Bank of Bluff City competed with the Greater Bank of Bluff City. The Bluff City Stable was at one end of the main thoroughfare, Bluff Street; at the other end was the one-room Bluff City School.

Bluff City was called the Queen of Silver, a shining beacon of raw greed. Many of her whiskey mills and houses of ill repute were open twenty-four hours and never lacked for customers. Games of chance drew the gullible and professional in droves. Doves paraded their carnal wares along Bluff Street from sunset to sunrise.

Into this sprawl of bedlam, on a morning in the early fall, rode a young man in a brown suit and a matching derby. He had black hair cropped close to his head and was clean-shaven. His shoes were polished to a sheen. He sat easy in the saddle and had an air of competence about him. His eyes were a penetrating blue.

The young man drew rein at the hitch rail in front of the *Bluff City Courier*. He lithely alighted, wrapped the reins around the rail, and stood regarding the hustle and bustle of Bluff City life. He turned to open the door and bumped into someone about to do the same.

"I beg your pardon."

Shock rooted the young man. Snatching his derby off, he blurted, "My apologies, ma'am. I didn't see you."

"Plainly not," said the object of his shock. She was about his age, with a wreath of blond curls, emerald eyes and ruby lips. Her dress was plain and prim, contrasting sharply with her llama jacket. "Well, are you going to stand there gawking or be a gentleman and open the door for me?"

The young man reacted as if poked with a sword. He stood aside as she swept past him, then followed her in but stayed well behind her.

A bellow from the back of the newspaper office heralded a stout man with remarkably thick muttonchops. He had his jacket off and his thumbs were wrapped around his suspenders. "Melanie! It's about time! Where have you been, girl? Taking a promenade about our fair city?"

"Bluff City is a harlot, not a maiden," the blond vision said. She pushed against a small gate that admitted her to the part of the room barred to the general public. "And how many times must I tell you not to call me 'girl'?"

"I am your employer and will do as I please."

"You are also my uncle, and I will kick you in the shins if you ever do it again." Melanie set down the parcel she was carrying and absently swiped at a stray bang. "Now then, do you want the details of the tunnel collapse or would you rather my morning be wasted?"

The man with the muttonchops noticed the young man in the brown suit and came over to a counter cluttered with a stack of newspapers, pencils, pens, ink, loose sheets of paper, and a Bible. "You must excuse my niece. Somewhere or other she got it into her head that the world must adjust its schedule to her and not the other way around."

"Sir?" The young man smiled sheepishly.

The blonde put her hands on her shapely hips. "How dare you carp about me to a complete stranger?"

"I can remedy that." Her uncle thrust out an ink-stained hand. "Jerome Stanley, at your service. This humble enterprise happens to be mine."

The young man shook.

"And you?" Stanley said.

"Me what?"

"Your name, sir. Your name. You do have one, I would imagine."

A look of bewilderment came over the young man. "Of course I do."

"Then what would it be, if you do not mind my prying?"

"Clay, sir. My name is Clay."

Jerome Stanley waited, then asked, "Would that be the first or the last?"

"What? Oh." The young man scanned the counter and his gaze fixed on one object in particular. "Adams. My name is Clay Adams."

"There, now," Stanley said. "That wasn't so hard, was it? And what can we do for you, Clay Adams?"

"I need a job," Clay Adams said. "I figured I would start here at the newspaper office."

"An excellent choice. We run a list of jobs wanted in the *Courier*. If you can part with five cents, I will sell you a copy of the latest edition."

"No. I mean I wanted to apply here," Clay Adams said.

Melanie had sat at a desk and was rummaging in a drawer. She did not appear to be listening, but suddenly she was on her feet, saying, "We do need someone at the counter, Uncle Jerome. Betsy had to quit on account of the baby."

"What?" Stanley said. "Oh. Yes. I forgot. But I usually hire a woman for that. It is tedious work, hardly befitting a strapping young man like Mr. Adams, here."

"Why don't we let him be the judge of that?" Melanie rebutted. "Ask him."

Stanley glanced from her to Clay Adams and back again. "Ah. As you wish. Would you be interested in a job at the *Courier*, Mr. Adams? Five dollars a week to start. Later, if you show aptitude, you could move up to typesetter, or perhaps journalist if you are as adventurous as my niece."

"It sounds suitable," Clay said.

"Can you read and write?"

"Tolerably. My ma taught me. It got so I could read from the Bible without having to say the words out loud. But my writing is more chicken scratch than cursive."

Jerome Stanley chuckled. "You should see mine. My niece writes impeccably, but then she prides herself on doing everything impeccably. It comes from being a natural show-off."

Melanie flushed and said, "Remember what I said about your shins, Uncle."

Ignoring her, Stanley said to Clay, "How is your patience? Do you have a little or a lot?"

"Sir?"

"The counterman has to deal with idiots and chuckleheads on a daily basis. Such as the gent who was in here earlier wanting us to do a story about his pet rat. Or the woman yesterday who wanted me to write an editorial proposing we ban pigs and hogs from the city streets."

"I reckon I can tolerate fools as well as the next man," Clay Adams said.

"Very well, then. I will ask you again. Are you interested in the job? My niece will teach you everything you need to know."

"I'll what?"

"Yes, I would like the job," Clay Adams said. "I only hope I can live up to your trust in me."

Stanley's brown eyes crinkled with amusement. "Son, it's not like you will be guarding a bank. You will be taking ads and subscriptions, and doing the lost and found; those sorts of things."

"And you expect me to show him what to do?" Melanie asked. "On top of all the other responsibilities I have?"

"Oh, my," Jerome Stanley said. "What was I thinking? It should take you all of fifteen minutes. We have hours yet before the next edition goes to press, so you have ample time to write your report on the cave-in."

"I can't thank you enough, Uncle."

Stanley winked at Clay Adams. "When she is polite like that, it usually means she is about to unsheathe her claws. I will take that as a hint to hie me elsewhere and leave you in her razor-sharp hands." He merrily made for a Washington Hand Press.

Clay laughed, earning a pointed glare from Melanie Stanley. "I'm sorry, ma'am. But your uncle is a hoot."

"If by that you mean a wise old owl, that he is. He is also the most scrupulously honest man I have ever known."

"Honesty means a lot to you, does it, ma'am?"

"I cannot abide deceit, Mr. Adams. Which explains why I ferret it out for a living. And why I respect honesty more than any other trait." Melanie looked at him. "Are you honest by nature, Mr. Adams?"

"I like to think so, ma'am."

"That's nice to hear. Otherwise we would not get

along. And please stop calling me 'ma'am.' It makes me sound old."

"If you will call me Clay instead of Mr. Adams, I will call you Miss Stanley instead of ma'am."

"We've only just met and you encourage such familiarity? Why, Mr. Adams, I am scandalized."

Now it was Clay who blushed. "If I have offended you in any way, ma'am, I mean, if I have hurt your feelings somehow, Miss Stanley, I mean—"

"Goodness gracious," she interrupted. "Do you always stutter so? I was teasing, Mr. Adams. Or shall I call you Clay? You can call me Melanie." She opened the gate for him. "Now that you are an employee, you are entitled to come on through."

Clay took a step, and stopped.

"What is the matter? Second thoughts?"

"No, ma— No, Melanie. It's just I have never had a woman hold a door for me before. Even if it is a little bitty one with slats."

Melanie laughed and placed her hand on his arm. "I get it now. You are doing this to entertain me. I must say, your impression of a yokel is remarkable."

Clay Adams wrung his derby and said, "I aim to please you."

While the rest of the staff went about their usual routine, the blond chronicler showed the new clerk how to go about his own. Which forms to use. Where the pencil sharpener was kept. Where the ink was stored. How to determine the rates for a given advertisement. Where to file subscriptions.

At length Melanie glanced at the clock on the wall above her uncle's desk. "Mercy me. Fifteen minutes,

he said, and I've been at this over an hour. How time
does fly."

"I didn't mean to keep you from your work,"
Clay said.

"It's all right. I can still file my report on the cave-
in at the Weaver mine. A new shaft they were digging
collapsed and two workers were hurt. One will be on
crutches for a while. Fortunately no one was killed."

"How long have you worked at this?" Clay asked.

"Here? Or elsewhere? I got my start in St. Louis.
When Uncle Stanley launched the *Courier*, he sent for
me. That was not quite a year ago."

Clay's blue eyes grew thoughtful. "Then you must
know all there is to know about this part of the
country."

"I would not go that far. But yes, I suppose I am
up to date on all that has happened since I arrived."

"That must be a considerable lot," Clay said. "I
would love to talk to you about it. Is there any chance
I can take you to supper later? That is, if you don't
have previous plans."

Melanie tilted her head and regarded him as a person might regard a polka-dot horse. "You are amaz-
ing. Do you know that? Most men take a week or
more to muster their courage, but you kick in the barn
door and barge on in. I don't know whether to be
flattered or worried."

"Ma'am?"

"There you are, doing it again." Melanie moved
toward her desk, but stopped and glanced back. "I
can't make up my mind whether you are exactly as
you appear to be or a wolf in sheep's clothing. But I

will go to supper with you if for no other reason than to figure you out."

"Thank you, ma'—" Clay caught himself. "Thank you, Melanie. I assure you my intentions are honorable."

The newspaper did not keep regular hours. The day started at seven sharp each morning and lasted for as long as was needed to get that day's edition out on the street. Each edition usually ran to several pages, at least one page of which was devoted to advertising. Subscriptions were delivered by wagon. Street urchins sold the bulk of the copies from assigned street corners.

It was past eight that night when Jerome Stanley came up to Clay Adams and clapped him on the back. "Congratulations. You have survived your first day. Head on home if you like."

"Did I do all right?"

"Fine, my boy. Absolutely fine. You were polite, and I can read your handwriting. Now get yourself some rest. Tomorrow is Friday, and Friday is a busy day for us because a lot of businesses only advertise in the weekend edition."

Clay took his derby from the hat rack and turned to Melanie's desk. Her chair was empty.

"She left a while ago," Stanley mentioned. "Something about needing her hair done up."

"Oh." Clay put on his derby and walked out. The street was clogged with a press of humanity. Townsmen in a variety of store-bought garb. Grimy miners in dirty overalls. Gamblers in frock coats, frontiersmen in buckskins, ladies in proper or too-tight dresses depending on their matrimonial status and how they earned a living. Clay observed the ebb and flow until a warm hand fell on his arm.

"Are you as hungry as I am?"

"Melanie!" Clay clasped her fingers and beamed. "I thought maybe you had changed your mind."

"Not on your life." Melanie hooked her arm in his and guided him into the flow of the human current. "I know the perfect place. They serve a delicious New England plate with corned beef and cabbage."

"You are from New England?"

"Heavens, no," Melanie said. "I like exotic dishes. How about you?"

"I'll eat just about anything."

They walked a block, and Melanie asked, "So what exactly did you want to ask me about?"

Clay Adams gestured. "About Bluff City. Whatever you think is important." He paused. "I hear tell that the outlaws hereabouts are as thick as ticks on a hound dog. One bunch has stolen so much money that they're on their way to becoming famous."

Melanie nodded. "The Jesse Stark gang."

Chapter 6

The restaurant not only served New England fare, it was called the New England House. Exceedingly popular, New England food, as it was called, included dishes like corned beef and cabbage, brown bread with a heaping bowl of baked beans, and all kinds of vegetables. Puddings and pies were favorite desserts.

When the majordomo saw Melanie Stanley enter, he fawned over her. He insisted on giving her a table near the window, and then snapped his fingers for a waiter to hurry and wait on them. Even more telling, no sooner were they seated than the owner came out of the kitchen to welcome her and ask how her father was doing and what was new at the newspaper.

When they were alone again, Clay Adams sat back and commented, "You are something of a celebrity, I see."

"I suppose. It comes from being the only female journalist in these parts. Plus, when you are out on the streets every day gathering information, you get to know a lot of people."

"Do you like it here?"

"I love my job. I would never think of doing anything else. There is always something new. One day I am investigating things like the cave-in, the next day I might be delving into a shooting or a robbery."

"Is there much in the way of gunplay in Bluff City?"

Melanie broke a bread stick and took a bite. "There is a lot of crime, period. Boomtowns are always wild and reckless, and Bluff City is one of the wildest. You saw the saloons. There must be twice as many fancy houses. Opium dens thrive in the Chinese section." She pointed the bread stick at him. "How about you?"

"Pardon?"

"Which vice is your cup of tea?"

"I'm partial to a drink and a game of cards now and then," Clay admitted, "but that is about it. How about you?"

Melanie laughed. "I guess I deserved that. But I limit my vices to a fondness for sweets and refusing to have a personal life. I spend nearly all my waking hours working."

"No men friends, then?"

"That is rather personal. But yes, there are a few who find me ravishing," Melanie said breezily, "and one who thinks I belong on a pedestal. But I thought you were more interested in outlaws and the like."

"Isn't everyone?" Clay rejoined. Then he casually said, "Earlier you mentioned something about the Jesse Stark gang. Who are they?"

"The talk of the territory. No one knows how many are in it. Some say fifteen. Some say twenty-five. They strike without warning, take what they want and shoot anyone who interferes. Banks, money shipments, stagecoaches—you name it. Fourteen killings to their credit that we know of."

"They sound like a tough bunch," Clay observed.

"The toughest. Places like Bluff City are magnets for the bad ones." Melanie studied him. "I notice you do not wear a gun."

"A lot of men don't."

"True. But a lot of men do, too, and they are the ones to watch out for. Ruffians and footpads are everywhere."

"I can take care of myself," Clay said. "Besides, you seem to get by just fine, and you are a woman."

"It's precisely because I *am* female that the rougher element tends to leave me alone," Melanie said. "Women are treated with special regard because there are so few of us west of the Mississippi, comparatively speaking."

The waiter brought their food. Melanie had ordered the corned beef and cabbage, Clay the baked beans and brown bread. As he was dipping a piece of bread into the beans, he asked, "This Jesse Stark. How is it the law hasn't thrown a noose around his neck yet?"

"Don't think they haven't tried," Melanie answered. "Three of those fourteen dead the gang is credited with were lawmen."

"Stark is out of Kansas, isn't he?"

"So they say. His early days are a mystery. He might have been born in Missouri. He might have come from Texas. When he first took to the outlaw life, no one can say. He was small potatoes until Whistler's Flat."

"Whistler's Flat?"

"You haven't heard of it? The story goes that Jesse Stark and his old gang tried to rob the bank there. Only Stark and Crooked Nose Neville Baine got away, and Baine was shot while riding off."

"Who is he?" Clay asked while dipping more bread.

"Something of a virtuoso with a pistol. Or he was. No one has seen anything of him since Whistler's Flat. Rumor has it he's dead." Melanie forked some cabbage. "Strange, though."

"What?"

"That he joined the Stark gang. Baine had a string of shootings to his credit but there was no record of him robbing anyone until the incident in Whistler's Flat. I read a few accounts about him when I was in St. Louis. A typical wild-and-woolly longhair except for his face. They say he was kicked by a horse once, and his nose was so terribly out of shape he was a fright to look at." Melanie chewed the cabbage while studying her new acquaintance. "You have a few scars yourself."

"A few."

"That tiny bump on your nose. Broken once?"

"Twice," Clay said, shifting in his chair.

"And that is all you have to show for it? You were lucky."

Clay Adams smiled wryly. "The luckiest man alive, I reckon."

"They lend character. Yours makes you appear a little tough yourself," Melanie said. "Maybe it will help protect you from the real toughs, the troublemakers who pick fights for the fun of it."

Clay was about to respond when spurs jingled and an odd apparition appeared beside their table. The man had a pasty complexion, no chin to speak of, and large, watery eyes. A slouch hat crowned his protruding forehead. He wore a brown vest, and on his right hip was a Starr revolver.

"Deputy Wiggins," Melanie said.

Clay stared at the badge pinned to the vest. His fingers tightened on his spoon.

"How do you do, Miss Stanley," Deputy Wiggins said in a high voice that did not fit his plump build. "I was passing by and saw you through the window."

"Forgotten your manners, have you?"

Wiggins appeared confused, then snatched the slouch hat from his head, revealing a bald pate, except for a ring of crinkly, rust-colored hair that ran from ear to ear. "Sorry. It has been a long day and I'm tired." His watery eyes switched to Clay. "Who is this you're with?"

"Mr. Adams works at the paper."

"I've never seen him before," Deputy Wiggins said.

Melanie smiled sweetly. "Was there something you wanted? Or do you make a habit out of interrupting a lady's meal?"

"If you are referring to the flapjack house yesterday, I just happened to be there."

Her smile still in place, Melanie said, "That must explain the other nineteen or twenty times. Would you care to join us?"

"No, thank you. I must report in. The Stark gang has struck again."

Melanie half rose and waved an arm to get the waiter's attention. "We need another chair here." To Wiggins she said, "You are not going anywhere until you give me the details."

The waiter brought a chair and set it between Clay and Melanie. Deputy Wiggins slid it closer to Melanie and plopped down. Setting his hat on the table, he shifted so he faced her.

"I can never refuse you. What is it you want to know?"

"Everything." Melanie had taken a pencil and pad from her bag and had the pencil poised to write.

"Well, let me see. Four days ago the Stark gang hit Calamity. Rode in whooping and firing their guns in the air and rounded up—"

"Is Calamity a town?" Clay broke in.

Deputy Wiggins gave him the sort of look that implied his question was not appreciated. "Calamity is one of about fifty mining camps higher up in the mountains. A collection of tents, mostly. Got its name last winter when a couple of prospectors were caught in an avalanche."

"What was worth stealing?" Clay asked.

"Not a whole lot. Oh, a few of the prospectors have made strikes. But piddling finds compared to Bluff City."

"Then why was Jesse Stark there?"

"Money. What else? He rounded up the prospectors and made them empty their pockets."

"Hardly sounds like it was worth his while," Clay said.

"Who is telling this? You or me?" Deputy Wiggins demanded. He grinned at Melanie. "There's more. It seems Harve Barker opened a saloon there just last week and—"

"Who is Harve Barker?" Clay asked.

Wiggins let out with an exaggerated sigh. "Keep interrupting me and there will be the devil to pay."

Melanie laughed. "You must excuse his curiosity. He is new to Bluff City." She turned toward Clay. "Barker owns the Bluff City Emporium, the largest and most luxurious saloon in town. He has also set up saloon tents in about half the mining camps. He is well on his way to becoming one of the wealthiest men in the territory."

"I've noticed he is rather fond of you," Deputy Wiggins said.

"Barker is fond of anything in skirts."

"I wish you wouldn't talk like that. It is unbecoming."

"Go on with your account," Melanie said.

"There is not much left. Stark robbed Barker's saloon tent in Calamity. The bartender lost a few teeth when he objected and Stark pistol-whipped him."

Clay Adams raised a hand to his face, but quickly lowered it again. "So how much did Stark end up with?"

"Two thousand, maybe," Deputy Wiggins said.

"Not much for a greedy slug like him," Melanie commented. "Rather brazen, to raid an entire camp. But then, he is becoming more and more bold as time goes by."

"That he is," Deputy Wiggins agreed. "But this time he might have overstepped himself. If I know Harve Barker, he won't take being robbed lying down. He's not the turn-the-other-cheek type."

"So you were up to Calamity?" Melanie asked.

Wiggins nodded. "I tried tracking the outlaws. But

that Jesse Stark is crafty. I lost the trail on a rocky point above the tree line." The deputy gazed out the window, then stood. "I had better be going. You know how Vale is always riding me about dawdling."

"I understand," Melanie said.

The deputy jammed his slouch hat on his head, looked down his nose at Clay and beamed at her. "It was a pleasure, as always. Maybe you and I can go to the theater later this week. That play you like is still being put on."

"Maybe."

Clay watched the plump lawman hurry from the premises. "I half expected him to shoot me."

Melanie grinned. "He's fond of me, no doubt about it. I suppose I don't discourage him because he is one of my best sources."

"You are using him?"

The grin was replaced by a frown. "You make that sound like an accusation. But yes, I am. I justify it by my gender."

"You've lost me," Clay Adams said.

"Only because you aren't female. If you were, you would appreciate how hard it is for a woman to make it on her own in a world ruled by men. It is twice as difficult for me because I am a woman. But I refuse to let that hinder me. I am educated and independent and proud of it. And yes, before you ask, I'm also a suffragist."

"I don't see any reason women can't have the vote," Clay said earnestly. "As for the rest, my own ma had a hard time of it after my pa died because jobs for women are so few. She worked as a seamstress, but she barely earned enough for us to get by."

"Where is she now?" Melanie inquired.

"She died when I was twelve, thank God. If she had been alive to see what I became, it would have broken her heart."

"What a strange thing to say. What were you before you showed up in Bluff City? A patent medicine salesman?"

Clay bent over the baked beans.

"Let me guess," Melanie bantered. "You were a highwayman. Or, better yet, you rode with Jesse Stark." She laughed and, when he did not reply, she said with mock sternness, "You better tell me or I am liable to think you really were a badman."

Clay said slowly, "It's just that I never made as much of myself as my ma would have liked."

"What son or daughter ever does? My father wanted me to marry and raise a passel of grandchildren. He was furious when I decided to work for Uncle Jerome." Melanie hesitated. "As for you, I should think your mother would be proud. You are a fine, upstanding, handsome young man."

Clay recoiled as if she had slapped him.

"What's wrong?" Melanie was bewildered by his reaction.

"You just called me handsome."

"Was I being too forward?"

"No, no, it's not that." Clay gazed at the window, at his reflection. He reached out as if to touch it, then drew his hand back. "No one has ever called me that before. It will take some getting used to."

Chapter 7

Over a week and a half went by. Clay Adams settled into his new job as a clerk for the *Bluff City Courier*. He took a room for rent in the shadow of the bluff. That it happened to be on the very outskirts of Bluff City did not strike any of his coworkers as unusual. Rooms were hard to come by. Nor did they wonder that he had wanted a place where he could also board his horse. Stable fees added up.

The elderly couple who owned the house kept to themselves. They rarely saw their new tenant. The room was at the rear and he always came in the back way.

Clay and Melanie ate supper together nearly every night. If the rest of the *Courier* staff thought anything of it, they kept their thoughts to themselves.

When Clay was not at work and not with Melanie, he made the rounds of the saloons. Nothing unusual there. A lot of men spent a lot of their spare time at watering holes. Clay soon showed a special interest in two: the Bluff City Emporium, owned by Harve Barker, and the Rusty Spittoon, considered to be the worst dive in Bluff City. No decent person, it was commonly held, ever set foot in the Spittoon because of the two-legged catamounts who considered it their private lair.

The proprietor of the Rusty Spittoon, a ferret of a man named Gressel, catered to the mean ones and to those who were not particular about how they acquired their money.

On his first visit to the Spittoon, Clay Adams walked to the bar and asked for a whiskey. He paid no heed to the unfriendly stares fixed on him.

"What have we here?" Gressel asked as he poured. He had greasy black hair and wore an equally greasy apron. "Did you take a wrong turn somewhere, boy?"

"Can't a *man* drink where he wants?" Clay responded.

"Sure. Trouble is, most folks want nothing to do with my place. Look around you. I get the dregs. The kind who would slit your throat for a dollar. The kind who don't wash but once a blue moon and wear their clothes until the clothes fall apart." He smirked at Clay. "Then we have you. Standing there in your clean, store-bought suit and hat. You are as out of place as an Apache at a quilting bee. Scat before someone takes it into their head to chuck you out the window."

"Are you demanding I leave?"

"Hell, no. If you want your skull busted, that's your business. But I sure as hell don't savvy what you're up to."

"Trying to have a drink in peace." Clay carried his whiskey to a table where four human wolves were playing poker. The fifth chair was empty. "Mind if I sit in, gents?"

"Yes," said the scruffiest and biggest of the players,

placing his foot on the empty chair so Clay could not sit.

"My money isn't good enough?"

They stopped playing. Contempt oozed from the big one's pores as he said, "Go away, boy. You are a lamb asking to be shorn."

"Who has the shears? You?"

"Brazen whelp," snapped another. "That there is Skagg Izzard you are talking to. He can break a pup like you over his knee without half trying."

"That would be something to see," Clay Adams said.

Skagg Izzard rose out of his chair and kept on rising until he towered over the table, the players and Clay Adams. "I've had enough of your sass." He balled his huge fists and rapped the knuckles together. "Can you guess what's next?"

"This," Clay said, and threw his whiskey into Skagg's bearded face. The hard case raised his hands to his eyes to clear them, and Clay unleashed an uppercut that started at the floor.

Skagg Izzard tottered. A look of blank amazement came over him as he gingerly rubbed his jaw. "That hurt."

"I'm still waiting for you to break me."

From over at the bar Gressel hollered, "He's poking fun at you, Skagg. Can't you see the son of a bitch thinks he can whip you?"

"I have never been whipped," Skagg Izzard boasted. "Not ever." He brought his fists up and lumbered toward Clay Adams. "You stung me, boy. I'll give you that. But now I'm ready for you. Your tricks won't work again."

"If you say so." Clay feinted to the right, and when Skagg swiveled and threw a punch, Clay dodged, slid in close and brought the heel of his right foot down on the toes of the bigger man's left foot.

Bellowing like a stuck bull, Skagg Izzard lowered his fists and staggered a couple of steps.

Clay went after him. He launched another uppercut. This one rocked Skagg on his heels. Skagg swung an open hand at Clay's ear, but Clay ducked and flicked two swift punches to his gut.

Skagg Izzard grunted and started to fold. He clutched at the table for support, spittle flecking his lips. "I must be dreaming."

"Some dream," Clay said. He drove his forearm into Skagg's stomach clear up to the elbow and Skagg Izzard collapsed like a ruptured water skin, to sprawl on his craggy face and not move.

"I saw it, but I don't believe it!" exclaimed another player.

Clay Adams smoothed his jacket and adjusted his derby, then claimed the empty chair. "Deal me in, gents."

Gressel came around the bar, walked up to Skagg and nudged him. "Hell in a basket." He leaned on the table and appraised Clay through slitted eyes. "Why here, mister? Of all the whiskey mills in Bluff City, why this one?"

"Don't let the clothes fool you," Clay said. "This is what I'm used to."

Gressel cocked his head. "Who *are* you?"

"Someone who likes a whiskey and a game of cards now and then. Someone who will come here when he wants and leave when he wants and mind his own business while he is here." Clay slid a wallet from his jacket pocket. "Bring me a glass of water."

"Water?"

"You heard me."

If Gressel was surprised, he was more so when Clay Adams accepted the glass and upended it over Skagg Izzard. The big man sat up and shook his shaggy mane, drops flying every which way. Izzard looked at the glass and then at Clay Adams. "I could shoot you."

"But you won't."

"Why won't I?"

"For the same reason you didn't go for your gun when I hit you. You have a fair streak, and I respect that."

"I didn't go for my gun because I didn't think I would need it, as puny as you are," Skagg said. He sat on the floor a while longer, his bushy brows puckered. Finally he said, "You sure are a strange one, but I like you. I reckon I won't kill you for now."

"I'm obliged." Clay patted the table. "Why don't you join us? I'll give you a chance to take my money."

An hour later Clay Adams left the Rusty Spittoon with twelve dollars more than when he went in. Bluff City's night life was in full, riotous revel. The churchgoing folk had retired for the day, leaving the streets to their less restrained brethren.

Clay walked three blocks east. He turned left, rounded a corner and ducked into the recessed doorway to a hardware store that was closed. His back to the door, he slid his hand under his jacket. He held it there until he was satisfied no one was following him, then he emerged onto the street.

That had been ten nights ago. On this particular evening, Clay Adams was in the heart of Bluff City. Here the buildings were grander, the pedestrians better dressed. The Bluff City Emporium was ablaze with light. Fine carriages constantly pulled up out front and disgorged occupants dressed in the height of fashion. The doorman wore a purple uniform. Purple, it was widely known, was the owner's favorite color.

Harve Barker liked to say that it took money to make money. He spent it with a complete disregard for how much he was spending. He had reaped a fortune and was growing richer. Vice was his trade. He offered for purchase every sin known to man, and then some.

His establishment was the premier gambling den not only in Bluff City but in that part of the Rockies. Paintings of naked women adorned the vaulted ceiling, cast in intimate relief by large chandeliers. The walls were paneled in mahogany and the floor was thick with plush carpet. The ground floor, which covered an entire city block, was devoted to games of chance, everything from poker to faro to roulette. In the galleries were lavish suites where those so inclined could indulge carnal tastes. Higher up were private rooms for private games and other doings.

Nightly the Bluff City Emporium was filled to overflowing. The rich and the almost rich came as a matter of course simply because it was "the" place to be. But many with far less money also dared its doors to spend an excited hour or three wallowing in luxury. Most went home broke, but considered the time spent well squandered.

The patrons were generally carefree and friendlier

than at, say, the Rusty Spittoon. Unlike some gambling dens, where fights and knifings and shootings were common, the Emporium was touted as the safest nightspot in town. Barker made it known that anyone who started trouble would be banned, and no one wanted to be banned from the Emporium. That, and his staff, which included the toughest bouncers anywhere, kept the Emporium largely violence-free.

Clay Adams nodded at the doorman and strode in with his derby at a jaunty angle. Hooking his thumbs in his vest, he made the rounds of the tables. He smiled at everyone and offered greetings if greetings were offered to him. His meandering eventually brought him to where the best of the professional gamblers and those with a lot of money to lose played high-stakes poker. The section was roped off from the rest of the floor. Admittance was by Harve Barker's invitation only. His private club, was how the people on the street referred to it.

Each night the purple rope was lined with gawkers who would point out the rich and the powerful to one another, and often applaud when large pots were won.

Clay joined the gawkers. He contrived to stand near the table reserved for Harve Barker and the select few who nightly joined Barker for friendly games that lasted well into the wee hours of the morning.

Barker always sat with his back to the wall in a chair that was more like a throne. A purple-clad minion was always at his elbow, ready to supply his every whim. Barker's age was hard to gauge. He looked to be in his mid to late thirties. His brown hair was fluffed in a crest, his chin clean-shaven. His suit was the pinnacle of tailored artistry. Gold rings gleamed on several fingers. His pocket watch and fob were gold.

Clay recognized two of the other players. One was the president of the First Bank of Bluff City, the other the owner of a prosperous mercantile. Neither showed the least interest in the onlookers.

Taking a quarter eagle from his vest pocket, Clay began flipping and catching it. He flipped it over and over, seemingly not paying much attention to what he was doing, so it appeared to be by accident when he flipped the coin high and missed, and it fell inside the purple rope and rolled toward the exclusive table.

Almost instantly, the man in the purple uniform at Harve Barker's elbow moved to pick up the coin and return it.

Clay said thanks more loudly than was necessary.

Play at the table had not been interrupted, but Harve Barker's gaze did drift toward the rope. Interest animated him when he saw Clay. Barker leaned toward his purple-clad minion and said something.

The minion came back to Clay. "If you would be so kind, sir, Mr. Barker would like to talk to you." He unhooked the purple rope.

"Me?" Clay said.

"Yes, sir. You."

"What for?"

"Mr. Barker did not take me into his confidence, sir," the man said. "Now please, if you would be so kind."

Clay followed the man over. The other players gave him a curious scrutiny but did not greet him.

Harve Barker was dealing. Pausing, he smiled and

said, "Mr. Adams. A pleasure to make your acquaintance."

"You know who I am?"

Barker's smile was lordly. "I make it a point to know most everything there is to know where Bluff City is concerned. For instance, the day you arrived you were hired at the *Courier*. Jerome tells me you are a diligent worker and have shown an interest in becoming a journalist. Or should I say, *in* a journalist."

"Sir?" Clay said.

Harve Barker looked up. "We'll let that pass for the moment. Right now, how would you like to sit in?"

Clay shifted his weight from one foot to the other. "I am afraid the stakes are too high for me."

"Well then, sit anyway, and we can talk while I play. Charles, bring my guest a chair."

The man in purple scurried to obey. Clay sat with the derby in his lap and commented, "This is quite an honor."

"Is it?" Barker finished dealing and leaned back. "I pull on my pants one leg at a time, the same as you do."

The president of the First Bank of Bluff City chuckled. "Modesty from you, Harve? I didn't think you had any."

"Next he'll start attending church," said the owner of the mercantile, and the players all laughed except for the professional gambler.

Barker smiled a polite smile while studying his cards. "Tell me, Mr. Adams. Where did you live before you came to our fair city?"

"Here and there," Clay said.

"How did you make your living?"

"This and that."

"I see. It's none of my business." Barker placed the cards facedown on the table and turned in his chair. "But there is something that *is* my business. Or should I say *someone*? A person I am quite fond of. And I do not take kindly to your intrusion. I do not take kindly to it at all."

"Would this have anything to do with Melanie Stanley?" Clay asked.

"It has everything to do with the delightful Miss Stanley, yes," Harve Barker said. "You will stop seeing her or I will have every bone in your body broken."

Chapter 8

Harve Barker waited for a reply. He drummed his fingers on the table. He arched an eyebrow. Finally he snapped, "Didn't you hear me?"

"I thought maybe you were pulling my leg," Clay Adams said.

"In case you were not aware of the fact, I have a personal interest in the beauteous Miss Stanley."

Clay flicked a piece of lint from his jacket. "I seem to recollect Deputy Wiggins saying as how you were fond of her."

"So you do know? Yet you have gone out with her anyway."

"Like you say, Melanie is right pretty," Clay said. "What man wouldn't leap at the chance to escort her out and about?"

"You are not paying attention," Harve Barker responded. "Melanie Stanley is mine to court, not yours. I have been wooing her since she arrived. God willing, she will one day become more than a good friend. Much more."

"I was thinking the same thing," Clay said. "She has a way about her I admire. A man could do a lot worse."

Barker resumed drumming his fingers. "I'm wise to

you now. You are doing this on purpose. You are trying to get my goat."

"All I am trying to do," Clay said, "is savvy why you think you have staked a claim to her. She's not wearing your ring, is she? She's not even your betrothed."

The other players had laid down their cards. They were listening but trying to act as if they were not. The only one bold enough to openly stare at Barker and Clay was the gambler, who was grinning.

"I don't need to propose to stake a claim, as you so quaintly call it," Harve Barker said flatly. "The mere fact she and I have gone out together a number of times is enough. Ask anyone in Bluff City and they will tell you Melanie Stanley is my woman."

"Does she know she is yours?"

"That's irrelevant," Barker said. "Her feelings are not the issue. The issue is you infringing where you are not wanted."

"She hasn't beaten me off with a broom yet," Clay said.

Harve Barker became a portrait in marble. When he spoke, he did so biting off each syllable as if it were a piece of jerky. "Enough of this. I will say it plain so you will understand. Before I do, let me make it clear to you that I am not a man to be trifled with. Nor do I have a forgiving nature. Continue to impose and the consequences are on your shoulders."

"I do believe that was a threat."

"Construe it as you will," Barker said. "The important thing is that you have gone on your last supper date with Melanie Stanley." He turned back to the table. "Our talk is at an end. Charles, see him off."

Clay Adams slowly stood and put on his derby. But instead of going with Charles, he leaned on the table. "You have had your say, Barker, so now I will have mine."

Harve Barker was too surprised to take exception.

"I have heard about you. I have heard how you lord it over everyone. That you do whatever you please and get away with it because you are the most powerful man in Bluff City. Most people are scared of you. Most would tuck tail if you told them to. But I'm here to stay, and I'll continue to see Melanie for as long as she lets me." Clay straightened and smiled and touched the derby's brim. "I thank you for the warning, though. It's always good to know who your enemies are."

The gambler's quiet laughter followed Clay as he merged with the throng and made his way to the ornate bar that ran the length of the north side of the palatial room. He ordered a whiskey, chugged it in two gulps, and ordered another. He watched the mirror behind the bar and saw Harve Barker storm from the private section to a flight of stairs that led to the galleries. Shortly after, the gambler rose and came to the bar. Clay pretended not to notice him.

"Buy you another, Mr. Adams?"

"I'd better not," Clay said. "But I thank you for the offer."

The gambler studied him from under a wide-brimmed black hat. The gambler's frock coat, his pants, his boots—they were all black. Only his frilled shirt was white. He had sandy hair with wisps of gray at the temples, and gray eyes. "That was something to see. It's not every day someone has the grit to stand up to Harve Barker. Be on your guard."

"The cock of the walk, is he?"

"Son, you have no notion of the hornet's nest you've stirred up," the gambler said. "He will make his move when he is good and ready, but mark me, he will make one, and it will be permanent."

Clay pursed his lips. "Barker will go that far?"

"He's no bluff," the gambler answered. "A whisper in the right ear, enough money changes hands, and you disappear."

"Why are you warning me? You must be an acquaintance of his to play at his personal table."

The gambler shrugged. "I know him, sure, but that doesn't mean I like him. I do like taking his money, though." He held out a slender, pale hand. "Wesley Oaks, but you can call me Wes."

Clay shook. "Been in Bluff City long?"

"About half a year now," Wes revealed. "The smart gamblers go where the money is to be had, and Bluff City is bursting at the seams with jackasses who think they know how to play cards." He paused. "How about you? Are you a gambling man?"

"I used to be but I've turned over a new leaf. You could say I've turned over a whole tree's worth of late."

"Any of those new leaves have to do with wearing a six-shooter on your hip?" Wesley Oaks asked.

"I'm not the only man in town who doesn't," Clay evaded the query.

"True. But you are one of the few who wears a shoulder rig. Don't look so surprised. In my line of work I have to be able to spot hide-outs. My point, though, is that those others who don't go heeled don't have Harve Barker out to nail their hides to the wall. It won't be him who pays you a visit. It will be men who are good with guns and aren't bashful about using them."

Now it was Clay who shrugged. "Better now than later, and better I know it is coming than wonder if the stories about him are true."

"I saw you flip that coin," the gambler said. "I saw you miss it. Nicely done. I hope your lady is worth the risk."

"Have you ever wanted to crawl into a woman's heart and stay there?" Clay bluntly asked.

A pained expression came over Wesley Oaks. "Yes," he said throatily. "As a matter of fact, I have."

"How did it work out, if that is not too personal?"

"She let me in and I stayed there for six years," Wesley said. "The six best years of my life. I wasn't a gambler then. I pushed a plow for a living. I married that gal. We bought a farm. One day she was out in the barn milking the cows, and when she bent down to pick up the stool a hornet stung the cow she was about to milk and the cow kicked her. Crushed her head like you would crush a grape. Can you imagine? A stupid damn cow killed the woman I loved. I shot it, after." He stopped and looked down at himself. "Why in hell am I telling you this?"

"I'm sorry for your loss," Clay said. "That woman of yours, she was to you as Melanie is to me."

"Have you told the young lady how you feel?"

"Not yet. I figure I shouldn't throw my loop until I'm sure the mare is mine to rope."

Wesley Oaks chuckled. "I like you, son. You are welcome to sit in on my games any time you want."

Clay was smiling when he left the Emporium half an hour later. He bent his steps toward the outskirts of town, and his apartment. He made a point of glancing at every storefront window he passed, and had gone a couple of blocks when he spotted the three men who were following him. He did not let on that he knew they were there but continued strolling along as if he did not have a care in creation.

The three held well back until the center of town, with its many streetlamps, was behind them, and Clay was passing through a quiet—and dark—neighborhood. They began to narrow the gap.

The trio wore townsman's clothes. Bowlers crowned their heads. Brogans were their favored footwear. They were perfectly ordinary, except that each was a brawny husky with shoulders as wide as a buffalo's and a neck as thick as a bull's.

Clay walked faster. He knew the area, having been through it many times on his way to and from work. Around the next corner was a house under construction. He took that corner, and the instant he was out of sight he broke into a run.

Stacks of lumber offered plenty of places to hide, but he was not trying to shake his shadowers. He was after a suitable board or a tool.

The frame and the floor had been erected. Lying on the floor near the edge was a three-foot length of wood. Hefting it, Clay smiled. He moved into the inky shadow of a stack of planking, and waited.

The three men were abreast of the lot when they stopped and glanced about in confusion.

"Where did he get to?" one wondered.

"He must have seen us and run off, but he can't have gotten far," said the second. "If we hurry we can catch him."

The third was the smart one. He proved it by saying, "Hold your horses. It could be that is exactly what he wants us to think. It could be that's exactly what he wants us to do." The man motioned at the construction site. "I say we check there first."

"What if you're wrong?" said the first man. "Then he gets away, and Mr. Barker has us strung up by our thumbs."

"I have an idea," the second man said. "I'll go on ahead while the two of you look around. If you find him, give a holler. If I find him, I'll trail him to where he is staying and come fetch you."

The two who were staying separated and entered the lot from different directions. One drew a short-barreled pistol from under his jacket. The other produced a dagger. Judging by how they carried themselves, and how silently they moved, they had a lot of experience at this sort of thing.

Clay might as well have been carved from wood. He did not move, did not twitch, did not blink. He held the club shoulder-high, his muscles bunched.

The thug with the pistol crept closer. He was staring at the frame, not the stack, and it was doubtful he knew what felled him.

Stepping into the open, Clay swung his club. It caught the man across the back of the head and the man's legs folded as if they were soggy cheese. Clay whirled, but the man with the dagger had not heard. Crouching, Clay stalked him. This one was more alert.

The man repeatedly glanced back. Taking him by surprise would be difficult.

Then Clay saw a wheelbarrow filled with dirt. Dropping to his knees and elbows behind it, he tapped the bottom of the wheelbarrow with his club. It was half a minute before a pair of brogans crept into view. Clay waited, and when the brogans were next to the wheelbarrow, he heaved erect and swung.

It should have worked. By rights, Clay should have knocked the hired cutthroat senseless. But the man happened to see him as he rose, and ducked. Clay was thrown off balance. Before he could recover, the man kicked at the wheelbarrow and sent it toppling against Clay.

Clay tried to spring to safety but slipped. He landed on his back with the heavy wheelbarrow across his legs and dirt spilling across his stomach and chest.

Voicing a howl of triumph, the man with the dagger lunged, spearing the double-edged tip at Clay's chest. Clay blocked it with the club. But he had only delayed the inevitable. Pinned as he was, he was as good as slain.

The man wielding the dagger thought so, too. Grinning, he skipped to one side and then the other. "I aim to whittle you done to the bone," he snarled.

"Don't you mean kill me?" Clay stalled.

"We're to persuade you, not feed you to the worms," the man revealed. "You don't rate higher than a petty nuisance."

"Those sound like Barker's words."

"Who?" The man smirked. "I've never heard that name before. But the gent we work for did want us to make sure you got his message."

"Barker's words again," Clay said. By now he had a handful of dirt, but he wanted the man closer.

"A few weeks laid up in bed might convince you to leave well enough be," the man related.

"When you see him," Clay said, "tell him it will take more than cheap toughs to scare me off."

"Cheap, am I? For that I'll cut your leg so you walk with a limp the rest of your days."

The man bent toward him, and Clay threw the dirt. With a bark of anger the man backed away and rubbed at his eyes. He was still rubbing when Clay reared and raised the club. "Don't forget to give your boss my message." His blow was precise and powerful.

No outcries had split the night. No lamps had been lit in adjacent homes. Clay bore left at the street. He held onto the club until he had gone far enough to feel it was no longer needed.

The claybank was dozing when Clay arrived at his apartment. Slipping inside, he inserted his key. His room was as dark as the bottom of a well. Fumbling with the lamp, he got it lit and adjusted the wick.

"About time you showed up."

Startled, Clay spun. He started to reach under his jacket but froze at the sight of a battered badge on the intruder's shirt. "Who are you? How did you get in here? What do you want?"

"Who I am should be obvious," the man replied, tapping his badge. He appeared to be in his fifties and had an air of weariness about him. "Getting in was easy. Your landlord gave me the spare key. As for why I'm here, that should be obvious, too."

"I must be stupid, then," Clay said.

"No, but you could very well soon be dead."

Chapter 9

"If you are fixing to gun me down I would like to know why."

"It's not me you have to watch out for," the lawman said. He smiled and held out his hand. "But I'm getting ahead of myself. I'm Marshal Vale. Tom Vale. You've met a deputy of mine, I believe. Deputy Wiggins."

"Pleased to meet you." Clay took the other chair and set his derby on the small table. "But I don't quite follow your meaning."

"Don't you?" Marshal Vale said. "When you make an enemy, you don't make puny ones, do you? Harve Barker isn't a weak sister. He thinks he is God Almighty but acts more like Satan."

"How did you find out so fast?"

"About half an hour ago a friend of mine came to see me," Marshal Vale said. "Seems he had taken a shine to you and doesn't want you back-shot."

"This friend have a handle?"

"Wesley Oaks." Marshal Vale tiredly rubbed his eyes. "He and I go back a ways. When he vouches for someone, I know that someone would do to ride the river with."

"I appreciate the compliment."

"I'm not done. Baiting Barker was stupid. You should have kept your mouth shut and quietly gone on seeing Miss Stanley instead of bringing things to a head."

Clay said, "I can take care of myself."

"Sure you can. Every hombre thinks the same. But the Wild Bill Hickoks of this world are few and far between, and it would take a man with Hickok's ability to stand up to a bastard like Harve Barker."

"Am I to take it you don't much care for the man?"

"Barker is poison. He does whatever he wants whenever he wants and crushes anyone who stands in his way. He will crush you over Miss Stanley, and drink a toast after you are dead."

"He will try," Clay said. "But I still don't get exactly why you have paid me a visit."

"Is there any chance I can talk you into leaving Bluff City?"

Clay Adams gazed out the window. "Not a chance in hell," he said quietly. "I haven't done anything wrong."

Marshal Vale sighed, then scratched his side. "I figured as much. Then the best I can do is give you my word that, whatever happens, I will deal with you fairly. I am always fair. Ask anyone."

"If you don't mind my saying, Wiggins seems a poor choice for a deputy," Clay remarked.

"There you go again. Sometimes it's best to keep certain notions to ourselves," the lawman said. "Wiggins has his faults, but who among us doesn't? He has his uses, too, not the least of which is that he takes his job seriously and I can count on him to always do what I ask him to do."

"Speaking of your job," Clay said, "how is it a town marshal sends a deputy up into the mountains to a mining camp to investigate a robbery? Isn't that rightly the county sheriff's job?"

"That it is," Marshal Vale agreed. "Only the sheriff went and turned in his badge and lit out for California. Bluff City never was much to his liking. He preferred the kind of town where the only excitement a lawman has is riding his rocking chair. Anyway, until an election can be held, the town council asked me to sort of fill in where I can, which is why I sent Wiggins to Calamity. But I would have sent him anyway."

"Why is that?"

"My job is to catch lawbreakers, and Jesse Stark is the biggest lawbreaker in these parts. He robbed the First Bank of Bluff City once, right under my nose. That's a humiliation I could have done without."

"You sure seem decent enough for a badge toter," Clay commented.

The marshal grinned. "And you sure say the damnedest things." He rose and stretched. "Well, I've said my piece. I need to catch a few hours of shut-eye so I'll be going. If the next time I see you is in the morgue, don't say I didn't warn you about being too pigheaded for your own good."

"I'll keep that in mind," Clay said dryly. "Thanks for the visit. And if you hear anything new about Jesse Stark, I would be obliged if you passed it on."

Vale had taken a step but stopped. "What on earth is Stark to you?"

"Didn't Wes tell you I work at the *Courier*?"

"As a clerk, I understand."

"I won't be a clerk forever."

Marshal Vale scratched himself again. "Mr. Adams, you worry me more and more. Having Harve Barker for an enemy is bad enough. Nosing after Jesse Stark's doings is worse. If you're trying to get yourself killed, you will likely succeed."

Clay Adams considered that, then said, "Marshal, do you believe in miracles?"

"How your mind works," Marshal Vale said. "I'm not all that religious, so I can't rightly say I do or I don't."

"Let me try a different way then," Clay said. "Do you believe in second chances?"

"We take all kinds of chances in life, son. Which particular chance are you talking about?"

"At living," Clay said.

"If you want to live, stay away from the likes of Harve Barker and Jesse Stark," the lawman advised.

"I would if I could. But you see, I was different once. A lot different than how you see me. I didn't much like what I had become but I didn't see how I could change, me being as I was."

"You are confusing me more and more."

"It's just that life gave me a second chance. I don't have to be who I was. I can live as I choose. I can do what I want. And I want to do it right this time."

"I'm all for doing things right," Marshal Vale said. "But what does all of that have to do with Barker and Stark?"

"Barker likes to boss people around, to tell them what they can and can't do. But my life is my own and no one is going to tell me how to live it. I won't let anyone spoil my second chance, no matter how rich and powerful they are."

"I respect your sentiments."

Clay Adams did not appear to hear and went on in that quiet manner of his. "The way I see it, there are two trails each of us can take. One is what they call the straight and narrow. The other is the wild and woolly. But maybe wild and bloody is a better way to describe it. I was on that trail once. I hated it and I hated myself, but I was stuck. Then came the miracle, and now I can give up the old ways if I want to. If I truly and really want to."

"That part I can understand. I think."

"If I back down to Barker, if I show yellow, then the miracle was for nothing. I won't have that. I won't have my life be worthless. But at the same time, if I stand up to him, I might need to be the me I don't want to be anymore."

Marshal Vale scratched his head this time. "Now you have cut the line and cast me adrift, son. I have no idea what in hell you are talking about."

Clay looked at him. "Maybe there is no getting away from the past. Maybe it always comes back, whether we want it to or not."

Vale gave the younger man a searching scrutiny. "You sure are a puzzlement if ever I met one. But I see why you impressed Wes. If I can be of any help, you let me know, hear?"

Clay Adams let the lawman out. After he closed the door he leaned his forehead against it and said, "God help me. What if the old urges come back? What if there is no escape?"

*   *   *

Melanie Stanley liked to eat breakfast at a small restaurant a block from the *Courier*. Her favorite was oatmeal with sugar and milk, and she had just started to eat when someone sank into the seat across from her without asking. "Well, this is a surprise."

Harve Barker was, as always, the pinnacle of sartorial splendor. But his face was pinched and drawn, and his eyes were quartz prisms. "Melanie."

"Can this be? The notorious night owl, up before noon?" Melanie poised her spoon over the oatmeal. "What has brought you out and about so early?"

"You have," Harve Barker said.

Melanie smiled. "I am touched. You got up just to have breakfast with me? I must say, you have kept your romantic nature well hidden until now."

"We need to talk, my dear."

Dipping the spoon into the oatmeal, Melanie asked, "About what?"

"Your betrayal."

The spoon stopped halfway to Melanie's mouth. "I beg your pardon?"

"Did you think I wouldn't find out about you and that clerk?" Barker stressed the last word so that the profession of clerking sounded like a job fit for half-wits. "About all the time you spend together? About the nights he has walked you home?"

Melanie set the spoon by the bowl, placed her elbows on the table, and laced her fingers together. "Who I see, and when, and what I do with them, is my own affair."

"I respectfully disagree," Barker said. "I have made

no secret of my interest in you. Everyone in Bluff City knows my intentions."

"Everyone in Bluff City can think what they want," Melanie said. "You and I are friends. That is all we have ever been."

"I was under the impression we were closer than that," Harve Barker said.

"You were mistaken."

Barker gazed out the window at the carriage that had brought him. It cost more than most people earned in a year. "I see. I can't tell you how disappointed I am to hear you say that. There isn't a woman anywhere who wouldn't relish my attention."

"Friends," Melanie stressed.

"This clerk is something more?"

"You overstep yourself."

Barker swung toward her. "He must be. Why else did he have the gall to confront me last night?"

Melanie's fingers came unraveled. "He did *what*?"

"You haven't heard? I should imagine it is the talk of the town by now. Your clerk came into the Emporium and mocked me to my face in front of some of my friends. He told me you are his."

"I don't believe it."

Harve Barker sniffed. "So now I am a liar as well as misguided? It appears I have misjudged you, rather severely, I am afraid. You are not the innocent I took you for. You trifle with men like any common—"

"Be careful," Melanie said. "Be very careful." Her hand closed on the spoon as if it were a knife. "It isn't my innocence that irritates you. It is what you once called my willful nature. I live my life as I see fit, and I am answerable to no one for my actions. Certainly to no man."

"You need to learn your place in this world."

Melanie's eyes flashed fire. "That's what this is really about. A woman's place. Not just mine but every woman's. You can't stand the thought that women want lives of their own."

"Let's not start that again," Harve Barker said.

"Yes, we have had this argument before, haven't we?" Melanie said. "And it always ends the same. You refuse to admit I am right and I refuse to be less than I can be. If that's willful, so be it."

"What about Clay Adams?"

"What about him?" Melanie rejoined. "I enjoy his company. He is bright and he is earnest and he never treats me like I am his property."

Barker pushed back his chair. "I might as well go. This is getting us nowhere."

"Yes. Go. Go and never impose on me again. Whatever we had, whatever friendship we shared, is over. I want nothing more to do with you."

"It's not that easy."

"Sure it is," Melanie said. "You walk out that door and never look back. In a few weeks or a few months you will find someone else. A woman willing to be ground under your boot heels. A woman who doesn't think for herself. A woman you can wear on your arm like you wear rings on your fingers."

"That was uncalled for," Barker said. "And harsh."

"The truth usually is."

Avoiding her gaze, Harve Barker rose. "Very well. When you are in one of your moods talking is pointless. I'll leave if that is what you want. But you have not heard the last from me. Neither has your clerk friend."

"You leave him be, Harve."

The door closed behind him. Melanie picked up the spoon and dipped it in the oatmeal, then set it down again. She fiddled with the tablecloth, and when the clatter of the carriage faded, she rose, paid for her meal, and hurried out.

The *Courier* staff was busy with various duties. Jerome Stanley was at his desk, lighting his pipe. Clay Adams was at the front counter, rifling through a pile of subscription forms.

"What on earth did you think you were doing?"

Clay did not stop rifling. "Good morning to you, too, Miss Stanley. I trust you slept well?"

Melanie came around the counter to stand next to him. "Harve Barker paid me a visit this morning. Are you insane? He is the most dangerous man in these parts."

"He's second on the list."

"Quit quibbling and answer me. Why did you brace him? Why did you tell him I am your woman?"

Clay looked up. "You are?" He grinned broadly. "I would like to take credit but I can't."

Before they could say more, a cloud of aromatic pipe smoke wreathed them. "Whatever you two are bickering about can wait," Jerome Stanley said. "The payroll to the Cavendish Silver Mine was stolen last night. Jesse Stark's bunch again. I want the two of you to find out all you can and get back to me in time for today's edition."

"What?" Clay Adams said.

"The two of us?" Melanie asked almost in the same heartbeat.

"Clay wants to be a reporter, doesn't he? And you, dear niece, are the best I have, which makes you the most qualified to teach him." Jerome Stanley puffed on his pipe. "Off you go, and for God's sake, watch yourselves. Stark should be long gone by now, but you never know. If he gets his hands on you, there's no telling what he will do."

Chapter 10

The mud wagon was stifling hot and thick with dust. The vice president of the Greater Bank of Bluff City could not stop coughing.

Clay Adams did not mind the dust or the heat. He was used to a lot worse. The mud wagon was climbing yet another steep grade on its way to the Cavendish mine when he turned to Melanie Stanley. "You don't mind being bounced up and down until your teeth rattle?"

Melanie grinned. "It comes with the job. And no, I don't mind at all. I will do whatever it takes to get news. It's what I do."

The vice president coughed some more. He had covered his mouth and nose with a handkerchief but it did not help. "This is awful. Just awful. I wish Mr. Winslow were here so he could handle it."

Clay arched an eyebrow at Melanie. "Winslow?"

"The Greater Bank's president. He is off in St. Louis on business and won't be back for two weeks yet, so Mr. Franks, here, has to fill in for him."

The vice president nodded. A spindly man with bony knuckles and knobby knees that pressed against his too-tight pants, he whined, "It's not fair. A disaster like this falling on my shoulders."

"The payroll was robbed, Mr. Franks," Melanie said. "If you ask me, it is not much of a calamity. Your bank is the second largest in Bluff City. It can absorb the loss."

"That's not the point, Miss Stanley," Franks said. "We don't want anyone to think we can't safeguard their money. Nervous depositors lead to a run, and a run on a bank can lead to ruin."

"But the Cavendish mine is responsible for getting the payroll from the bank to the mine," Melanie noted.

"You know that and I know that, but most people do not," Franks said worriedly. "As sure as I am sitting here, they will blame the bank. Then there is Sam Cavendish. That ornery old coot has been threatening to take his business to the First Bank of Bluff City, and this might be the shove he needs."

Again Melanie explained. "Sam Cavendish was prospecting down in Arizona when he heard about the silver on Bluff Mountain. He wasn't here a week when he struck it big. Now he owns the third largest mine around, right after the Jones Silver Mine and the Barker Silver Mine."

"Harve Barker owns his own mine?"

"He won it in a high-stakes poker game," Melanie said. "The previous owner couldn't hold his liquor. One night he had a hand he was sure couldn't be beat and bet the deed to his mine. He lost."

"If Barker had his way," Franks mentioned, "he would own all the businesses in town, if not the entire territory. I have never seen anyone so money hungry.

The man has bought every square acre that isn't spoken for."

"You sound like you don't much care for him," Clay remarked.

"I never implied any such thing," Franks said, "and I will take an oath to that effect if you should spread word that I have."

The mud wagon came to a switchback. The crack of the driver's whip was like the crack of a pistol. The wagon swayed and jounced, and it was all they could do to stay in their seats. Beyond the switchback was a meadow, and for a short span they rode in relative comfort. Then another grade canted the wagon bed, and Clay and Melanie were thrown against one another. Clay quickly pulled back, and she smiled.

Franks was clinging to the door. "I hate mountain travel. Given my druthers, I would much rather be at my desk."

"I've been meaning to ask," Clay said. "How much was the payroll for?"

"A few hundred short of twenty thousand dollars," Franks disclosed. "The biggest payroll for the mine ever. Sam Cavendish added a third shift a month ago."

"What's he like, this Cavendish?"

Franks smiled. "You will find out for yourself soon enough, Mr. Adams. We should arrive at the mine in about half an hour."

The prediction proved true. Several plank buildings were clustered on a broad bench within a few hundred feet of a dark cavity that marked the entrance. Workers were bustling about. One building bore a large sign that read CAVENDISH SILVER MINE. TRESPASSERS WILL BE SHOT. On the porch stood a grizzled older man bellowing orders. He wore a flannel shirt and overalls that had not seen soap and water in a month of Sundays, and a straw hat with a split brim.

"That there is Cavendish," Franks said. "Be careful he doesn't bite your head off."

"He doesn't even know me," Clay said.

"That's never stopped him before."

Another man, his rotund bulk clothed in ill-fitting clothes, scampered to meet the mud wagon. Nervously wringing his hands, he displayed a mouth full of yellow teeth. "Mr. Franks! Grand of you to get here so quickly. Mr. Cavendish is fit to be tied. He expected someone sooner."

Franks had the look of a man who had swallowed a cactus. "He is aware the bank president is out of town?"

"Oh, yes, indeed." The man bowed slightly to Melanie and said, "As always, ma'am, a pleasure. The last time you were up here was when you did that series on mine owners."

"You have a good memory, Mr. Teckler."

"It's why I'm the company bookkeeper," Teckler said.

Sam Cavendish was striding toward them and glowering fiercely. "It's about time you showed up," he lit into Franks. "Some bank you work for!"

"We take pride in the services we offer," Franks answered. "Just as we take pride in helping our friends."

"I may be many things," Sam Cavendish said, "but gullible is not one of them. The only friend a bank has is the money in its vault. And the only reason you are here is because you are afraid I will switch from your bank to that other one." Franks went to speak but Cavendish hushed him. "We'll chew the fat directly. Right now I must greet my other guests."

"You remember me, then?" Melanie said.

"I would have to be six feet under to forget a fine filly like you, girl." Cavendish switched his attention to Clay. "Is this one with you or is he looking for work? I already have one dandy working for me"—he pointed at Teckler—"and I don't need another."

"I work for the *Courier*, sir," Clay said.

"They sent two of you? One would have been enough. All we know is that Jesse Stark is to blame. His gang opened fire on my boys as they were coming up the switchback. Blasted five of them from the saddle. The sixth was hit but crawled into a deadfall. He saw Stark—saw them take the strongbox—so there is no doubt who to blame."

Melanie bestowed her most ravishing smile. "We would very much like to talk to him."

"He's in the infirmary," Cavendish said, pointing again. "The sawbones says he'll live but he won't be on his feet for a month or more. The slug nicked his lung." As an afterthought he added, "The guard's name is Ward."

The infirmary consisted of three cots and a medicine cabinet. The wounded guard lay on the middle cot with his eyes closed and a blanket pulled to his waist. Half his chest was swathed in bandages and he was ungodly pale.

"Maybe we should come back," Clay suggested.

"Nonsense." Melanie lightly shook the guard's arm and, when he did not come around, she pinched him.

Ward's eyes snapped open and he looked about him in confusion. "What is it? Who are you?"

Melanie introduced them. "If you don't mind, we would like to ask you a few questions about the robbery."

Ward weakly fluttered his fingers. "Not now, lady. I'm awful tired and I hurt like hell."

"We've come all the way from Bluff City," Melanie said pleasantly. "Surely you can spare a minute or two."

"Talk to Mr. Cavendish," Ward said. "I have already told him all there is to know." He closed his eyes.

"Please, Mr. Ward," Melanie said, placing a hand on the man's shoulder. "We understand you saw the whole thing. What can you tell us about Stark and his men? How many were there? Can you describe Stark for me? Is there anything you did not tell Cavendish that you have remembered since?"

"Go away," Ward said.

"Details are important," Melanie persisted. "The more the people of the territory know about Stark's wild bunch, the sooner the outlaws will be taken into custody." She gently shook him when he did not reply. "Mr. Ward?"

The door opened and in walked a stoop-shouldered man in a black suit, carrying a black bag. He took one look and exploded, "What in God's name do you think you are doing, young lady? You will desist this instant. That man is not to be disturbed."

"We are with the *Bluff City Courier*," Melanie said.

"I don't care who you are, you are leaving this instant." He held the door open for them. "I am Dr. Johnson, by the way, and Mr. Ward is my patient."

"We only wanted to ask a few questions."

"Do your ears function as they should, young lady? If they don't, I can examine them and establish why your hearing is impaired."

Clay took Melanie's elbow. "We should listen to the doctor."

"But—" Melanie began.

"There are no buts, miss," Dr. Johnson said firmly. "Ward came close to dying. A slight infection has set in, and unless we are extremely careful, the infection can get worse." He impatiently motioned for them to leave. "In case you haven't heard, more gunshot victims die of infection than from being shot."

Melanie walked with Clay to the door, but paused. "When will I be able to talk to your patient?"

"In a week or so, I should say," Dr. Johnson answered.

"A *week*?"

"Come on," Clay said. The sunlight was bright after the inside of the infirmary, and he squinted as he guided her toward the main office. A horse was at the hitch rail, a horse that had not been there before, and as they reached the steps, the office door opened and out came Cavendish, Franks and another man. The newcomer wore a brown leather vest, a badge and a leer.

"I just heard you were here, Miss Stanley," Deputy Wiggins said. "Imagine my delight."

"I'd rather not," Melanie said. Then, to Cavendish, "Your man won't talk. How about if you and I sit down and go over everything he told you?"

"We can do it on the ride down, if you like," Cavendish said. "The deputy wants to see where the robbery took place. I am taking him there."

The company bookkeeper, Teckler, appeared out of the shadows. "Is that wise, sir? Surely one of the men can do it."

"I never have the men do anything I wouldn't do myself," Cavendish said. "And I can use the exercise. I'm tired of sitting on my backside. Have someone fetch horses for us."

"No horse for me, thanks," Franks said. "I'll stay here, if you don't mind."

"I'm not exactly dressed for riding," Melanie said, "but I will take you up on your offer."

"We both will," Clay said.

Teckler insisted that two company men with rifles accompany them, and Cavendish relented. He rode alongside Melanie. Clay rode next to Deputy Wiggins. They descended from the bench and were winding along the rutted track when Wiggins shifted his pasty complexion from the surrounding woods to Clay.

"You are working with Miss Stanley now, are you?"

"Looks that way," Clay said.

"Lucky you."

High above, a bald eagle soared on outstretched pinions. In the nearby firs a squirrel spotted them and squatted on a branch to chatter its displeasure. Lower down flew a pair of ravens, their black feathers glistening.

"I heard about your tiff with Harve Barker," Deputy Wiggins remarked. "That wasn't very smart."

"I think it was."

"You are new to Bluff City. You don't realize how powerful he is. He crushes those he doesn't care for like you or me would crush an eggshell."

"Are you scared of him, Deputy?"

"Anyone with half a brain would be," Wiggins said. "No one bucks Barker and goes on breathing."

"He's killed before? You're sure?"

"As sure as I am that you're too headstrong for your own good."

"Then why hasn't he ever been arrested?"

"Men like Harve Barker are above the law. They never do the deed themselves. They hire it done, and there is never any evidence they were involved. If I were you I would light a shuck. Nothing in Bluff City is worth losing your life over."

"That depends on your notion of worthwhile," Clay said.

Presently they came to the meadow. Wildflowers grew in profusion. Deputy Wiggins idly swatted at a bee and remarked, "I can't wait to get back to Bluff City. I could use a whiskey right about now."

Clay breathed deep of the scents of the flowers and the earth.

At the top of the serpentine switchback they reined up. Pines hemmed them on both sides.

"The exact spot is about halfway down," Sam Cavendish announced. "We can't miss it. There are bloodstains, and the ground is all trampled."

"No need to go any further, old-timer," declared a gruff voice from out of the woods.

Clay Adams stiffened.

"Who's there?" Sam Cavendish asked. "Who is that?"

"I am," said the gruff voice, and into the open strolled Jesse Stark.

Chapter 11

Clay Adams smiled fiercely. His right hand flew under his jacket. But the next moment more figures came out of the forest on both sides of the switchback. The two guards started to level their rifles, but stopped when Jesse Stark warned, "Try that and you'll be shot to pieces."

The guards had no choice. They were covered by over a dozen gun muzzles. They mimicked trees, their arms the branches.

Sam Cavendish's mouth was opening and closing like that of a fish out of water. "What is the meaning of this outrage?" he sputtered. "Who are you?"

"Can't you guess, old man?" Jesse Stark rejoined. "I'm the gent who relieved your men of twenty thousand dollars."

"So you're Stark," Cavendish spat in contempt. "You have your gall. What are you doing back here? Come to rob me again?"

"We never left," Jesse Stark said. "We've been in hiding, waiting for you to show yourself."

Sam Cavendish could not hide his confusion. "Whatever for?"

Jesse Stark was gazing at Melanie. His thumbs hooked

in his gun belt, he walked up to her mount. "What have we here? As I live and breathe, the prettiest gal I've set eyes on in a coon's age." He went to put his hand on her leg.

"Do that and I will kick your teeth in," Melanie warned.

Jesse Stark laughed. "You've got spunk. I like that." He glanced sharply at the guards. "What are you two waiting for?" Their rifles clattered to earth, and Stark moved to the next horse in the line. "Who is this, then?"

"He works at the *Courier*," Melanie answered on Clay's behalf, "the same as me. Lay a hand on either of us and my uncle will see to it that the governor calls out the militia to exterminate every last one of you."

"My, my," Stark said, still staring at Clay Adams. "Sounds to me, lady, like you have an awful high opinion of yourself." He stepped closer to Clay. "What's the matter, mister? Cat got your tongue?"

"No," Clay said. He did not look directly at the outlaw leader but slightly off to one side, his chin low to his chest as if he were fearful of being struck.

"I reckon you just always let women do your talking, is that it?" Stark chortled and began to turn, then stopped. "Do I know you?"

"No," Clay said.

"You sure? There's something about you. I can't say what." Stark scratched his anvil jaw. "Where have you been of late?"

"Bluff City."

"No. It was somewhere else." Stark might have gone on asking questions but Sam Cavendish twisted in his saddle.

"Quit pestering him, you pip-squeak. It's me you have to deal with. Let us go or my men will hunt you to the ends of the earth."

"I have no doubt they would try," Stark said, facing the mine owner. "But I'm afraid you are stuck with my company for a spell, old man." He stabbed a finger at the two guards. "Lose the six-shooters, too. You've got until the count of three." He didn't pause. "One."

Their revolvers landed near the rifles.

Stark puffed out his chest and nodded. "Yes, sir. This worked out better than I reckoned. Not only the old coot but the gal and the dandy, besides. They're bound to pay up."

"What are you babbling about, you sawed-off slug?" Cavendish demanded.

"Just this." Jesse Stark moved so fast that he had hold of the older man's leg before anyone could blink. With a brutal wrench, he heaved upward, spilling Cavendish from his saddle. Cavendish thudded on his shoulder and rolled onto his back, startled but otherwise unhurt. That changed when Stark took several swift steps and savagely kicked Cavendish in the ribs, not once but several times. Aglow with bloodlust, Stark drew back his boot to do it again.

"Amigo, no!" A stocky outlaw wearing a sombrero, a short jacket, flared pants and two black-handled pistols darted forward. "We need him alive. Without him there will be no money, eh?"

Jesse Stark slowly lowered his boot and the red drained from his face. "I'm obliged, Bantarro. Sometimes I forget myself." Wheeling, he stalked over to Deputy Wiggins, who had sat as rigid as a board the entire time, his hands in the air. "You thought I'd forgotten about you, huh, pudgy? Think again."

"You don't want to kill a lawman," Wiggins said.

"Why not? I've done it before," Stark boasted. "But I will let you live on one condition."

"What might that be?"

"I want you and the two guards to take a message to the mine for me. Tell whoever is in charge now that we have the old man, and if they ever want to see him again they are to fork over a hundred thousand dollars."

Melanie blurted, "You're holding Mr. Cavendish for ransom?"

"Him," Stark said, "and you and your friend. Your being along was a lucky break for me. They won't let a woman come to harm."

"You are despicable."

"So folks say," Stark replied to her barb. "But I will also be a hundred thousand dollars richer." He hastily amended, "Me and my boys, here."

Deputy Wiggins did not try to talk the outlaw out of it. He did not protest, argue or debate. He simply lifted his reins and said, "Can we leave now? Or is there more?"

"Fan the breeze," Stark said. "But once you give my message to the lunkheads at the mine, you're to stay there with everyone else."

Sam Cavendish had sat up and was holding his side. "You are the lunkhead, you little weasel!" he snapped, "if you think I keep a hundred thousand dollars in my office."

Stark smiled. "Not at your office, no, but you have

deposited every cent you made from your mine at the Greater Bank of Bluff City."

"I have an account there, yes," Cavendish admitted, "but there is barely thirty thousand in it."

"You're a liar, old man. You see, I slip into Bluff City any time I feel like it. And I overheard a gent who works at the Greater Bank say how much you have on deposit."

Cavendish was flabbergasted. "Someone from the bank was talking about my private account in public?"

"He was drunk and bragging how the Greater Bank has more assets than the First Bank, or some such nonsense," Jesse Stark imparted.

Livid with fury, Sam Cavendish declared, "I will gut them! I will roast them! I will bring their bank crashing down around their ears."

"You sound like me," Stark said, and laughed. To Deputy Wiggins he said, "Off you go."

But Wiggins did not move. "Aren't you forgetting something? If no one can leave the mine, who gets word to the bank?"

"The old buzzard, here, has a tub of lard working for him by the name of Teckler."

"The bookkeeper," Deputy Wiggins said.

"That's the one. Have him go to the Greater Bank and bring the money. If he rides like a bat out of hell he can be back by midnight."

"Where will you be?"

"Right here. Watching the trail so no one tries to slip off. Because if anyone does, Cavendish dies."

"You have this all thought out."

"Don't I, though?" Stark said, and laughed.

Deputy Wiggins looked at Melanie. "I'm sorry, Miss

Stanley. I don't want to leave you in this man's clutches, but if I don't do as he says, you are liable to be harmed."

Melanie was glaring at the outlaw leader. "Spread the word that he is holding me against my will. Every man in Bluff City will be out combing these mountains in no time."

"No, they won't," Stark said. "Not if they want you to go on breathing." He motioned at Wiggins and the guards. "Quit dawdling, gents. Remember. Do exactly as I say or these three become maggot fruit."

Clay and Melanie and Sam Cavendish watched the deputy and the guards depart. Clay started to knee his horse closer to Melanie but stopped when Bantarro whipped out one of those black-handled pistols.

"No moving unless we tell you, gringo."

Jesse Stark smiled at Melanie and bent in a mock bow. He indicated the trees. "Climb on down, lady. My camp isn't far."

"If I refuse?"

"Then I will have a couple of my men carry you, real gentle-like." Stark chuckled. "I'm trying to be hospitable. The least you can do is cooperate."

"You are a slug."

"Calling me names is just plain childish," Stark said. "I can gag you if you can't think of anything nice to say." He waited, and when she did not reply or move, he asked, "Which will it be?"

Her shoulders slumping in defeat, Melanie dismounted. Clay followed suit. Cavendish had to be prodded by a rifle before he would budge.

Four members of the gang were left to watch the trail.

Stark was in marvelous spirits. He beamed like a cat about to eat a cage full of canaries. "Yes, sir. I'll be famous after word of this gets out. It will be in all the newspapers."

"That's important to you, is it?" Melanie asked sarcastically.

"Being famous? It sure as hell is. It beats being a nobody. Look at Jesse James. Or Billy the Kid. Pretty soon folks everywhere will be talking about me, just like they talked about those two. Hell, if I play my cards right, I can be bigger than they ever were."

"You have a twisted sense of values, Mr. Stark."

"What's that supposed to mean? Who doesn't want to be famous? I sure wouldn't amount to much if I was a no-account like your friend, there." Stark turned and stared at Clay. "I still say I know you from somewhere, mister. Help me out. Where was it?"

"If we've met, I don't remember it," Clay said.

A small fire crackled in a clearing. Two outlaws were minding it and their horses, which were saddled and ready for a swift getaway.

Stark stopped at a log that had been placed near the fire. "Make yourself comfortable, lady," he directed. "It's going to be a long wait."

"I'd rather stand."

"You sure are one pigheaded female." Stark squatted and began to fill a tin cup. "How about you gents? Do you have more sense than the filly?"

Clay sat at one end of the log. Cavendish sat on the ground. An outlaw handed them cups of coffee, which they accepted without comment. The outlaw held out a cup to Melanie but she shook her head.

Jesse Stark laughed. "I swear. Females! If you were any sillier, you would be five years old."

"Quit riding her," Cavendish said. "You have as little respect for womanhood as you do for human life."

"I'll admit I don't put women on pedestals," Stark said, and took a sip. "They're nuisances, every blamed one. The moodiest cusses alive. They gripe all the time." He bobbed his head at Melanie. "Look at this one. Pretty as a sunset on the outside but a bitch on the inside."

Clay switched the tin cup he was holding from his right hand to his left. "I will thank you not to speak of Miss Stanley that way."

"Will you now?" Stark rejoined, and he and some of the other outlaws chortled.

"Should we tie them, amigo?" Bantarro asked.

"No need," Stark answered. "They wouldn't get ten feet and they know it. They will behave like little lambs until the money is brought."

"A hundred thousand dollars will break me," Sam Cavendish said. "It's nearly all the money I have."

"You still have the mine," Stark said. "You can make more."

"Not fast enough to pay my debts and make the payroll," Cavendish said. "I might stay afloat a month or two, but then all the people I owe money will come pounding on my door. I'll have to sell out."

Melanie abruptly took a seat on the log near Clay. From her handbag she took a tablet and pencil and placed the tablet on her knees.

"What in blazes do you think you're doing?" Stark asked.

"I might as well make the best of this. As much as I hate to admit it, you are newsworthy."

"Now you want to write about me in your newspaper?" Stark cackled. "Lady, you are as changeable as the weather. A minute ago you didn't want anything to do with me."

"The *Courier*'s readers will be interested in learning about you and your men," Melanie said.

"I don't know," Stark said.

"You're the one who wants to be famous," Melanie reminded him. "Can you think of a better way?"

Some of the outlaws had sat down. Others were standing around talking, their rifles cradled in their arms. Bantarro had slid his revolver back into his holster.

Clay placed his right hand on his knee.

"Suppose you tell me a little bit about yourself," Melanie said to Stark. "Where you were born. What it was like growing up. When and why you turned to a life of crime. Those sorts of things."

"I grew up on a farm," Stark said. "I left when I was eleven after I stabbed my pa with a pitchfork."

As casually as could be, Clay slid his right hand under the edge of his jacket.

"You murdered your own father?"

"He was a bossy bastard. Always smacking and beating me when I didn't measure up. One day he had me sweep out the barn and I didn't do it good enough to suit him, so he hit me. Hit me so hard he knocked me down. Right next to the pitchfork. You should have heard him squeal when I stuck it in his belly."

"Dear God."

"He had it coming," Jesse Stark said.

Clay started to raise the cup to his mouth. Suddenly lunging, he threw the coffee into Stark's face while simultaneously streaking a short-barreled Smith and Wesson from under his jacket and jamming the muzzle against Stark's head.

Chapter 12

The outlaws were too stunned to do anything. All except for Bantarro, who started to draw his revolvers but thought better of the notion at the *click* of the Smith and Wesson's hammer.

"Don't anyone move!" Clay warned.

Jesse Stark was curiously calm. Chuckling, he remarked, "When will I learn? This is what I get for being nice."

Clay gouged the muzzle against his temple. "Not another word," he warned. His hand shook as he said it, and his trigger finger curled and uncurled.

"Look at you," Stark scoffed. "You're so scared, you can't hold your pistol steady. Shoot him, boys. He annoys me." His eyes swiveled to Clay. "On second thought, if this dandy doesn't drop his hardware, shoot the female. Shoot her in the head so it's permanent."

"You wouldn't!" Sam Cavendish exclaimed.

Bantarro palmed a pistol and pointed it at Melanie. "*I* would, senor. A woman or a man, it is all the same to me. Dead is dead."

Stark grinned up at Clay. "What's it going to be? Kill me and she dies? Or hand me that six-gun and take your medicine?"

Clay Adams was a study in contrasts. His face was set in fierce lines of animal savagery, yet his hand and his arm shook as if with palsy. He looked at Melanie, then at the hard faces of the pack that surrounded them, then at Jesse Stark. "I reckon I'll have to take my medicine." With a deft twirl, he reversed his grip on the Smith and Wesson and held it for the other to take.

Jesse Stark's brow knit. He accepted the revolver, hefted it, twirled it twice on his finger, and then, still seated, he rammed it into Clay's groin.

Doubling over, Clay clutched himself and sank to his knees. The veins on his neck swelled. He clenched his teeth but made no sound.

Stark set down his tin cup and slowly rose. He twirled the Smith and Wesson a few more times, wedged it under his belt and contemplated the man at his feet. "Mighty slick of you to get the drop on me like that. It's my own fault for not having you frisked." Drawing back his right leg, he kicked Clay Adams in the ribs.

"Stop it!" Melanie cried, and leaped to her coworker's defense, only to be grabbed by Bantarro and held by her wrists. "Quit hurting him, damn you!"

"Now, now," Stark chided. "Try to remember you are a lady."

Another outlaw, a rangy man with a shock of sandy hair poking from under his hat, stepped up to Clay and drew a revolver. "Want me to finish off this yack for you, Jesse?"

"I'm tempted, Gorman," Stark said. "But it's best if we keep them alive until we get the money. Tie him, though, hands and feet."

Once that was done, Bantarro let go of Melanie and she immediately knelt beside Clay, her arm over his shoulder. "Is there anything I can do?"

Clay shook his head. He lay with his arms bound behind his back and his legs bent so his hands were inches from his ankles.

"Thank you for trying to save me," Melanie said. "It took great courage."

"I didn't do much good."

"It's the attempt that counts," Melanie flattered him. "I've never had a man risk his life on my account before. It's touching. Wait until my uncle hears. He would never forgive himself if anything happened to me."

Shifting so he faced the fire, Clay remarked, "Most any man would do the same. Don't make me out to be more than I am."

His rebuff, spoken harshly, caused Melanie to draw back as if he had hit her. "I'm sorry. You're in pain, and here I am chattering away. I'll leave you be so you can recover in peace." She moved to the log.

Jesse Stark hunkered beside it. "Ready to start asking me questions?"

"I've changed my mind. I know all about you that is worth knowing. You are a despicable coward, and I, for one, will celebrate the day you are hung."

"There you go again with the insults," Stark said. "What about your readers? What about making me famous?"

"You're no Jesse James and you're no Billy the Kid and, if I have my way, you never will be."

"Damn all women," Stark said. "If it wasn't for making babies you would be next to worthless."

Over the next half hour the camp quieted. Some of

the outlaws rested. Some played cards or dice. Jesse Stark, Bantarro and Gorman moved off by themselves and huddled, swapping whispers.

Melanie stayed on the log, her features downcast. Every so often she glanced at Clay Adams, whose eyes were closed.

"I reckon he's sleeping," Sam Cavendish commented as he sat down on the other end of the log. "Although how he can is beyond me." He smiled at her. "I'm sorry you are involved, missy."

"Stark is to blame, not you."

"I hope to God the bank doesn't pay him," Cavendish said. "I'd rather be dead than lose the mine."

"No one wants to die," Melanie said.

"I was poor and starving most of my life, and I don't hanker to be that way again. I'm too old to start over." Cavendish sighed. "I might have to take Harve Barker up on his offer. He's been after me to sell for months but I've always told him to go jump off a cliff."

"Word is, he has been buying a lot of property," Melanie mentioned.

"I don't doubt it. That there is one ambitious gent. He had the gall to offer a pittance, then got all huffy when I turned him down."

One of the outlaws who had been left behind to watch the trail burst into the clearing. He made straight for Jesse Stark, who whooped and slapped his leg with his hat.

"Teckler must be on his way down the mountain," Cavendish guessed. "And here I sit, unable to lift a finger to protect my interests."

The mine owner lapsed into morose silence. Melanie rested her forearms on her knees and her forehead on her forearms. The outlaws left her alone. She stayed on the log as long as she could, until her frayed nerves demanded that she get up and walk about. She had only taken a few steps, however, when a guttural growl brought her up short.

"Where do you think you're off to, missy?"

"I just want to stretch my legs," Melanie answered.

"You sit back down and you stay down until I say different," Jesse Stark said. "It's for your own good. Some of my men haven't been with a woman in a month or more, and you sashaying around showing your wares is the last thing they need."

"I never!" Melanie heatedly declared.

"Save your breath. No woman ever owns up to it except doves. You ask me, saloon gals are more honest than you Bible-thumping types, and whores are more honest than both of you."

"Must you always be so vulgar?"

"Must you always be such a pain in the ass?" Stark mimicked her tone. "I'm only saying how things are. You're the one walking around with her nose in the clouds."

"Can it be that you have as low an opinion of me as I do of you?" Melanie marveled.

"Probably lower," Stark said. "I don't think much of them that acts like they are better than everyone else."

"You have just described yourself."

"I don't think I'm better. I think I'm meaner. Hell, I *know* I'm meaner. I've left a string of bodies to prove it."

Melanie shook her head in disbelief. "How can you be so proud of being so violent? What kind of man are you?"

"The kind who takes what he wants, when he wants. The kind who doesn't live by rules others make. The kind who won't be stepped on or pushed around."

"You almost make it sound commendable."

Jesse Stark gazed at a distant snowcapped peak. "I'm just being me. I can't help how I am, and I have no desire to change. Until the day I die I will be true to my nature. If that's wrong, so be it."

"What about all the people you've killed? What about all the money you've stolen? Doesn't any of that matter?"

"I don't lose any sleep over it. I do what I have to, and if somebody is hurt, it's their tough luck."

Sam Cavendish interjected, "That's as convenient an excuse as I have ever heard."

"Go to hell."

The outlaws went on playing cards and dice and sleeping. Melanie reclaimed her spot on the log and placed her cheek on her forearm. Gradually, her eyelids drooped. She was aware she was falling asleep and she did not want to, but it would not be denied. When she opened her eyes again the sun was on the west rim of the world and the shadows were three times as long as they had been.

"Another six hours and we should have the ransom," Jesse Stark was saying to Gorman and Bantarro.

Stifling a yawn, Melanie lowered her cheek. Belatedly, she noticed that Clay Adams had rolled over and now had his back to the fire and was facing her, and that his eyes were open. She started to say that she was happy to see him alert and unhurt, but he gave a barely perceptible shake of his head and closed his eyes.

As sunset approached, the outlaws put on a fresh pot of coffee to brew. Several went off to hunt and returned with a doe. Gorman skinned it and skewered a haunch on a spit. Like starved wolves, the outlaws gathered around to watch the juicy meat cook and lick their lips.

Melanie refused a piece. "I'm not hungry," she lied. The truth was, she could not stop her stomach from rumbling.

Night fell abruptly. From out of the dark came a hideous chorus of bestial cries: the throaty howls of wolves, the high yips of coyotes, the short barks of a fox and the shriek of a mountain lion. Once, from not too far off, came the rumbling roar of a prowling bear.

Melanie nearly jumped out of her skin when fingers brushed her ankle. She looked down and discovered Clay had inched closer. None of the outlaws were paying attention. Most were hungrily tearing at the venison.

"I'm getting you out of here," Clay whispered.

"Are you crazy?" Melanie retorted. "How far will we get with you tied up and without your gun?"

"Tell Cavendish," Clay directed, and closed his eyes.

With a nervous glance at Stark, who was greedily devouring a slab of meat, she sidled along the log until she was close enough to the mine owner to whisper, "Clay and I are going for a stroll. Care to join us?"

"Need you ask, girl?" the feisty silver king whispered.

Fully two-thirds of the outlaws stretched out on the ground to rest after gorging themselves. Jesse Stark was one of them. He lay on his back with his hands folded on his chest and his hat brim pulled low over his eyes.

Bantarro was pouring a cup of coffee and had his back to the log.

Gorman and two others were over by the horses. They, too, had their backs to the log.

Clay Adams picked that moment to slowly stand. The ropes fell away as he rose. With feigned nonchalance he stepped to the log. Smiling at Melanie, he offered her his arm as if they were at a cotillion and he was asking her to dance. She cast an anxious gaze about the clearing, then hooked her arm in his. Together they moved toward the edge of the clearing.

Sam Cavendish fell into step beside them. "This is plumb loco," he whispered. "We'll never make it."

But they did. They gained the cover of the trees, and the instant the night swallowed them, Clay said, "Run!" He did so, holding onto Melanie.

The woods were thick with undergrowth and presented obstacles in the form of downed or partially downed trees, and deadfalls. Clay picked his way with an ease that baffled his companions, and it was not long before Cavendish whispered, "How in hell can you tell where we're going?"

"By the north star," Clay revealed. "I took a fix on it in the clearing. We're heading northwest toward your mine."

"It will take a month to get there on foot," Cavendish exaggerated.

"With any luck we won't be on foot for long."

"I have a question," Melanie whispered. "How did you get those ropes off? I saw Gorman tie them. The knots were good and tight."

Clay's right hand rose and something glinted dully in the starlight. "I keep a knife strapped under my right pant leg."

"A revolver, a knife," Melanie said. "What kind of clerk are you?"

"The kind who hopes to go on living a while yet," Clay said.

"That's no answer."

"Save your breath for running."

She did. They all did. They ran as fast as the terrain permitted, repeatedly avoiding calamity only by virtue of Clay's extraordinary ability to navigate in the dark. He spotted logs and thickets and tangles before they did.

Suddenly, from the vicinity of the clearing, there rose hard yells and angry curses.

"They'll be after us now," Sam Cavendish said.

"But they don't know which way we went," Clay said. "They'll have to scatter. Only a few will come in this direction."

"What can you do with just a knife?" Melanie asked.

"A lot," Clay said.

With alarming rapidity the clamor of pursuit spread as riders plunged into the forest. They shouted back and forth to one another, which made pinpointing them easier.

Presently Clay stopped and turned his head, listening. "Hear that?"

The crash and crackle of undergrowth had grown ominously loud. Some of the outlaws were coming right toward them.

Chapter 13

"Stay close," Clay whispered, and led them to a dead-fall. Scores of saplings had been felled by the hand of nature, either in a storm or during one of the powerful chinook winds that tore through the mountains during the winter months.

"We can't get across that," Cavendish said.

"We don't have to." Clay came to a gap wide enough for two people. "Here will do. Stay put until I come fetch you."

Melanie held onto his arm. "What are you up to?"

"Getting us horses."

"Be careful. They have guns."

"I'll have surprise on my side," Clay said. He helped her into the space, and when she had hunkered and was next to invisible, he touched her arm and whispered, "Whatever you hear, whatever you think you hear, stay put. Don't come to help me, no matter how much you want to. If I'm not back by morning, head northwest and you will strike the trail to the mine."

"We won't desert you," Melanie said.

"See that she listens to me," Clay said to Cavendish.

"You heard the man, girl."

Clay whirled and retraced their steps for perhaps twenty-five yards. Then he darted behind a low pine. No sooner did he crouch than two outlaws appeared, riding half a dozen yards apart.

"See anything yet?" one man asked the other.

"Not unless you count trees."

"They might not even have come this way. If you ask me, this is a waste of time. But we can't turn back until Jesse signals."

"It doesn't matter which way they went," the other outlaw said. "Even if they slip by us, Stark sent four men up the trail to keep them from reaching the mine."

By then the pair were close to the pine. For a moment Clay thought they would go by on his left, but each reined wide, one to the right, the other to the left. They were scanning the terrain ahead. Neither looked down.

Like a giant spring uncoiling, Clay launched himself at the outlaw on the right. The man had his hand on his revolver and went to jerk it even as Clay was in midair. Clay was quicker. With a swift thrust he buried his knife in the man's ribs. The outlaw stiffened and cried out and sought to use his spurs, but Clay, grabbing the man's shirt, gave a fierce pull.

Down they went. Clay alighted on his feet but the outlaw hit on his side and cried out a second time.

Clay spun. The other outlaw had reined toward them and was in the act of drawing a revolver. Clay could not possibly reach the man before the revolver went off, so he did the only thing he could; he threw the knife.

The man howled as the blade bit into his arm. Clay

had thrown the knife at the man's chest but it imbedded itself in the man's rising arm. Almost in the same motion Clay hurtled forward so that he reached the man barely a second after the knife. Launching himself like a two-legged battering ram, Clay slammed the outlaw from his horse. Both of them tumbled hard but it was Clay who regained his feet first.

The outlaw rose as high as his knees and tugged on the knife to yank it out. It came free as Clay sprang, and suddenly Clay was confronted by his own weapon in the hands of a killer who very much wanted to repay him for the pain he had caused. Clay avoided a stab to the throat and dodged a slash to his thigh.

Hissing like an enraged bobcat, the outlaw feinted to the right and lanced the knife to the left. Again Clay saved himself, but by the merest whisker. Backpedaling so he would have space to move, Clay did not see the small boulder he tripped over until he was falling.

Clay landed on his back. The outlaw reared above him, the knife upraised. "Now I've got you, you damned jackrabbit!"

Clay kicked out. He hoped to knock the man's legs from under him. His right foot connected with a kneecap and there was a loud *snap*. The man yelped and staggered, then cut at Clay as Clay, a shade too eager, pushed erect. Clay winced as the blade sliced into his arm. It did not slice deep, but it drew blood.

Hopping on his good leg, the outlaw gloated, "I got you that time! I felt it! Come closer and I'll cut you again!"

Staying just out of reach, Clay circled. Twice he sprang, only to be driven back by the knife.

The outlaw never took his eyes off Clay. Holding the blade close to his body so Clay could not grab his arm, he matched Clay step for step. Suddenly he glanced over Clay's shoulder and a suggestion of a grin quirked his mouth. He quickly caught himself but it had been enough of a warning.

Clay leaped to the right, and twisted.

The other outlaw was still alive. Bleeding profusely, one hand pressed to his chest, he had his six-shooter in his other hand, and he fired at the exact split instant that Clay leaped aside. The slug intended for Clay's back cored the chest of the outlaw with the knife, whose face was etched with astonishment as he fell.

Before the man with the revolver could fire again, Clay was on him. He got hold of the man's wrist and wrenched, seeking to force him to drop it, but the outlaw desperately clung on. Throwing a leg behind him, Clay pushed. It had the desired effect. The outlaw sprawled onto his back, and in a twinkling Clay had a knee on the man's chest and landed several punches in swift succession. At the third blow the outlaw went limp.

Clay pushed to his feet. The fight had left him winded but he could not rest. He unbuckled the man's gun belt and was strapping it around his waist when footfalls pattered and out of the greenery rushed Melanie and Cavendish. Clay frowned. "I told you to stay put."

"We heard the shot," Melanie said. "We were worried."

"One of us was, anyhow," Cavendish said.

"I was hoping to take them quietly," Clay mentioned. "That shot will bring others." He examined the revolver, a standard single-action, long-barreled Colt Army model. "Catch their horses while I finish here."

"Finish?" Melanie said.

"Come on, girl," Cavendish prodded. "Now's not the time to be asking questions. We have to light a shuck or we won't see the morning sun."

Clay replaced the spent cartridge in the Colt. He spun the cylinder, then thumbed back the hammer and pointed the Colt at the outlaw who was still alive. All it would take was a slight squeeze. Clay stood there pointing the Colt for over a minute; then he slowly lowered it, let down the hammer, and shoved it into the holster, saying softly, "Not like this or it will all be for nothing."

A whinny drew Clay to where Sam Cavendish had hold of the reins to one of the mounts and was seeking to calm the skittish animal. "Where did Melanie get to?" Clay asked.

"Over yonder," Cavendish said, with a vague gesture to the southwest. "After the other horse."

"Wait here." Clay ran in a zigzag pattern to cover more ground. He expected to come on her any moment but he went twenty to thirty yards and no Melanie. He cupped a hand to his mouth to shout but lowered it.

A short jog brought Clay to a clearing. In the center, struggling to hold onto the reins of a spirited dun, was the object of his concern. Hurrying to help her, he snatched at the bridle just as the dun pranced from her grasp. Inadvertently, his hand brushed Melanie's body. "Sorry."

"For what? Touching me? Don't be ridiculous."

Throwing an arm over the animal's neck, Clay grasped the bridle and held on tight. "I was being polite."

Melanie faced him. "How do you intend to explain yourself?"

"It was an accident. I bumped you."

"Don't play the innocent," Melanie said. "I wasn't referring to that. I have seen a new side to you tonight, Clay Adams."

"I don't know what you are talking about."

"You pulled a gun on Jesse Stark, of all people. The way your hand was shaking, I figured you were scared. But then you went and bested two badmen all by your lonesome. Now I don't know what to think."

"They weren't much as badmen go."

Melanie's skepticism was transparent. "Don't give me that. You can handle a six-shooter. You can handle a knife. Strange skills for a would-be journalist."

At that juncture the brush crackled and into the clearing rode Sam Cavendish. "Why is it the young never use the brains God gave them? The Stark gang is after us and you stand around jawing!"

Clay swung onto the dun and lowered his arm to Melanie. "We'll have to ride double. If you don't mind, that is."

"I can't very well walk back to the mine, now, can I?" Melanie allowed him to swing her up, then wrapped her arms tight around his middle. "Ride like the dickens. And don't worry about me. I'm not fragile."

Clay was not wearing spurs but his heels sufficed. He rode faster than was prudent but not so fast as to endanger the dun. To lose a horse now increased the chances of being recaptured. "I'll be damned if I'll let him get his hands on us again," he thought out loud.

"What was that?" Melanie asked in his ear. "I didn't quite catch it."

"Nothing," Clay said. He prevented her from asking more questions by bending forward so she had to shout to be heard above the drum of hooves, and she would not shout when there was a chance the outlaws would hear.

After half an hour of riding Clay drew rein to let the horses rest, and to listen. He did not dismount, and when Cavendish went to do so, he said, "Stay in the saddle. There's no telling how close they are."

"I haven't ridden this blamed hard in a coon's age," the older man said. "I've got aches in places I've never ached before."

"I don't do much riding, either," Melanie said, "but I've noticed that our friend, here, is right at home in the saddle."

"I noticed that, too," Cavendish said to Clay. "You ride like a Comanche, son. And you can see in the dark almost as good as they can."

"I have good eyes," Clay said.

Sam Cavendish snorted. "Sonny, when word gets out that you outwitted Jesse Stark, you'll be the talk of the territory."

"In that case," Clay said, "I have a favor to ask."

"Anything, son," Cavendish said. "You saved my bacon, so whatever you want is yours."

"I would be obliged if you and Miss Stanley would keep this to yourselves," Clay requested.

"That's a mite peculiar."

"It's more than that," Melanie said. "Why do you

want us to keep quiet? If the eastern papers pick up the story, and a kidnapping is always big news, you will be halfway famous, like Stark wants to be."

"I'm not Jesse Stark," Clay said curtly.

"No, but you just helped us escape from him. That in itself is newsworthy. I have a responsibility to my uncle and to the *Courier*'s readers to report everything that has happened."

"You couldn't just say we escaped together?"

"It wouldn't be the truth," Melanie said. "We couldn't have done it without you. Whether you like it or not, you are a hero."

"Hush!" Sam Cavendish abruptly raised a hand.

Clay rose in the stirrups. To the south a considerable piece hoofbeats rumbled like thunder. "They are still after us."

"Then what are we twiddling our thumbs for?"

It soon became apparent that the countryside was crawling with outlaws. They heard riders to the north, to the east, and to the west. Once they thought they heard Gorman shout and Bantarro answer.

Again and again Clay stopped to probe the night for enemies. When Melanie complained that they should simply press on, he retorted with, "Would you rather enjoy Jesse Stark's hospitality again?"

"He's right, girl," Cavendish came to Clay's defense. "The closer we get to my mine, the more of those owlhoots there are. We have to be like mice in a barn full of cats."

"Stark sent most of his men on ahead to cut us off," Clay said. "He expects us to strike straight for the mine. So I propose we swing to the northwest and come up on it from above the mine shaft."

"It will take a lot longer," Cavendish noted.

"But be a lot safer," Clay responded, with a flick of his eyes at Melanie that only Cavendish noticed.

Time crawled. Every moment was spent in tense expectation of being discovered. They never knew but that they might blunder on hidden outlaws and be forced to fight their way through.

The position of the North Star was as reliable as a timepiece. By Clay's reckoning it was past one in the morning when they drew rein on a slope that over-looked the Cavendish mine. The buildings were ablaze with lamp and lantern light. Miners milled near the office, evidently awaiting word.

"You did it, son," Sam Cavendish said. "We're almost there."

"I wouldn't put it past Stark to have riflemen ready to pick us off as soon as we break cover," Clay said. "I'll go first by myself. If I don't draw fire, it should be safe for the two of you to follow."

"Nonsense," Melanie said. "We have come this far together. We will stick with you the rest of the way."

"I agree with the girl this time," Cavendish said.

Clay argued but they refused to heed. And so, lashing the dun's reins, Clay flew down the steep slope at breakneck speed. Melanie clamped hold tighter than ever, her cheek pressed to his shoulder, her warm, excited breath fanning his neck. But not a single shot shattered the night. Just whoops and hollers as the miners swarmed to meet them.

"Mr. Cavendish! Mr. Cavendish!" Teckler clasped his employer's calloused hand as Sam Cavendish dismounted. "Praise the Almighty you are all right! They let you go as they promised they would."

"Like hell they did," Cavendish said, and grabbed the smaller man by the shoulders. "My money! Tell me my money is safe!"

The bookkeeper frowned. "I don't understand. We paid the ransom over an hour ago."

Chapter 14

The *Courier* had the details.

Teckler had ridden to Bluff City alone, as Jesse Stark had demanded. The bookkeeper rushed into the Greater Bank of Bluff City and shoved a note from Gary Franks, the vice president, under the nose of the head teller. The head teller wanted to send someone to fetch Marshal Vale but Teckler talked him out of it. "For all we know, the outlaws are spying on us as we speak. If we don't do exactly as Jesse Stark wants, Mr. Cavendish's life is forfeit."

Every employee at the bank was pressed into service to help count the money. A guard was sent to the mercantile for sacks to stuff it in. Most of the one hundred thousand was in the form of National Bank notes and United States notes. The counting took hours but was completed with time to spare.

Since Teckler had about ridden his horse into the ground, a fresh mount was obtained. He immediately headed back up the mountain and reached the switchback an hour early. On not seeing sign of anyone, he called out.

None other than Jesse Stark came out of the trees and cheerfully took possession of the ransom.

"What about Mr. Cavendish?" Teckler had asked.

"Your boss will be let go as soon as I make sure all the money is there," Stark responded. "You can go on to the mine and wait there for him."

The loyal bookkeeper had not liked the arrangement but he had done as the outlaw commanded. He was shocked to learn he had been duped.

But Teckler's shock was as nothing compared to Sam Cavendish's. He was out nearly every cent he owned. He had to lay off most of his workers, and his mine was in danger of going under. He scrambled to secure financing to keep the mine operating but no one was willing to help. The only offer he received was one already tendered—Harve Barker's pittance to buy the mine outright.

The *Courier* related the financial dealings. It also covered the abduction of Sam Cavendish in remarkable detail. Every aspect was covered. Every word Stark uttered was set down for posterity.

But when it came to the escape, Melanie Stanley suffered a lapse of memory. She reported that the three captives snuck off when Stark was not looking. She made no mention of the part played by Clay Adams. To hear her version, one would think he did nothing at all.

The morning after the newspaper came out, Clay sat on the edge of her desk and placed a copy in front of her. "I'm obliged."

"Go away. I have pencils to sharpen."

"What changed your mind?" Clay inquired.

"I don't know," Melanie said a trifle angrily. "I guess I decided it wouldn't hurt to honor your request, although why you want to keep what you did a secret is beyond me."

"I have my reasons."

"Which you are unwilling to share. And here I thought we were friends."

"There is no one in this world I like more," Clay said matter-of-factly.

"You have a strange way of showing it."

Clay sighed and stood. "Think what you want. But I do appreciate what you did. I know it went against your principles."

"Who are you, Clay Adams?" Melanie unexpectedly asked.

"What?"

"Just this morning it struck me that I know next to nothing about you. Where you are from. What you did before you came here. You are secretive about your past. But you are clever about it, so no one realizes how secretive you are being. Why hide who you have been unless there is something worth hiding?"

"We have all done things we would rather forget," Clay remarked.

"True. But I suspect there is more to it than that. And since you won't willingly confide in me, I have decided to do some digging."

"Please don't," Clay said.

Melanie made a tepee of her hands. "You can stop me. All you have to do is tell me what I want to know."

"I never took you for a snoop."

"How could you not? Look at what I do for a living." Melanie gestured to encompass the newspaper office. "Snooping is in my blood."

"Please leave well enough alone," Clay tried again.

"I'm sorry. I can't. There is nothing I like more than digging for information, and you are a gold mine of facts waiting to be unearthed. I will get to the bottom of the mystery that is Clay Adams. Just see if I don't."

Melanie said it lightheartedly but there was nothing lighthearted about Clay's expression. "Do what you have to," he said, and returned to the front desk.

The rest of the day was uneventful. Melanie left early to see about a woman who had been run over by a buggy after a hornet spooked the horse. Clay stayed until near eight, when Jerome Stanley told him he could go home.

"Thank you, sir. See you tomorrow." Clay donned his derby, stepped outside, and was immediately wreathed in cigar smoke.

"I have been waiting for you," Marshal Vale said. He came out of the shadows, puffing contentedly on a cheroot. "Let's walk."

Without saying anything, Clay fell into step.

The marshal went on puffing until they came to the end of the block. Then he casually gazed over his shoulder, presumably at a young woman in a tight dress. "Who are you?"

"The question of the day," Clay Adams said.

"I've read the newspaper account," Marshal Vale remarked. A carriage clattered past and they crossed behind it. "It leaves out a lot, which strikes me as strange. Usually Miss Stanley is more thorough."

"Maybe you should be talking to her, then."

"Sheathe your claws, son. I'm not out to find fault with either of you. But I would like to know what you are up to."

"You're speaking in riddles," Clay said.

"Don't do this," Marshal Vale said. "I can be your friend if you'll let me." He removed the cigar from his mouth and flicked ashes to the street. "I had a long talk with Sam Cavendish. He told me a lot that wasn't covered in the newspaper. Most of it was about you."

"I told him not to make more of it than there was."

"That's the point, son," Marshal Vale said. "No one is making nearly enough of it. Certainly not Miss Stanley. I only got Sam to talk after he made me promise to keep what he told me to myself." Vale stared at Clay. "You're no clerk. I'm not sure exactly what you are, but that suit you're wearing is a disguise. You're up to something. You came to Bluff City with a purpose in mind. I'd like to know what that purpose is."

Clay's lips pinched together. "You don't miss much, do you?"

"No, son, I don't. It's why I've lasted so long. For instance, I haven't missed the two men who are following us. Or should I say following you, since they both work for Harve Barker?"

"I'd forgotten about him," Clay said.

"An oversight like that can get a man buried," Marshal Vale commented. "But your squabble with Barker is your affair. He likes Miss Stanley. You like Miss Stanley. Two men fighting over a pretty woman. It happens all the time. So long as neither of you spray lead in public, there's not much I can do."

"I hope it won't come to that."

"He's not the reason you're here, though. From what Miss Stanley tells me, you didn't know Barker existed until you came to Bluff City. Which brings us back to where we started. Who are you and what are you up to?"

Clay said, not without irritation, "You are fishing without bait."

"Am I? Well, I have been wrong before. Maybe you are what you seem to be. If that turns out to be the case, I'll be man enough to apologize." Marshal Vale smiled. "I'll quit badgering you now. But I'll leave you with a few words of advice." Vale glanced at a storefront window they were passing, a window that showed the street behind them. "Have a care, my young friend. You have made powerful enemies. Enemies who might take it into their heads that the only good Adams is a dead Adams. Savvy?"

"All too well," Clay said. "And, Marshal?"

Vale had started to turn up a side street. "Yes?"

"Thanks."

"Just doing my job, son," Marshal Vale said. "It's best to keep on top of things. Fewer nasty surprises that way."

Clay resumed walking. It was dark and the street-lamps had been lit. He came to an intersection and paused. To the right would take him to the Emporium; to the left, the outskirts of town and the Rusty Spittoon. He went to the right.

It was early and Bluff City's premier gambling den was not as crowded as it would be later. Clay threaded through the poker and roulette tables to the roped-off section, and Harve Barker's private table. No one was there. He made for the bar and heard his name called.

Wesley Oaks was at a poker table, winnings piled high in front of him. "It has been a few days."

"I've been busy," Clay said.

"So I've read." The gambler indicated an empty chair. "You are welcome to sit in."

"I'm looking for Barker. Is he here?"

"I spoke to him about noon," Wesley said. "He was in good spirits. Something to do with the Cavendish mine."

"Sam Cavendish sold out to him."

"Give Barker ten years and he will be the richest man in the territory," the gambler predicted.

From behind Clay came a familiar voice. "Make that five years, and the richest man west of the Mississippi, and you will be closer to the mark." Harve Barker was the epitome of fashion in a flawlessly tailored suit. Flanking him were the two men who had been shadowing Clay.

"Just so I get to win some of it," Wesley Oaks said.

"You can try." Harve Barker sobered and wagged a finger at Clay. "Wasn't I clear enough the last time you paid me a visit? The Emporium is off limits to you so long as you draw breath. This time you get off with a warning. The next I won't be so charitable."

"I go where I want, when I want," Clay said. "Try to stop me and you will find that out."

"Brave words for a clerk."

"I have more. Stop having me followed. I should think you would know better after the other night."

Barker turned to the two toughs. "Did you hear

him, boys? He doesn't like you. Why don't you show him the door and the bottoms of your boots?"

"Is that really called for?" Wesley Oaks asked.

The two underlings were cast from the same mold: husky, muscular and obedient. Without saying a word they closed on Clay.

And just like that, a derringer was in the gambler's hand. It was not pointed at anyone in particular but there was no denying his intent as he said, "You are distracting me from my game, gentlemen, and I can't have that."

The two toughs stopped and looked at their boss.

Harve Barker was not pleased. "You walk a fine line, Mr. Oaks. I don't presume to tell you how to play cards."

"As a favor," Wesley said.

Clay stepped between them. "It's all right. I wasn't planning to stay. I only wanted to deliver the two messages."

"Two?" Barker repeated.

"The other is this. I will also see who I want, when I want. The sooner you accept that, the less wear and tear on your hired help."

Harve Barker glowered. "The arrogance."

"Listen to the kettle call the pot black," Clay said. "But I guess you can afford your temper tantrums."

"I can indulge my every whim," Barker boasted. "You would do well to keep that in mind."

"There you go again. Haven't you heard? All our stupidities eventually catch up with us. I know that better than anyone. You'll learn it too, someday, and you won't like the lesson."

"Listen to you. You should be a preacher."

"People aren't always as they seem," Clay Adams said. Nodding to Wesley Oaks, he walked off. At the glass doors he looked back, smiled at Harve Barker, and gave a little wave.

Barker did not smile back.

Hurrying across the street, Clay turned right at the next intersection. He stopped and waited, but no one came after him.

Whistling cheerfully, Clay ambled west. High on the bluff and surrounding mountains the lights from mines and camps sparkled like land-bound stars. Two men on horseback came up behind him and his hand drifted under his jacket. But they were townsmen on their way home after a long day's labor.

The Rusty Spittoon was elbow to elbow. Clay shouldered through to the bar and found himself next to Skagg. The giant smiled and pounded him on the back.

"Good to see you again! How about a game of cards? I'm low on money, so we can't play for high stakes."

"How would you like to earn a hundred dollars?" Clay asked.

Skagg's craggy face split in a grin. "Who do I kill?"

Before Clay could answer, Gressel came down the bar, wiping his hands on his greasy apron. "Well, if it isn't the bundle of surprises."

"How so?" Clay asked as Gressel slid a bottle toward him.

"Someone was in here asking about you this afternoon. If I had charged by the question, I would be rich."

"Let me guess. It was one of Harve Barker's men."

Gressel chuckled and winked. "Who said it was a man?"

Clay froze with the bottle halfway to his mouth.

"It was as pretty a gal as you'll find anywhere. I told her I don't talk about my customers behind their backs, but she wouldn't take no for an answer. Showed credentials from the *Courier*. Her name was Melanie Stanley."

Chapter 15

The next day at the *Courier*, Clay went about his tasks as he normally would. He was polite to Melanie. For her part, her friendliness had been replaced by an aloof reserve. Clay did not think anyone else noticed, but along about the middle of the afternoon, after Melanie had left to cover a fire, Jerome Stanley came to the counter, puffing on his ever-present pipe.

"How are things, my boy? Have you recovered from your ordeal in the mountains?"

"As ordeals go, sir," Clay answered, "it wasn't much."

"My niece has certainly recovered," Stanley said. "Where that girl gets her energy is beyond me. She never stops. It's work, work and more work."

"So I've noticed," Clay said.

"I have tried to persuade her to enjoy herself more. But there is no talking to someone her age. They think they know everything."

"I'm her age."

Jerome Stanley chuckled. "That you are. And for a while there, I had high hopes you were just what she needs. She could do worse. In my opinion you are a fine young man."

Clay shifted his weight from one foot to the other and sheepishly mumbled, "Thank you, sir."

"I should thank you. She hasn't shown an interest in men since I can remember. Watching the two of you brought back memories of my own courtship. Always smiling and laughing and giving each other those special looks." Stanley took the pipe from his mouth. "But something has happened. I can tell. She is not acting the same toward you." Stanley held up a hand when Clay went to speak. "Never you mind. It is between you and her and I would not presume to stick my nose in. But I am troubled. Doubly so after her admission to me last night."

"Sir?"

Stanley glanced around the office, then lowered his voice. "I shouldn't be telling you this, but she has been following you around. Asking questions of everyone you know. Trying to find out more about you."

"Has she, now?" Clay shammed innocence.

"She wouldn't tell me why. All she would say was that she was investigating you because she likes you." Stanley fell silent as the typesetter walked past, then said, "Now I ask you, isn't that just like a female? Her logic is no kind of logic at all, but there you have it."

"Why are you telling me this, sir?"

"Because I would like for the two of you to get back together. It's her I'm thinking of. She needs more in her life than work. Hell, we all do." Stanley clamped his teeth on the pipe stem and puffed. "Well, back to work."

It was shortly after two when a short, scruffy man in a slouch hat, wearing a revolver tucked under his

belt near the buckle, slunk into the *Courier*. On seeing
him, Clay slid his right hand under his jacket. "Can I
help you, mister?"

"Would you be Adams?"

"If I am?" Clay rejoined.

"Skagg sent me. I'm a friend of his. They call me
Rat."

Clay made sure no one was near, then crooked a
finger. "I'm listening."

Rat leaned across the counter. He had yellow teeth
and fetid breath. "Skagg says to tell you he found out
what you wanted to know. He says you're to come to
the stone bridge over Pine Creek at ten tonight."

"Why did he send you instead of coming himself?"

"He says he has to be careful. That the gent you
have had him asking about is as dangerous as a wol-
verine. Skagg doesn't want to be seen anywhere
near here."

"I would rather meet him at the Rusty Spittoon,"
Clay said.

"The bridge is better. That late, and that far out,
no one will be around." Rat turned to go, then
snapped his finger. "I almost forgot. Skagg says to be
sure to bring the money you promised."

"I will have the hundred with me. Tell him not to
worry."

The rest of the afternoon crawled by. Clay glanced
at the clock above Jerome Stanley's desk a score of
times. Twice he caught himself impatiently tapping his
fingers, and stopped.

Shortly after five Melanie returned. She ignored
Clay, sat at her desk and set to work on her story
about the fire, consulting her notes when she had to.

Every now and then she gazed out the front window, but only when Clay's back was to her.

It was almost seven when Jerome Stanley, puffing on his pipe, announced that Clay could go home. Clay promptly donned his derby, but instead of heading for the door, he stepped to Melanie's desk.

"Might I have a word with you, Miss Stanley?"

"I'm busy," Melanie said without looking at him.

"I wanted to let you know I'm leaving," Clay said.

"I heard my uncle. Off you go. I have work to finish."

"Should I wait outside?"

Melanie's head snapped up. "Whatever for? We don't have a supper date tonight, if that is what you are implying."

"I just wanted to make it easy for you to follow me as you have been doing," Clay said.

Melanie sniffed and continued writing. "I am sure I have no idea what you are talking about."

"Remember Gressel from the Rusty Spittoon? He remembers you. Remembers the questions you asked about me. And he's not the only one, is he?"

Her eyes flashing, Melanie said, "You have only yourself to blame. I asked you to be honest with me and you refused. If you had been more forthcoming I would not need to unearth the truth about you by other means."

"What have you found out so far?" Clay asked.

"That I was right. There is something peculiar about you."

"Name one thing."

Sitting back, Melanie folded her arms. "For starters, how about the fact that you spend a lot of your free time at the worst saloon in Bluff City. And by worst, I mean it's the haunt of some of the most vicious characters on the frontier. Yet you mingle with them as if you are one of them."

Clay shrugged. "They accept me, is all."

"Don't be coy. Mr. Gressel told me that you beat the toughest man in the saloon with your bare fists."

"I landed a lucky punch."

"Was it luck when you helped Cavendish and me escape from Jesse Stark? Was it luck when you killed two of his men? Was it luck that kept us out of their clutches and brought us safely to the mine?"

Clay leaned on the edge of her desk. "I thought you liked me."

Taken aback, Melanie replied, "I do. I like you a lot. Well, more than a little, possibly. Why else would I be so curious about your past?"

"Because your nose is twitching," Clay said. "Because you like to bite into a mystery and worry it until you have bled it dry."

"You think you have me all figured out, but you don't," Melanie said stiffly.

"It wouldn't be the first time a woman has confused a man," Clay said. "I suppose it's pointless to ask you to leave well enough alone?"

"It most definitely is. I love a challenge. And you, Mr. Clay Adams, are proving to be a most interesting one."

On that note Clay walked out. He was mad but he was also flattered. "Her uncle did say she likes me," he said aloud in wonderment, then glanced quickly around. No one had noticed.

On this particular night Clay did not bend his step

to the Rusty Spittoon or the Emporium. He hurried to his apartment. From a valise he stored in the bottom of the closet he took an entirely different set of clothes and laid them out on the bed: buckskins and knee-high moccasins. At the bottom of the valise were a gun belt and holster. He unwrapped the belt and palmed the pearl-handled Colt nestled in the holster. With a skilled flourish he twirled the Colt forward, then backward, then forward again. He flipped it high into the air and caught it by the grips, his trigger finger curling around the trigger in a single smooth motion.

"I've missed you," Clay said to the revolver. Grinning happily, he slid the Colt into the holster and proceeded to change clothes. When he was done, he examined himself in the full-length mirror attached to the closet door. The pearl-handled Colt rode high on his right hip, the cartridges gleaming brightly in the lamplight.

"Now that looks more like the real me," Clay addressed his reflection. "One thing is missing, though." He went to the closet. From a shelf near the top he took the article that completed his transformation: a wide-brimmed black hat.

About to leave, Clay did a strange thing. He ran a finger up and down his nose several times, and laughed. Then he snatched his saddlebags from off the table, slid a Winchester from under the bed and walked out humming.

His saddle, saddle blanket and bridle were in a shed next to the picket fence. He slid the bridle on the claybank, threw the saddle blanket over its back and smoothed the blanket, and reached for the saddle. After tightening the cinch he tied his saddlebags on, shoved the Winchester into the saddle scabbard and informed the claybank, "We're ready."

Leading the horse by the reins, Clay opened the gate, looked both ways and led the horse into the side street. It was deserted. He quietly closed the gate, then forked leather, the saddle creaking under his weight. The claybank stomped a hoof.

"I know, I know," Clay said. "You have been cooped up too long. I don't blame you."

A jab of his heels and Clay was on his way. Pine Creek was a mile to the south of Bluff City. The stone bridge where he was to meet Skagg Izzard was another half mile past the junction. He rode slowly, relishing the sense of being himself after weeks of being someone else.

To the west reared Bluff Mountain and the chain of peaks the bluff was part of. They bulged gigantic against the sky. Several were crowned with snow.

The Rockies in the autumn were magnificent. A blaze of vivid colors put to shame efforts by artists to capture Nature's beauty on canvas. The leaves of the maples and oaks and others changed from green to vibrant hues of red, orange and yellow. But it was the aspens for which the mountains were noted. People made a holiday of traveling to the high country to admire the leafy spectacle.

Clay's regret, as he rode south, was that it was night and not day, so he, too, could enjoy the scenery.

Once away from the lights of Bluff City, a legion of stars filled the firmament. So many stars that it took the breath away. As Clay marveled at the celestial display, a shooting star streaked across the heavens.

"Some Indian tribes say that brings good luck,"

Clay told the claybank. "Others say it's a bad omen. Me, I never did believe in four-leaf clovers or get spooked by black cats."

A buckboard appeared, coming the other way. Clay automatically placed his hand on his pearl-handled Colt and angled to the side of the rutted dirt road. The driver wore homespun and waved in greeting.

"Howdy, friend. Nice night."

"That it is," Clay replied as the buckboard rattled by. "That it is," he said again, even though the man could not hear him.

Most people preferred the comforts and safety of Bluff City to a settler's life. But here and there Clay glimpsed cabins, their windows aglow. He wondered about the settlers inside those cabins, about their families and whether they were happy.

Clay encountered no one else after the man in the buckboard. Country folk generally turned in a lot earlier than their city cousins. They had too. They were up with the crowing of the cock and toiled until the setting of the sun.

At the junction Clay drew rein. He was early, on purpose. He rose in the stirrups and looked and listened, then reined to the right, off the road and into the trees. He stayed there a spell, acquainting himself with the rhythms of the night, with the rustle of the wind and the cries of the wild creatures.

Every nerve tingling, Clay rode on, paralleling the road. When he spied the stone bridge, he stopped. It had been built so that wagons bound for the mining camps would not bust their wheels and axles on the boulders that littered the bed of Pine Creek.

Clay reckoned he had half an hour yet. He stayed

in the saddle. He occupied himself with thoughts of Melanie, and how she would feel if and when she discovered the truth.

It was about ten minutes to ten when pebbles clattered, and a rider came up out of the creek bed onto the far side of the bridge. Clay did not need daylight to tell that the rider was an uncommonly large man. "Skagg?" he called.

"Who else would it be?" was the surly retort. "Come out in the open where I can see you. I'm not no owl."

Clay gigged the claybank to the near end of the bridge. The creek was as black as a well. Had it not been for the gurgle of the water he would have thought it was dry. "What are you waiting for? Cross on over."

"On this side, not that side," Skagg said.

To Clay it made no difference. He crossed the stone bridge and reined up yet again only a few feet from the giant.

"What the hell?" Skagg exclaimed. "Where did you get those clothes? You don't look anything like yourself."

"I am more me now than I have been since you met me." Clay waved a hand. "Forget about my clothes. Were you able to do as I wanted?"

"Why else would I have sent for you?" Skagg gruffly responded. "I let it be known all over town that I was interested in joining the Stark gang. I didn't think it would work, but just like you figured, someone got in touch with me." Skagg held out a huge hand. "Our deal was fifty dollars in advance and fifty more when I found out what you wanted to know."

Clay fished for his poke. "It's money well spent if you can tell me where to find Jesse Stark."

"I can do better than that." Skagg's other hand rose from his side holding a revolver.

Chapter 16

Where others might have grabbed for their six-shooter in panic, Clay Adams calmly stared at the leveled revolver and asked, "What is this, Skagg? We had a deal."

"I did agree to help you for the hundred dollars, yes," the big man rumbled. "But then I got to thinking about how you used me and it made me good and mad."

"How did I use you?" Clay asked.

"By pretending to like me. By pretending to be my friend. But the whole time all you really wanted was someone to find the Stark gang for you. Probably so you can write a story for that newspaper you work for."

"It's not like that," Clay said.

"All those nights we played cards at the Rusty Spittoon. All the drinks you bought me. You were playing me for a damn fool." Skagg grinned a sly grin. "But I've been put wise to you."

"Someone fed you the notion that I was using you?" Clay studied him. "Did you find out where Stark is holed up?"

"No. But I've met one of his men. I had been to

every watering hole in Bluff City, and I was about ready to give up, hundred or no hundred. Then last night a gent named Gorman came up to me and offered to buy me a drink. He said as how he heard I was asking around about Stark, and was it true I wanted to join Stark's outfit. He said Stark is always on the lookout for the right kind of men. Men who can squeeze the trigger without batting an eye."

"You didn't tell Gorman about me, I hope."

"Hell no," Skagg said. "Not after he told me that if I joined up with Stark, I'd get an equal share of the loot. That promises to be more money than I've seen in all my born days."

"So you decided to break your deal with me and join up with Stark for real," Clay said.

"That's about the gist of it," Skagg said. "Except I can't leave you alive to tell folks I've joined up with Stark." Skagg's tone softened slightly. "You can see how it is, can't you, Clay? A man has to do what's best for his poke."

"What now?"

Skagg Izzard kneed his mount closer. "There is only one way to keep you from talking. I'm sorry it has to be like this but I'm not partial to the notion of gurgling at the end of a rope." As an afterthought he added, "I asked a friend to help me."

"A friend?"

"That would be me," said the man called Rat as he came riding out of the shadows with a revolver in his hand. "Any last words, mister, before we send you to hell?"

"Amateurs," Clay said in mild disgust.

"Who?" Skagg asked.

"You and your friend. When you have to kill someone, kill them. Don't talk them to death. And you
make damn sure you disarm them before you do anything else."

Skagg wagged his revolver. "We have you covered.
Your pistol is still in your holster. What do you think
you can do?"

"This," Clay Adams said, and his Colt was in his
hand, spouting lead. He fanned it four times with
lightning rapidity, putting three slugs into Skagg Izzard
in the time it took the big man to blink, and then
sending the fourth slug into Rat's scrawny chest before
Rat could squeeze the trigger. Rat toppled backward
and his horse spooked and bolted past the claybank.
Clay let it go. He had his Colt trained on Skagg, who,
incredibly, still sat his saddle, wheezing loudly, his
arms limp, his revolver dangling.

Clay gigged the claybank alongside the bigger man's
mount. "I wish you hadn't done that."

"That makes two of us," Skagg Izzard gasped.
"You've done shot me to pieces."

"Where can I find Jesse Stark?"

Skagg's mouth curled in the suggestion of a grin.
"Gorman never told me." Sounding like a bellows on
its last gasp, he sucked air into lungs. "He was to meet
me later tonight and take me to meet Stark." Scarlet
froth dribbled over his lips and his big frame twitched.
"That was mighty slick, that draw of yours."

"I've had a lot of practice."

Skagg managed to raise his head and look Clay in
the eyes. "You're fast. Maybe the fastest I ever saw."

Clay said nothing.

"Tell me the truth." Skagg sucked in more air. "No

scribbler could beat me with his fists and a six-gun. Who are you really?"

"No one in particular."

"I'm asking nice. I don't have long, and I'd like to know your name. The name of the man who killed me."

Clay Adams sighed. "In another life I was known as Crooked Nose Neville Baine."

Skagg's eyelids fluttered. He seemed about to keel from his saddle, but somehow he steadied himself and said, "I heard tell you were dead."

"I am. I go by Clay Adams now, and only Clay Adams."

"But your nose?"

"It got fixed."

"I'll be damned." And with that, Skagg Izzard died, his huge form oozing to the ground in a tangle of limbs.

Clay stared down at the body. "I'm trying not to be," he said. Shaking himself, he replaced the spent cartridges, twirled the pearl-handled Colt into his holster and reined the claybank around. He started onto the stone bridge but had only gone a few yards when he saw a rider at the other end. Instantly, his hand flew to his Colt. "Who's there?" he challenged.

"Who do you think?" came the soft reply.

"Please, no." Clay flicked his reins and was across the bridge in moments. His eyes confirmed what his ears had heard, and in his anxiety he blurted, "What in God's name are you doing here?"

"What else?" Melanie Stanley said. "I was following you." She had on a black riding outfit, with a black hat and a black quirt. Unlike a lot of women, who rode sidesaddle, she rode as a man would ride, her dress hitched up halfway to her knees.

They stared at one another, neither showing an inclination to speak. Melanie's face was in shadow and impossible to read; Clay's a mirror of torment. Finally he said, "It's dangerous for a woman to be on her own this far out from town at night."

Melanie motioned with her quirt at the sprawled forms. "It's dangerous for men, too, I see."

"You don't seem as shocked as I expected."

"It's not as if you haven't killed before," Melanie said. "Or have you forgotten those two outlaws you knifed to death?" She bit her lower lip. "I wonder how many more."

"I'm not Jesse Stark. To me, people aren't bugs to be squashed whenever I have the urge."

Melanie motioned with her quirt again. "Is that what this was about? Does it have something to do with Stark?"

"It has everything to do with him," Clay said. Impulsively, he gripped her wrist. "Promise me you won't tell anyone."

"Let go," Melanie said.

"Please," Clay beseeched her. "You don't realize what is at stake. You don't know how much finding Stark means to me."

"I won't ask you again."

Clay looked at his hand on her arm. "Oh. Sorry. I didn't mean—" He broke off, his features downcast.

"Let me see your pistol," Melanie requested.

"What?"

"You heard me."

"Why?"

"Humor me." Melanie held out her hand.

Reluctantly, Clay slid his revolver from its holster and placed it on her palm. "Don't cock it. It has a hair trigger."

"I know a little about guns," Melanie said. She examined the Colt with great care, running her hand over the cylinder and along the barrel. "Pearl handles. Nickel-plated. Etching. And a hair trigger? They don't get any fancier than this."

"I suppose," Clay conceded.

"Only one kind of person carries a pistol like this," Melanie said. "Some people call them leather slappers. Pistoleros, the Mexicans say. Gunslingers, gunnies, gun sharks. Need I go on?"

Clay held out his hand. "May I have it back now?"

"What's the matter? Feel uncomfortable without it?" Melanie pointed it at him. "I just saw you commit two murders. Legally, I am obligated to turn you over to the marshal."

"Do whatever you want," Clay said, and as he said it, his right hand became a bolt of living lightning and relieved her of the Colt. Shoving it into his holster, he slapped his legs against the claybank.

It was a full minute before Melanie caught up. "You and I have a lot to talk about, Mr. Adams."

"What do you want to know?"

"Everything."

"My real name is Baine. Neville Baine. I was born in Indiana. When I was eleven my folks went to visit my mother's sister and left me home. It was the middle of the winter, and right after they left, it snowed for five days. They couldn't get back and I couldn't get out. I was in the hayloft, forking hay down for the horses, when I slipped and fell. I hit my face on the ladder and broke my nose in three places. I didn't know what to do so I didn't do anything, and a week later, when my folks showed up, the bone had started to mend so they left it be. Only thing was, my nose was bent in the middle. Bent bad. The other kids took to calling me Crooked Nose. One day when I was fifteen I was talking to a girl I liked and a neighbor boy started poking fun at me, calling me Crooked Nose and teasing the girl for liking someone so ugly. I hit him. I hit him hard, again and again and again. I hit him so many times, I thought I had killed him. So I lit a shuck. Ended up in Kansas. I worked at all sorts of jobs, and everywhere I went, I was teased about my face. Then I met Dave Mather. Mysterious Dave, they call him. A leather slapper. A pistolero. A gunslinger. Gunny. Gun shark. Shootist. He took a shine to me and taught me how to use a pistol. How to use it so no one would tease me ever again. I was in a few shooting scrapes and word got around. After that, everyone left me alone." Clay abruptly stopped. He had not meant to tell her so much, but once he started he could not stop.

"Dear Lord," Melanie breathed.

"There is more if you want to hear it."

"There is nothing I want to hear more."

Clay grimly continued. "Jesse Stark tried to rob the bank at Whistler's Flat. You know about that. What you don't know is that I tried to stop him. The townsmen mistook me for one of his men and shot me. I made it out of Whistler's Flat but Stark found me and beat me until I was dead. Or so he thought. Then he rode off."

"So that's it," Melanie said.

"I didn't die, though. I healed. So did my nose. He broke it worse than that time I fell from the loft, but when it mended, my nose was a normal nose again. I was like everyone else. Crooked Nose Baine was gone."

Clay drew rein in the middle of the road. Taken unawares, Melanie was a shade slow in doing the same. She twisted in her saddle and asked, "What's wrong? Why did you stop just when I was beginning to understand?"

"Do you? Do you realize how important this is to me? I have been given a new chance. Call it a miracle, call it the hand of the Almighty, call it blind luck, but I can start my life over."

"When do you intend to begin?"

"I already have. I cut my hair short. I shaved my mustache. I bought new clothes and a new hat and took a new name."

"Was all that before or after you came to Colorado to kill Jesse Stark?" Melanie asked.

"Does it make a difference?"

"Indeed it does. Yes, your nose is as it should be. Yes, you changed everything about you that you could. But you are still the same man you were before. You are still a killer."

"Only when I have to be."

"Wrong, Clay. You are completely, utterly wrong." Melanie gazed at the stars and at the road and finally back at him. "You're deceiving yourself, is what you are doing. You are out for revenge. You want to kill Jesse Stark for what he did to you." She gave a sharp intake of breath. "My God. Now I understand why your hand was shaking when you held that gun to Stark's head. It wasn't that you were scared. It was because you wanted to kill him so badly. Why didn't you?"

Clay's answer was barely audible. "I couldn't."

"The same question. Why?"

"I couldn't risk you taking a stray slug when his men shot me down. I would never risk your life."

"Oh."

Clay clucked to the claybank and Melanie clucked to her mare and they rode side by side, the breeze caressing their faces.

"I am grateful you felt fit to confide in me."

"Do you still aim to report me to Marshal Vale?"

"I don't know what I am going to do. To be honest, I am so confused right now, my head is spinning."

"But I just explained everything," Clay said.

"It's not your past I'm confused about," Melanie clarified. "It's me. My emotions are in a whirl. I can't get over the fact you have slain four men since I met you, and now I learn you hope to kill a lot more—"

"Only Jesse Stark," Clay interrupted her. "He's the one I want."

"But don't you see—" Melanie began, and was interrupted yet again, this time by the sudden pounding of hooves as seven or eight riders swept down on them from out of the night and one of the riders bawled, "Kill the man and grab the woman, boys! And be quick about it!"

Chapter 17

Clay recognized the voice. It was Gorman. Evidently Gorman had followed Skagg, just as Melanie had followed him. He figured Gorman had witnessed the shooting and shadowed them.

"Ride!" Clay bellowed, and smacked Melanie's mare.

A glance showed Clay the outlaws were in a crescent, the nearest a mere fifty feet away. He was furious with himself for letting them get so close. He had been careless, letting his talk with Melanie distract him.

The outlaws whooped and hollered. Several shots boomed and leaden hornets buzzed past Clay's head. Drawing his pearl-handled Colt, he swiveled in his saddle and fired twice. The nearest badman cried out and clutched at his saddle horn to keep from falling.

"He shot Roy!"

"I can keep up!" the man named Roy yelled. "He only winged me."

More slugs sought Clay and Melanie. He bent low, his mind racing faster than the claybank. If he stayed with Melanie she might be hit. But if he veered off he could lead the outlaws away, provided they all came after him.

One of their pursuers made up Clay's mind for him by gleefully bellowing, "Remember! We take turns with the woman and I get to go first!"

Clay stayed with Melanie. Gorman and his friends stopped wasting lead and stayed far enough back to discourage Clay from wasting lead, too, but not so far back as to lose sight of them.

Melanie rode superbly. Clay had known she was competent but now she impressed him even more. She was exceptional. Strong-headed, yes. Impulsive, yes. More independent than most females, yes. But for all that, he liked her more than he had liked any woman, ever.

Clay glanced back. He would rather it was Jesse Stark who was after them. One shot, and he could end it. End Stark's spree of mayhem and murder. End, finally and forever, a part of his life he would rather not think about.

Clay had felt uncomfortable revealing his secret to Melanie. He had not wanted anyone to know that he once—

A shout from Melanie shattered Clay's reverie. He looked back again. They had gone almost a mile. The outlaws, to his surprise, were falling behind. They were giving up too easily. Then he noticed the riderless horse. The man he shot had fallen off.

Clay and Melanie galloped for another half mile. By then their horses were winded and they slowed to a walk. Clay kept glancing back, but evidently the outlaws had given up.

"Thank you," Melanie said.

"I didn't do anything."

"If you hadn't shot that man they would still be after us. And you winged him. You didn't kill him."

Clay did not point out that he had shot in the hope of doing just that. But firing from horseback was always an iffy proposition, more so at night.

"I also want you to know I have come to a decision."

"About?" Clay asked, checking behind them yet again. He would not consider them safe until they reached Bluff City.

"You."

"So soon?" To Clay it did not bode well.

"You can thank Gorman and his friends. They would have killed us if they caught us, after violating me. Stark and his men are wicked clear through and must be stopped."

"What does that have to do with me?"

"I'm getting to that," Melanie said. "The law has been trying for almost a year now to stop Stark, and can't. Single-handedly you have done more than all the posses sent out after them."

"It just happened, is all."

"There is more to it than that. You are determined enough to succeed where so many others have failed." Melanie regarded him thoughtfully. "You will be happy to hear that I am not going to tell Marshal Vale who you really are and what you are up to."

Clay's smile was heartfelt. "Thank you. You have made the right choice. I promise you that after I settle accounts with Jesse Stark, I will hang up my Colt for good."

"I wasn't done," Melanie said.

"Pardon?"

"I won't tell Marshal Vale on one condition." Melanie waited for him to ask what the condition was, and when he didn't, she said, "I won't tell him if you let me help you."

Clay was dumbfounded, and it must have shown.

"Hear me out. In one respect I am as determined as you are. That's when it comes to my job. I will go anywhere, do anything, for a newsworthy story. You might say the newspaper life is in my blood."

"So?"

"So Jesse Stark is newsworthy. He sells papers. The robberies, the shootings, they make headlines. Heck, the *Courier* sold out three days running after Cavendish was taken for ransom, because everyone wanted to read about it." Melanie's voice had grown increasingly excited. "Think of how many papers we can sell when I do an exclusive series of articles about the capture or death of Jesse Stark. Told by someone who was there."

"If you mean yourself, you won't be," Clay said.

"Don't be so hasty. You can use my help in tracking Stark down. I have contacts you don't. We will hunt him together. I want to be on it at the end, and in exchange I will keep quiet about you. That strikes me as more than fair."

"You don't happen to have one of those magnifying glasses on you, do you?"

Melanie blinked. "Why would I need one of those?"

"To find your common sense." Clay shook his head. "I have heard some addlepated notions in my day but that one beats them all."

"Give me one good reason why we can't work together."

"I can give you six. One for each of the bullets in Jesse Stark's six-shooter. Or those in Gorman's. Or Bantarro's. If not the bullets, then how about a knife or a rope or their bare hands? They can kill you in a hundred ways."

Melanie said, "You are trying to scare me, but it won't work."

"Listen to yourself. This won't be like covering a fire. We have barely escaped with our lives two times now. Why invite a third?"

"Because I'm a woman."

Clay mulled that over and said, "I grant you, females are peculiar, but how does being a woman explain your harebrained idea?"

"Have you forgotten our talk at the restaurant? Women have it harder than men. There aren't as many jobs for women, for one thing. We're expected to stay at home and be good mothers and dutiful wives. Those of us who want something different, who want a job and a career the same as men, find ourselves having to work twice as hard to prove we are worthy."

"I will grant you all that."

"Then grant me this. Think what it will mean to my career, Clay, if I get a story no one else can. The end of the Jesse Stark gang. Newspapers all over the country are bound to carry it. It will open doors for me. I will have opportunities I never would have had otherwise. Maybe I'll land a job with a prestigious newspaper in Washington or New York City. Wouldn't that be wonderful?"

"If that is what you want," Clay said.

"All I ask is that you think about it," Melanie requested. "I'm not stupid. I won't do anything to put you or me in danger. But I am sure I can help you and, in the process, help myself."

Clay thought about it. For three days it was about the only thing he thought about. On the fourth day, attired once again in his store-bought clothes and the derby, he arrived at the *Courier* and walked to where Melanie stood near the printing press. "I've made up my mind."

Melanie eyed him expectantly.

"You can help me. But I have conditions of my own. You must share everything you find out. You are not to go anywhere without me if it involves Stark. And at night, every night, I walk you home."

"Why, Mr. Adams, can it be that you are using our pact as a pretext to get to know me better?" Melanie asked with an impish chuckle.

"I only want to protect you, is all."

"I'm flattered, sir," Melanie teased. "And I agree to all your conditions, even the last. But I should warn you. Start walking me home every night and people will start to talk."

"I never have much cared what people think," Clay said, but later, when he was at the counter, he realized it wasn't true. He did care. He had cared ever since that fateful fall from the hayloft. The fall did more than disfigure his nose. It made an outcast of him. It set him apart from the common herd. He became an object to be gawked at. A monstrosity to be gossiped about. A loner, but not by choice.

Clay touched his new nose, and smiled. Then he

shook himself and thought about something else, specifically, the deaths of Skagg Izzard and Rat. Their bodies had been found by a miner on his way into town. Both were buried in pauper's graves. Marshal Vale and Deputy Wiggins had asked around but no one knew what the pair were doing at the stone bridge. The official verdict: death by person or persons unknown.

Melanie made no mention to anyone of being there, or of being chased by Gorman.

The Stark gang appeared to have vanished off the face of the earth. They robbed no one. They killed no one. They were not seen by anyone. After several weeks people speculated that maybe Jesse Stark had left Colorado for Wyoming or the Badlands, or perhaps California.

True to his word, each and every night Clay walked Melanie home after work. He was spending most of each day in her company, and he liked it that way. Usually they arrived at the *Courier* at seven, and except when she was off gathering news and he was off running errands, they were together.

The nights were exceptions. Clay spent at least three nights each week at the Rusty Spittoon playing cards and keeping his ears open for hints to Stark's whereabouts. He visited the Emporium now and then, mainly for Wesley Oaks's company. The two had become friends, and if the gambler suspected there was more to Clay than Clay let on, Oaks kept his suspicions to himself.

The first cold snap brought a few snow flurries. Higher up, more peaks were mantled in white.

A chill tang was in the air on the afternoon of the

fifteenth when Jerome Stanley sent Clay to meet the stage. Stanley was expecting important papers in the mail and wanted them brought right over.

The stage was late, a not infrequent occurrence. Clay was gazing to the east, looking for the telltale cloud of dust that always preceded its arrival, when a purple-clad figure stepped from out of the knot of people on hand to greet the stage and held out an envelope.

"For you, sir."

"Charles, isn't it?" Clay said. He scanned the boardwalk and the street, but saw no sign of the manservant's employer or of any of the toughs he had tangled with.

"Yes, sir. I am flattered you remember me."

Accepting the envelope, Clay suspiciously asked, "What is this?"

"I am sure I don't know, sir," Charles answered. "Mr. Barker gave it to me to give to you. I am to await your reply."

Clay slit the envelope with a fingernail and opened it. Inside was a short sheet of paper with gold-embossed lettering. He read it, then read it again. "Is this some sort of practical joke?"

"Sir?"

"It's an invite to have supper with Barker tomorrow at his place. You must have given it to the wrong person."

"Oh, no, sir, Mr. Barker was quite explicit. I was to give one to you and then one to Miss Stanley."

"Barker is inviting Melanie too? Why the two of us? What is he up to?"

"Again, sir, I couldn't say. Mr. Barker does not take

me into his confidence in such matters." Charles coughed lightly. "What shall I tell him, sir? Will you be there?"

"I would like to hear what Melanie has to say."

"I am afraid I must insist on a reply, sir. Mr. Barker is waiting down the street in his carriage."

Clay hesitated. It had been so long since their last clash that he had begun to think Barker had forgotten about him.

"Sir?" Charles prompted.

"Tell your boss I would rather swallow a cactus, but I will be there if Melanie says she wants to go."

"Yes or no, sir," Charles said with exaggerated forbearance. "Mr. Barker undoubtedly wants a definite answer."

Clay's features clouded and he clenched his fists. "Don't push me, mister. I don't like being prodded."

Charles took a step back. "I am sorry, sir. It was not my intention to be rude. I will relay your answer to Mr. Barker."

"You do that."

Clay was pacing with impatience when the stage eventually clattered to a stop in a swirling cloud of dust in front of the company office. It did not help his disposition any that there was no mail for Jerome Stanley. He hurried to the *Courier*.

Melanie was at her desk. He dropped his invitation on it and asked, "Did you get one of these too?"

Picking it up, Melanie read it, her eyebrows arching. "Interesting. So he invited you, as well."

"What did you tell him?"

"That I would be delighted to accept."

"Why did he invite me when he wants me six feet under?"

Melanie bestowed her sweetest smile. "There is only one way to find out. We will enter the lion's den and pray we make it out alive."

Chapter 18

As much as Clay disliked Harve Barker, he had to admit one thing. Barker was not a miser. The man spent his money as if there was no end to it. The Barker estate, like the Emporium, oozed luxury. The first inkling was the high wall and wrought-iron gate. Once the carriage was admitted by a guard, it wound up a gravel drive lined by stately trees to an imposing mansion.

Gold and silver barons were famous for building homes to rival Solomon's temple. Not to be outdone, Barker had made his not just the largest in Bluff City, but the largest in the territory.

"I had no idea!" Melanie breathed in awe. "I had heard stories but I had no real idea."

Wide marble steps flanked by Grecian-style columns led to an ornate door. The central section was four stories tall. Wings, two stories high, spread to either side. Dazzling white, the mansion was fit for a king.

"There must be a hundred rooms in that place," Clay marveled.

Charles admitted them. He accepted Melanie's shawl and hung it on a bronze hook next to Clay's derby. "Right this way, if you please."

The hallway was paneled. Plush carpet was underfoot. At intervals hung paintings. Originals, not copies. The sitting room into which they were ushered was brightly lit by whale-oil lamps. The furniture was rosewood with thick upholstery. Melanie perched on a settee, but Clay stayed on his feet and paced the room like a caged tiger, going from the window to the doorway and back again.

"You will wear out the carpet."

"We should not have come," Clay said sourly. "Why you accepted is beyond me."

"Don't start that again."

A grandfather clock in the corner chimed eight. Somewhere off in the mansion a door closed.

Clay reached under his jacket and adjusted his shoulder holster. "Whatever happens, stay close to me."

"I keep telling you," Melanie said. "He won't dare touch us. Too many people know he invited us, my uncle among them."

"You don't know Barker like I do. He won't let a little thing like that stop him. He thinks he can do anything and get away with it."

"You gnaw your worries to death, don't you?"

"Poke fun. Just remember I warned you when our host unsheathes his claws. Out of the corner of an eye Clay became aware of a figure in the doorway. Spinning, he started to slide his hand under his jacket.

It was Charles. "If you would be so good as to follow me?" he requested with a polite smile.

The dining room was spacious enough to feed fifty. There was a door at each end as well as the one they came through in the middle of the room. A long mahogany table lined by mahogany chairs glistened with fresh polish. Sterling silverware gleamed under the light of a chandelier. Several servants stood around waiting to serve.

Charles escorted them to two places near the head of the table and pulled the chairs out for them.

Clay smoothed his jacket so the bulge did not show. "Where is our host?"

"Mr. Barker will be here presently, sir," Charles said. "In the meantime, what would you and Miss Stanley like in the way of refreshments? You may have any drink you like."

"Is there any chance I can get a Cherry Do or a Peach Do?" Melanie asked. "They are weaknesses of mine."

"You may have either. Which do you prefer?"

Melanie giggled. "How about a Cherry Do to start? When I finish it, I'll have a Peach Do."

"As you wish. And you, sir?"

"Water."

"That's all, sir? We can make over a hundred mixed drinks. Or you can have straight whiskey. I seem to recall you drank that at the Emporium."

Clay was tempted, but he wanted to keep his head clear and his reflexes sharp. "Just water."

"Very well." Charles bowed and departed.

Melanie ran a hand over the tablecloth. "You should indulge yourself. A treat like this doesn't come along often."

"A gilded cage is still a cage," Clay reminded her.

"Oh, posh. I refuse to let you spoil my mood. Harve Barker is many things, not all of them praiseworthy, but he is not and has never been a fool."

"I'll remember you said that when the wolf shows just how rabid it can be," Clay responded.

A pretty young woman in a short purple dress brought the Cherry Do and the water.

"Delicious," Melanie said after taking a sip. "I can tell I am going to enjoy myself immensely."

A door at the other end of the dining room opened and in strolled the man of the manor. He wore a tailored jacket, vest and pantaloons, all his favorite color, a striking purple shade, and gray pumps. By the time he reached the chair at the head of the table, Charles was there to hold it out for him. Barker sat with a flourish and bestowed a warm smile on Melanie. The smile evaporated when he looked at Clay. "Greetings to you both. I am glad you accepted. I hope I haven't kept you waiting long."

"Not at all," Melanie said.

"Mind telling me why I'm here?" Clay bluntly demanded.

Harve Barker fiddled with the hem of his sleeve for a moment. "Direct and to the point. I like that. You are here, Mr. Adams, so that we might clear the air, as it were. But that can wait, can it not, until after we have eaten? I am sure Miss Stanley would rather we hold our personal business until the end."

"That I would," Melanie said. "And since when do you call me Miss Stanley? My first name has always been good enough."

"It has," Barker conceded, "but that was before a certain entanglement presented itself." He cast a pointed glance at Clay.

"Please, Harve," Melanie said. "I'd rather you didn't."

"I am being as gracious as I know how," Barker said. "You can't hold a slight bitterness against me. I had high hopes regarding you at one time, if you will recall."

"We can still be friends," Melanie said. "And before we go any further, I should make it clear to you that is all Clay and I are. Good friends."

"Is that so?" Barker said. "I should think you would be more by now, given how much time the two of you spend together."

"Why, Harve, have you been spying on us?" Melanie asked with a grin.

Barker did not answer. He clapped his hands and servants scurried to their tasks. China plates were set out. Neatly folded napkins were placed at their elbows.

"Your servants are marvelously efficient," Melanie complimented them.

"They better be," Barker said. He clapped again and tray after tray of food was brought in. Platters of beef, pork and venison. Two kinds of soup. The vegetables included corn, string beans and peas. Fried, sliced potatoes were offered, as were corn bread and pudding. A tray of cheeses contributed to the elegance.

"All this for us!" Melanie exclaimed.

"You should know by now," Barker said, "I spare no expense in anything I do. When I want something, I do whatever it takes to acquire it."

Clay did not take part in the idle talk that followed. He picked at some venison, nibbled on a slice of Swiss cheese, and ate a little corn and pudding. Whenever servants came near the table he placed his right hand in his lap, his fingers under his jacket.

Melanie and Barker chatted and laughed. Barker seemed to have forgotten Clay was there. Not once in the entire meal did Barker look at him.

Over an hour was consumed. Then the servants cleared the trays and plates, and Charles produced a cigar that Barker snipped and lit, saying out the side of his mouth to Melanie as he did, "I trust you won't mind? You have indulged me in the past."

"My father and my uncle both smoke pipes, so I am accustomed to the smoke," Melanie said.

Barker motioned at his manservant. "That will be all, Charles. See that the staff goes to their quarters and stays there until I send word they may come out. Then tell Mr. Train I will see him."

"Very well, sir."

"Train?" Melanie said. "Is he another guest?"

"No, someone I have hired. A very special individual. One of the few who pursue his line of work."

"How mysterious."

"A lot of what I do is not for public scrutiny," Barker informed her.

Clay stayed silent no longer. "Would Marshal Vale be interested in any of your doings?"

"Don't start," Melanie chided. "You will spoil the evening."

"That's all right," Barker told her. He turned toward Clay. "Interesting that you mentioned our good town marshal. He came to see me about you. It seems he had heard you and I were at odds, and that you and some of the men who work for me were in a few scrapes. Vale wanted to impress on me that he would not take it kindly if anything were to happen to you."

"He did?" Clay was genuinely surprised.

"Ah. Then you didn't put him up to it?" Barker pursed his lips. "Not that his wishes matter in the least. I do what I think best for me. I always have. I always will."

"Don't you ever get tired of crowing about yourself?" Clay fired a verbal salvo.

"I wasn't boasting, Mr. Adams. I was stating fact." Barker inhaled on his cigar and leisurely blew a smoke ring. "Now then. Suppose we get to why I asked you here. I would imagine you are both quite curious."

"I was hoping it was to mend fences," Melanie said.

"In your case I would like nothing better," Barker replied. "But circumstances being what they are, I am afraid that's not possible."

"What circumstances? Are you referring to Clay and me? I told you we're good friends."

"The circumstance I refer to has nothing to do with you carrying on with him and everything to do with that nose of yours."

The door at the far end opened and in came a square block of a man dressed all in brown, including a low-crowned brown hat and brown leather boots. His neck was exceptionally thick, his chest extraordinarily deep, yet his waist was slim. He carried himself with catlike grace. Flat eyes as dark as pitch regarded Clay and Melanie with fleeting interest. "Are these them?" He had an accent that was difficult to place, with a trace of both a French and a Spanish influence.

"They are," Barker said. "Mr. Train, permit me to

introduce Clay Adams and Melanie Stanley of the *Bluff City Courier.*"

"Pleased to make your acquaintance," Melanie said. "Mr. Barker mentioned earlier that you are in a unique line of work. What might it be?"

Clay was taking note of Train's sun-bronzed skin, of the Whitney revolver on Train's right hip and the bowie on his left.

"I hunt men."

Clay snapped his head up. "You're a bounty hunter?"

"No."

"But you just said—"

Harve Barker bent forward. "Permit me to explain. Mr. Train hails from New Orleans. He was raised in the bayou country but has been all over plying his craft. He hunts men, yes, but not for the rewards on their heads. Once he has found his quarry his job is done. He does not take them into custody."

"He does this out of the goodness of his heart?"

"There is a fee involved," Barker said. "A substantial fee."

"Then you do not kill those you hunt?" Melanie asked Train.

Barker answered her. "He is a manhunter. Not a man killer. The best there is, some say. Which is why I sent for him. Why I have paid a considerable sum to retain his services."

"You hired him to hunt someone for you," Melanie said. "Who in the world can it be?"

"It is not just one person. I want him to find the Stark gang."

Clay and Melanie looked at one another in mutual consternation. It was Clay who found his voice first.

"Why this sudden interest in Jesse Stark? Do you aim to collect the bounty on him and his men?"

"Oh, please," Barker said. "I earn more in a day than the entire bounty being offered. I wouldn't hire a man of Mr. Train's caliber for such a pittance." He paused. "And my interest isn't sudden, by any means. Or have you forgotten that the Stark gang raided Calamity, a mining camp, and stole several thousand dollars from one of my saloons?"

"That was months ago," Clay said. "Why wait so long to go after him?"

"Because I believe in doing things right, Mr. Adams. I asked around to find out who is the best in the manhunting business. That took time. I sent a letter to Mr. Train and waited to hear back. That took time. Now he is here and everything is in place, and two days from now he heads up into the mountains after Jesse Stark. It is rumored that Stark has a hidey-hole somewhere. When Mr. Train finds it, he will bring word to me, and I will personally pay Jesse Stark a visit. Along with twenty or so hired guns." Barker smiled. "When I take revenge on someone, I like to see their face."

"In other words," Melanie said, "you are taking the law into your own hands."

Barker shrugged. "Call it what you will."

"Why have you told us all this?" Melanie wanted to know.

"I should think it would be obvious," Barker replied. "Word has reached me that you and Mr. Adams have been discreetly asking around, trying to find Stark yourselves. Oh, don't look so surprised. Little goes on in this town that I don't find out about. I am offering you a golden opportunity, the chance to do what you could never accomplish on your own."

Melanie glanced at the inscrutable manhunter. "You can't be saying what I think you are saying."

"But I can, my dear. When Mr. Train rides out in two days, you and Mr. Adams are welcome to go along."

Chapter 19

Clay tried to talk Melanie out of it. He used every argument he could think of. He stressed the danger. He pointed out that trusting Harve Barker was foolhardy, and trusting Mr. Train even more so. When that failed to persuade her he threatened to go to her uncle.

Melanie laughed him off. She told him that if he went to Jerome, so would she, to tell her uncle that the clerk he had hired was none other than the notorious Neville Baine. "Do you really want that?"

No, Clay did not. The only edge he had in his campaign to put an end to Jesse Stark's owlhoot spree was the fact Stark had no idea who he was. If Stark found out, he might light a shuck for other climes. Or come gunning for Clay with his entire gang to back his play. "We will do it your way. But it's a mistake you might regret."

"It wouldn't be the first time," was Melanie's outlook.

She had to go to her uncle anyway. She explained about Barker, and Mr. Train, and painted a rosy verbal portrait of the exclusive reports she would write of the manhunt and its aftermath. "Think of it, Uncle Jerome. We will sell more papers than ever."

Clay was by her side when she made her plea. She insisted he be with her. "For moral support," was how she phrased it. Several times she looked at him as if expecting him to come to her defense when Jerome balked, but Clay refused to say a word. It did no good. She convinced her uncle without his help, and daybreak of the second day after their supper at the mansion found them in front of the Emporium to meet the manhunter.

Harve Barker was there, as well, to see them off. At that hour the street was nearly deserted. The clomp of hooves as Mr. Train came around the corner leading a pack horse was unnaturally loud.

"You have enough supplies to last a month," Barker said. "Longer if you live off the land as much as possible."

"It is not too late to change your mind," Clay said to Melanie.

"And pass up the chance of a lifetime?"

Barker moved closer to his hired hunter. "You know what to do. Do it well and you will receive the other half of the money."

"I get the other half no matter what happens," Mr. Train said. "You agreed to that."

"Yes, I did." Barker moved over to Melanie. "I trust this redeems me somewhat in your eyes?"

"It has raised my opinion of you a few notches," Melanie said. "You will be doing the entire territory a favor by eliminating Stark."

"Be sure to mention that in your newspaper."

Barker came over to the claybank. "I bet right about now you wish you had never met me."

"This is your brainstorm. If anything happens to Miss Stanley it will be on your shoulders."

"Meaning you will blame me should she come to any harm?" Barker grinned. "Is that supposed to worry me?"

"No more than you worry me," Clay countered.

"For a clerk you are awful uppity."

"For a millionaire so are you."

Harve Barker laughed. "Unlike you, I have cause. I am richer than you will ever be. I am more powerful than you can imagine. I have the ear of the governor. If I want something done, all I have to do is snap my fingers and it gets done."

"That's the big difference between us," Clay said. "You hire others to do your work for you. Me, I ride my own broncs."

"That I would like to see," Barker scoffed. "I doubt you have ever been on one your whole life."

"I might surprise you," Clay said.

Mr. Train lifted his reins. "Are we going to sit here all morning or do what I am being paid to do?"

"Lead the way," Melanie said.

They reached the outskirts of Bluff City before the sun was half an hour high. Mr. Train turned south and before long they were at the junction. Train took the right fork.

Clay kept his thoughts to himself as they went over the stone bridge. Once on the other side he asked, "How is it you picked this way?"

"I do as Mr. Barker tells me," Train said.

"The rumors he mentioned about Stark's hidey-hole," Clay said. "How come I have never heard of them?"

"People are more likely to tell you things when you offer them money," Mr. Train answered. "And money is one thing Barker has plenty of."

The road climbed. Steep slope after steep slope, with heavy timber on both sides. At noon they rested the horses on a grassy shelf. The middle of the afternoon found them at the first of the mining camps. Silver had been discovered along the upper reaches of Pine Creek. A small strike, yet it drew the greedy like carrion drew vultures.

"We will stop here for the night," Mr. Train announced.

"But it's early yet," Clay objected. "We can cover a good many more miles before nightfall."

"I am to meet a man here," Mr. Train revealed. "He has information about Stark that will help us find Stark's lair."

The Pine Creek Camp, as it was called, had a tent saloon and a tent church and a tent where canned goods and tools where sold. A few lean-tos were scattered among the tents.

There was nowhere they could put up for the night so Clay and Mr. Train erected a tent of their own in a dry wash. Not for them; for Melanie. The wash afforded them some degree of privacy, and shelter from the wind.

Mr. Train excused himself to go look for the man he was to meet. "Don't wait up for me. I might not be back until late."

"I don't trust him," Clay said after Train walked off.

"Follow him, then," Melanie suggested. "See if he really meets someone."

"And leave you here alone?"

"I'm a grown woman. I can take care of myself."

"You are the *only* woman in this camp, as near as I could tell," Clay said. "Or didn't you notice how all the men were staring?"

"I thought they were admiring my dashing outfit," Melanie replied, making light of the attention.

They were not the only ones. Clay liked how her new riding garb accented the shapely contours of her figure. The trouble was, just as a flame drew moths, her figure might draw unsavory sorts who were not above imposing on a female. "I'll stick close anyhow."

"Do you cook, too?" Melanie teased.

As it turned out, Clay did do the cooking; they flipped a coin and he lost. He heated beans and made johnnycakes, simple fare they hungrily wolfed down. By then the stars had blossomed, and from the mining camp came the tinkle of a piano and merry laughter.

"It would be a shame to sit here all night doing nothing," Melanie remarked. "Why don't we take in the sights?"

"Tents, tents and more tents?"

"Come on. If anyone gives us a hard time, you have my permission to beat them senseless."

"The altitude has made you bloodthirsty," Clay said.

But he took her.

The camp was awhirl with activity. The saloon was the hub, with prospectors and others constantly coming and going. The reek of liquor reached Clay and

Melanie from fifty feet away. Taking her elbow, he steered her away from the press of women-hungry wolves and along a narrow aisle between the tents that brought them to Pine Creek.

Tucking her legs under her, Melanie sank to her knees and dipped a hand in the water. "It's ice-cold!"

"Runoff from higher up," Clay said. "From the snow on the peaks."

"There will be a lot more before too long," Melanie mentioned. "I hope an early winter storm doesn't drive us back down." She patted the ground next to her. "Have a seat, why don't you?"

Clay probed the veil of darkness. "It's not safe. I shouldn't."

"Will you listen to yourself? I swear, sometimes I think you think everyone is out to get you."

"Old habits," Clay said.

"Have we heard one gunshot since we got here? Has there been a disturbance of any kind?" Melanie patted the ground again. "We are as safe here as we would be in Bluff City. Sit before I drag you down."

"Since you put it that way." Clay complied, his left arm across his knees, his right hand brushing his jacket.

"Now take some deep breaths and appreciate the stars and the night," Melanie said, placing her hand on his leg.

Clay stared at the hand and then at her. "What are you doing?" he asked, more huskily than he intended.

"Something you need to do more of. They call it relaxing."

Putting his hand on hers, Clay said, "I was talking about this."

Melanie averted her gaze. "You make too much of a friendly gesture." She removed her hand and folded her hands in her lap. "I wonder if Mr. Train has found the man who was to meet him here."

"I wonder if there even is a man."

"There you go again. Always so suspicious. What will it take to break those old habits of yours?"

Clay took the question seriously. "Maybe when I can finally put my past behind me."

"You could do that now."

"Not with Jesse Stark still alive. Not when I wake up every night in a cold sweat from the nightmares. He nearly beat me to death."

"Killing him will make the nightmares go away?"

"I don't know," Clay said. "But it might help. Even if it doesn't, I can't let him get away with what he did."

"There is such a thing as turning the other cheek."

"Not for me. When I think of him—think of what he did—my insides twist and my head pounds. When he is gone, the twisting and the pounding will stop."

Melanie bent her legs and wrapped her arms around her knees. "I hope so, for your sake. I hope you can wipe the slate clean and start over."

"I have never wanted anything more," Clay said.

"Except to kill Jesse Stark."

Clay tried to lighten her mood with, "You gnaw a bone to death, don't you?"

"I have habits of my own. I'm pigheaded. Don't snort. I admit that when I sink my teeth into something I don't let up. But if I were like most women, if I acted fragile and demure, I would not be where I am today."

"Sitting high on a mountain in the middle of nowhere?"

Melanie's teeth showed white in the dark. "I would not be a journalist. I would not have come half as far as I have. I would be married, with nine kids, and be chained to a stove."

"That's harsh," Clay said.

"Oh, I'll marry one day. When the right man comes along. A man who won't mind my pigheadedness. A man who will let me go on working until I don't want to work any more. A man who will let me make my own decisions and not make them for me."

"I don't mind your pigheadedness."

"Really?" Melanie gazed heavenward. "I don't mind yours, either."

They sat in silence a while. Then Clay reached out and gently ran a finger from her chin across her cheek to her ear.

"Why did you do that?"

"It sort of did itself."

"You can do it again if you want."

Clay did it again. "You shivered. We can head back if you are cold."

"No. Can I lean against your shoulder?"

"Need you ask?"

Melanie leaned, and after another while she coughed and said, "You sure are a shy cuss, aren't you?"

"Touching your cheek took all the courage I have."

"Then I guess it is up to me." Melanie shifted toward him.

"What are you—"

A long silence ended with a sigh and a shifting and

Melanie saying, "That was nice. I thought you were never going to do it."

"I didn't. You did."

"A gentleman should not nitpick when a lady is flattering him with her attention," Melanie scolded.

A shooting star blazed in the firmament. To the north rose the ululating wail of a wolf.

"So what now? Are we . . . ? Do we . . . ? I mean—"

"You are having an awful time finishing a sentence tonight," Melanie said.

"Blame your lips," Clay said. "What I am trying to ask you, in my bumbling way, is if this changes anything."

"It changes everything unless you don't want it to change anything, in which case you will crush my heart."

"I hold your heart in high regard."

"Then it changes everything."

"I was hoping it would," Clay said. "So if I ask you to forget about Stark and forget about the newspapers your story would sell and go back to Bluff City in the morning, what would you say?"

"I would say yes if you are willing to forget about Stark and give up your revenge and go back with me."

"I can't do that."

"Pardon my unladylike language," Melanie said, "but then there is no chance in hell that I will, either."

"So much for changing everything," Clay said.

Chapter 20

Mr. Train did not return to their camp until well past midnight. Clay and Melanie had only been back a short while and heard him turn in. Clay did not let himself fall asleep until he was sure Train was sleeping.

Shortly before first light, Clay awoke. The smell of brewing coffee brought him out from under his blankets. The manhunter was already up, hunched close to the fire warming his hands. Clay jammed his derby on his head and shuffled over, his legs a little stiff. "You must like worms."

"We have a long day in the saddle ahead of us," Mr. Train said. "Best we get an early start."

"Did you find the man you were supposed to meet?"

"Yes." Mr. Train did not elaborate.

Clay hunkered and held his own hands close to the crackling flames. Soon the whole front of him was warm. He poured a cup of coffee and sat back. "I'll wake Melanie in a few minutes."

"She is an attractive woman, that one," Mr. Train remarked.

"I think so."

"So that is how it is."

"That is how it is," Clay said.

"There were hints. I wanted to be sure. Not that I have a personal interest. I have a woman. She pleases me and I am content with her."

"You don't fool around ever?" Clay asked.

"Would you?"

That ended their conversation until Clay was almost done his coffee and Mr. Train looked at him.

"Why do you wear those clothes?"

"Folks would talk if I ran around naked."

"They are the clothes of a city man. But I have seen how you move, how you ride, how you carry yourself. You are not a city man."

"I've spent some time outdoors," Clay hedged.

"It is more than that," Mr. Train persisted. "But if you do not want to tell me that is your right."

"Since we're asking questions," Clay said, "how did you ever get started in the man-hunting business?"

Train's flat, dark eyes glittered. "I have always liked to hunt. When I was a boy I hunted every creature in the forest and swamp. Birds, snakes, deer, everything. I became good at it. So good, it was too easy. When I was twelve I started to hunt bears, cougars and alligators. I became good at that, too. And when it became too easy, like before, and there was no challenge, I started to hunt the only thing left."

"Men."

"I started with runaway slaves and escaped convicts. There was money in that, a lot of money. Word spread. Offers came from all over and have kept coming."

"So this is just another job to you?"

"What else would it be? I never know those I hunt so it is never personal, if that is what you mean. I have heard of this Jesse Stark, though. He has been in the newspapers. A little man with much blood on his hands."

"That's him, sure enough," Clay said. He swallowed the last of his coffee, then asked, "Do you trust Harve Barker?"

"He is paying me."

"That's not an answer. Do you trust him? Trust him enough to put your life in danger?"

"He has hired me to hunt a man for him. Trust has nothing to do with it. I will find Stark, and Barker will pay me, and that will be that."

"Has anyone ever double-crossed you? Hired you and then refused to pay you?"

Mr. Train put his hand on the hilt of his bowie. "Only once. Are you suggesting Barker would do that to me? I do not see it. Not with all the money he has." Train's eyes narrowed. "You try to turn me against him, is that it?"

"Would you help someone you hate? Someone who has taken up with the woman you cared for?"

"No."

"Me either."

Mr. Train stared at the tent. "Barker and her?"

"He staked a claim but nothing ever came of it."

"Are you sure he hates you?"

"Some of his men tried to kill me."

"It appears there is more to this than I was told," Mr. Train said. "But it does not change my purpose. I will do as I am being paid to do. I have given my word and I never go back on my word."

"Just so you know," Clay said.

"You have done me a favor," Mr. Train said. "I will not forget it."

Clay was in slightly better spirits when they headed out. But he still rode with his hand on his thigh, close to his jacket.

The new day brought a change in Melanie. She was a fount of happiness. She smiled a perpetual smile. She hummed. Where the trail permitted, she rode beside the claybank.

"This mountain air must agree with you," Clay remarked at one point.

"After last night everything agrees with me," Melanie said. A look of concern came over her. "Don't you feel the same way?"

"Giddy and silly?"

"Like you are as light as a feather. Like you could fly. Like everything is right with the world." Melanie glanced at him, and when Clay did not comment, she said, "Well? Don't you?"

"What do you want me to say?" Clay rejoined. "Last night you made me the happiest I have ever been. But we are in the mountains. There are hostiles on the prowl. Outlaws are as thick as fleas, and we are after the worst outlaw there is. I'll save the giddiness for later."

All morning they climbed, wending along a pockmarked and rutted trail that led ever higher and ever deeper into the vastness of the Rockies. Midday brought them to an overlook that afforded a spectacular vista of the lower reaches. They drank from their canteens and chewed jerky and were soon under way again.

That night they camped in heavy timber. Somber

ranks of fir enclosed them in a protective phalanx, blocking out much of the sky but also screening their fire from unfriendly eyes.

Six days of hard travel carried them ever higher. They passed through two more mining camps, some of the many that had sprouted since the silver boom began. Most would wither and fade once the ore that gave them life ran out.

On the sixth day they arrived at yet another. Clay did not like some of the looks they were given, especially the hungry gazes fixed on Melanie.

Mr. Train led them beyond the camp to a hummock. At the top, amid huge boulders, was a clear space. It was early yet, only the middle of the afternoon, but they stripped their horses and Mr. Train kindled a fire. "I was told I might learn more about Stark here. I will ask around."

"Unless I'm mistaken," Melanie said, "this is Calamity, the mining camp Stark raided a while back."

"Is it, now?" This was news to Clay. "I'd like to do some asking around myself."

"You two go ahead," Melanie said. "Someone has to watch our things. I will be all right."

"No."

"Really and truly, I will be fine," Melanie said. "Give me a rifle if you are worried. I know how to use one."

When Clay still hesitated, Mr. Train said, "Why don't I go and come back, and then you go?"

"We'll do that," Clay said.

The manhunter drew his Whitney revolver, checked that it was loaded and slid it back into its holster. With a nod he was gone.

"He must expect trouble," Melanie commented.

"We should all expect it."

"What makes you say that? Stark and his cutthroats could be anywhere in these mountains."

"West of us is nothing but wilderness," Clay said. "A perfect place for Stark to hide out. But we know Stark and his men visit the camps and Bluff City from time to time. Some of them might be in this camp right this minute."

"Surely not. Not after they raided it and robbed the saloon."

"Who would stand up to them? The prospectors? They are not gun hands." Clay shook his head. "And there is no law. The outlaws can come and go as they please, at this camp or any other."

"At least Stark doesn't know we are looking for him," Melanie remarked.

"We want to keep it that way," Clay said. "We must be careful about the questions we ask. I hope Train remembers that."

They drank coffee and nibbled on biscuits they had left over from the night before as the shadows lengthened and the air chilled.

"He's taking an awfully long time," Melanie commented.

The last of the day faded. A gray mantle shrouded the forest, darkening by gradual degrees.

"Maybe you should go look for him."

"I won't leave you alone," Clay said.

"I am beginning to feel like a wife," Melanie chided. "I am not helpless, and I wish you would not treat me as if I am."

Clay set his tin cup on a flat rock and rose. He shucked his Winchester from the saddle scabbard, worked the lever to feed a cartridge into the chamber and held the rifle out to her. "It's loaded."

"I saw." Melanie placed the Winchester across her lap. "If you're going to be grumpy about it, then stay."

"I won't be a minute longer than I have to." Clay turned and hurried down the hummock. He did not look back.

The camp was the sole oasis of light and noise in a world gone dark and silent. The most noise came from the largest tent. The flap was tied open, and the clink of glasses and the tinkle of chips greeted Clay. To his left a long plank balanced on barrels served as the bar. To his right, poker and faro and roulette were the vices of choice.

Conscious of being stared at, Clay waded through the press of unwashed prospectors to the bar. In his derby and suit he stood out like a well-groomed dog thrust among timber wolves. He ordered a whiskey and, when the barman brought it, he slid a dollar across the plank and said, "I'm looking for someone."

"There are a lot of someones here."

Clay described Train.

"Can't say as I've seen him." The barman pocketed the dollar and went to serve someone else.

Clay swirled the whiskey in his glass, downed it in a gulp, smacked the glass on the plank and was turning to go when a heavy hand fell on his shoulder.

"I couldn't help but overhear, mister. I know where your friend is."

The Good Samaritan did not look the part. He had

no more flesh on him than a skeleton. His face, his beard and his clothes were dirty. On his large bulb of a nose had sprouted a correspondingly large wart.

"You do?" Clay said.

The Samaritan repeated Clay's description of Mr. Train. "If that's the gent you're looking for, I saw him not an hour ago over at Charlie's."

"Who would Charlie be?"

"He has a tent yonder," the Samaritan said with a vague wave of a dirty hand. "Always has a card game going."

"He's a gambler?"

"Not exactly. He just likes cards." The Samaritan stepped past Clay. "Want me to show you where it is? I was going back there later anyway, so it's no bother."

"Sure," Clay said. But he stayed a few steps behind the man, and when they were outside and at the corner he looked back, but did not see anyone following them.

The Samaritan was a talker. "We don't see a lot of dandies like you hereabouts. What do you do? Work at a bank or someplace like that? You're sure as hell not an ore hound."

"I work at the *Courier*."

"What's that?"

"The Bluff City newspaper."

"You don't say?" The Samaritan found that amusing. "You're a far piece from Bluff City."

"I'm investigating the Stark gang. Were you here when they helped themselves to the saloon's money?"

The Samaritan slowed and looked over a shoulder at him. "I might have been. I forget."

They came to the last of the tents. The canvas had more than a few holes in it and was as filthy as the Samaritan. The Samaritan went right in.

Clay pushed the flap aside but did not enter. A table occupied the center and three men were playing poker. More prospectors, from the look of them.

"This here is Charlie," the Samaritan said, indicating the filthiest of the players. "The one I was telling you about." He told Charlie about Clay working for the newspaper.

"I don't see my friend," Clay said.

"He was never here."

"What? Then why did you bring me?"

The Samaritan turned. In his hand was a cocked revolver. "Fact is, boy, you're as dumb as a stump. But don't feel bad. You are not the first to fall for it, and you won't be the last. Now hand over your valuables."

"And be quick about it," said the man called Charlie, "or we will kill you and take them anyway."

Chapter 21

Clay Adams wanted to curse, to fume, to vent a surplus of fury. But not at the men in the tent. He wanted to curse and fume and vent fury at himself for being so damnably gullible. The Samaritan was right; he *was* as stupid as a tree stump.

Charlie and the other cardplayers rose and unlimbered their hardware. "We're waiting," Charlie said, and from behind his back drew a bone-handled hunting knife with a long blade.

Clay thought about the revolver under his jacket. He stared at the four muzzles pointed at him, at the cocked hammers and the curled thumbs, and he did the only thing he could under the circumstances. He tossed his poke to Charlie.

"Well now." Charlie hefted it and grinned. "Listen to those coins jingle, boys. How much is in here?"

"One hundred and four dollars," Clay said. "About all I have left to my name."

"You don't say," the Samaritan said. "I reckon this will teach you not to carry so much money around. You never know but when you might be robbed."

Peals of coarse mirth filled the tent.

Charlie came up and gouged the barrel of his revolver into Clay's gut. "Here's how it works, boy. Tell anyone about us, anyone at all, and you die. Tell the law, and when we get our hands on you, you will die as slow as can be and in more pain than anyone has been in since Adam. Believe me. We have done it before, many times. Leave the camp by morning and don't let us ever catch you here again."

"You're letting me live?" Clay blurted, and wanted to beat his head with a rock.

The Samaritan laughed. "Listen to him! He sounds disappointed! Don't he beat all!"

Charlie laughed, too, and poked Clay with the barrel. "Damn, boy. Do you have any brains in that noggin of yours? Or do you just use it for a hat rack?"

"I'm beginning to wonder," Clay said.

"You're a reporter—isn't that right?" Charlie said. "If we blow out your wick, it could mean more bother than you're worth. More busybodies will come snooping around. The law, maybe, too. We can do without that. So yes, you go on breathing."

"I'm obliged."

"I bet you are," Charlie replied. "But don't thank us just yet. I said you get to live. I didn't say you get to walk out of here."

Too late, Clay saw the Samaritan's arm arc toward him. He tried to duck but his temple exploded in agony. A great emptiness gripped him, and then there was nothing, absolutely nothing at all.

The sun on his face restored Clay's senses. But he did not open his eyes right way. He had to cope with waves of nausea that churned his stomach and brought bitter bile to his throat. Only after he had swallowed the bile and the nausea had dwindled did he cautiously raise his head and look about.

Clay was on his back in a stone-strewn gorge. In the distance rose the murmur of voices. Judging by the sun, it was nine or ten in the morning. He rose on his elbows, but did so too quickly and paid for his mistake with pounding waves of pain. Sinking back, he waited for the torment to become bearable.

A jay flew over him, squawking noisily. He would gladly have shot it to shut it up. The thought caused him to slide his hand under his jacket. He exhaled in relief when he discovered his six-shooter was where it should be. He could not understand how they had missed finding it until he rose on his elbows and felt the pain in the back of his head and across his shoulders, and saw that his left shoe had been pulled nearly off. They had dragged him by the feet.

Clay gingerly felt the back of his head and discovered a hen's egg. He let a suitable interval go by and then slowly sat up. The contents of his stomach tried to climb out his throat but he swallowed, then grimaced. His derby lay in the dirt beside him. Someone had stomped on it. Picking it up, he went to put it on his head but was content to hold it.

Standing took a lot out of him. He had to try several times before his legs would bear his weight. Swaying, he started toward the mouth of the gorge, but had to stop when the sky and the ground changed places. He braced himself, thinking he would pass out, but he didn't.

His legs were wooden. They would not bend as they should. He shambled stiffly until movement restored some of his vitality, and after that he moved a little easier and a little faster. Even so, the gorge mouth seemed impossibly far away. He was breathing heavily when he reached it and stopped to catch his breath.

Clay nearly groaned aloud when he saw how far off the mining camp was. They had dragged him a long way over rough terrain. He was lucky all he had was the hen's egg and the soreness.

Girding himself, he set out. There were not a lot of trees but the ground was littered with boulders and a misstep might cost him a broken leg. He pressed on. He was careful, but he slipped every now and then. He always recovered his balance before gravity could bring him crashing down, but several times it was a close thing.

Clay occupied his mind with thoughts of the Samaritan and the men in the tent. He would never forget their faces. They believed they had him cowed; believed they had put the fear of dying into him. Little did they know. They had taken his poke but they had made mistakes. Mistakes a man like Jesse Stark would never make. Mistakes that would prove costly.

The sun was wonderfully warm. Clay broke out in a sweat, and sweating helped restore him even more. Still, he could not shake the pain or the throbbing or the queasiness that roiled in the pit of his stomach. It came and went, came and went, like surf crashing on a shore.

Then the tents were close, too close, and he got his bearings and skirted them. The Samaritan and Charlie and the others must not see him until he was ready for them to see him.

Clay spied the hummock and his pace quickened. He climbed to the top and wound through the boulders to the clear space, and stopped short. The horses were there, and the saddles and gear and packs, but not Mr. Train, and not the person who had come to mean more to him than anyone had meant in more years than he cared to recollect.

"Melanie?" Clay called, wincing, and received no reply. He turned and took several steps but again stopped short. "What am I doing?" he asked out loud. He was in no condition to go charging into the mining camp after them.

The fire had gone out. Clay rekindled it, and once the flames were high enough, put on a fresh pot of coffee to boil. He placed several strips of bacon in a frying pan and soon the bacon was sizzling and giving off an aroma that made his mouth water and his stomach rumble. He was so hungry that he speared a strip with a fork and bit off a piece without waiting for it to cool. It was so hot he nearly spit it out again, but he steeled himself and chewed.

Between the bacon and the coffee, Clay almost felt like a whole man again. He was almost done eating when footsteps pattered and he rose just as Melanie swept into his arms.

"Here you are! Thank God! Where have you been? We were so worried!" Melanie pulled back and inspected him and said, "You look pale. And what is that gash on your temple?"

"I was hit over the head," Clay said, overcome with embarrassment.

"Who did it?" Mr. Train had come out of the boulders. "She was scared Stark had gotten hold of you."

"Speaking of which," Clay said, "did you find anything out?"

"I might know where their lair is," Mr. Train revealed. "We can be there by nightfall if we leave right away."

"There is something I must do first."

"What would that be?" Melanie asked. "You still haven't explained who hit you, or why, or where you have been."

Instead of answering, Clay moved to the packs and selected his. With it under his arm, he moved off into the boulders, saying, "I will be back in a minute." When he was out of sight, he placed the pack down and began stripping. He folded the jacket, shirt and pants and placed his derby on top of them and his shoes beside them. He no longer had a use for the shoulder holster, so he draped it over the derby. Then he opened the pack and took out the other him: his buckskin shirt, his buckskin pants, his knee-high moccasins, his black hat and his gun belt.

Ten minutes later Clay rejoined them, dressed as he had been that fateful day he rode into Whistler's Flat, the pack over his shoulder.

"What's this?" Mr. Train asked.

Melanie put a hand to her mouth. "Oh no."

Clay set the pack down. He drew his pearl-handled Colt. He twirled it forward and back and flipped it into the air and caught it by the pearl handles and twirled it into his holster in one smooth motion.

"Interesting," Mr. Train said.

"Must you resort to this?" Melanie asked, placing a hand on Clay's arm. "Whatever happened to you, must it be this again?"

"I was robbed," Clay said. "I was robbed and beaten because they took me for a sheep."

"So what now? You teach them they had a wolf by the tail?"

"Something like that." Clay went to go but she held on to his arm.

"Someone might suspect the truth. What if Stark finds out? I thought you didn't want that."

"The other me is of no use up here," Clay said.

"And this you is?"

Clay gently pried her fingers off. "No man could let them get away with what they did and still look himself in the mirror."

"I'm going with you," Melanie informed him.

"No, you are not. It won't be something you should see. Keep her here, Train. However you have to."

"I can't," Mr. Train said.

"Why not?"

"Because I am going too." The manhunter smiled. "If you think I will miss this, you're loco. I knew there was something about you. I'll stay out of your way and I will watch her for you, but I am coming."

"You're as pigheaded as she is." Clay strode off down the hummock and across to the tents and in among them until he came to the saloon tent. Although it was not yet noon the tent was half full. Men lounged at the plank bar or played poker.

Clay stood in the open flap and raked those inside with a look that caused those who noticed him to stiffen and nudge their companions. He figured the four would be there spending his money and he was right. He shouldered past several men and one opened his mouth to object, but after a glance at Clay he changed his mind.

The four had a table to themselves. Each had a whiskey bottle. They were talking and smiling and Charlie was dealing.

Clay stopped and waited for them to notice him. His thumbs were hooked in his gun belt, his right hand near his Colt. His hat brim was low over his eyes.

The Samaritan was the observant one. About to take a swig, he crooked his head and said, "Care to sit in, mister?"

"No."

"Something we can do for you then?"

"You can die," Clay said.

That got their attention. They stopped drinking and playing and looked at him. Charlie's eyebrows met over his nose and he said, "Why did you go and say a thing like that?"

"You step on toes, you get kicked."

"What the hell?" Charlie said. "We'd never tangle with the likes of you. It's as plain as the nose on your face that you're a gunny."

"You thought it was healthy when you took my poke."

Charlie started, and the Samaritan swore, and one of the others nearly dropped his whiskey bottle.

"I came for my poke, and however much of my money you haven't spent," Clay said.

"It can't be!" Charlie blurted.

"But first there's the other thing," Clay said. "Sitting down or standing up, it makes no difference to me but it might to you, so you can stand if you want."

"All four of us?" the Samaritan said. "No one is that good. Not even Hickok."

"How would you know?" Clay rejoined. "You ever meet him? You ever see him shoot?" He lowered his arms.

Word was spreading and men were backing to the bar or the other side of the tent. The bartender said, "This is no place for a lady. What are you doing here?"

"Never you mind," Melanie replied.

Clay did not take his eyes off the four. "Don't take all day making up your minds. I have somewhere to be."

Charlie was the smart one. He stalled. "Can't we make this right? We'll pay back your money and extra besides." He spread his hands on the table. "How were we to know? In that suit and that silly hat, how were we to know?"

"I'll count to three," Clay said. "You can sit there or you can slap leather. It's all the same to me." He paused. "One."

With an inarticulate cry, the Samaritan heaved up out of his chair, his revolver sweeping from under his belt.

Clay drew and put a slug into the Samaritan's chest, then pivoted and put another into the man on the left, and fanned his pearl-handled Colt and the third man's face erupted in a spray of scarlet. That left Charlie, who had his six-shooter out and was smiling because he thought he had Clay beat. Charlie died with that smile on his face and a bullet hole between his eyes.

The saloon was deathly still until someone exclaimed, "Dear God in heaven!"

Clay reloaded, twirled the pearl-handled Colt into his holster, and collected his poke and his one hundred and four dollars. He did not take the rest of their money. All eyes were on him as he walked out.

Melanie said as he passed her, "You enjoyed that, didn't you?"

"I know I did," Mr. Train said.

Chapter 22

The remote vastness of the Rockies. Mile after unending mile of upthrust slopes, steep and severe, in places covered with treacherous talus or impassable deadfalls. Mile after mile of dense timber. Man rarely penetrated this far. Even the Indians only came on occasion, usually to hunt elk or mountain sheep, or to collect eagle feathers.

Crowned by the Continental Divide, the higher reaches of the mountains were the last bastion of unexplored land on the continent. There were no Indian villages, no towns, no cities. There were no roads or trails except game trails; but there was plenty of game. Here dwelled the majestic elk, giant grizzlies, fierce wolverines. Here roamed the big cats, the lions named after the high country they roamed.

For Clay Adams, Melanie Stanley and Mr. Train, the next phase of their search took them into the heart of the unknown. On foot they could not have done it. The terrain was too harsh, the strain on human muscle and stamina too relentless. Only on horseback could the upper reaches of the mountains be traversed, and even then it taxed them and their mounts to their limits. They were fortunate in that the weather had briefly warmed. Indian summer, some called it.

Four days of it, four days of pushing themselves minute by minute and hour by hour, and the three of them and their horses were close to exhaustion. Their nightly rest was not enough. They were always tired, and tired people and tired animals were prone to mistakes. So they had to go slower than they might otherwise, and always, always, watch that their horses did not suffer a misstep, for without their horses they would be at the mercy of the relentlessly cruel mistress known as Nature.

The morning of the fifth day found them camped beside a turquoise lake half a mile below a snow-capped peak. A waterfall fed the lake, its spray rising in a fine mist in rainbow hues.

Clay had not changed back to his store-bought clothes. He enjoyed being able to wear his old clothes again, and to openly wear his Colt.

They were about finished breakfast when Mr. Train said, "If what I was told is true, the Stark gang is holed up in a canyon south of here. I will go alone to scout around. The two of you stay with the horses and rest up."

"I'll go with you," Clay offered.

"They are bound to have a lookout, and one man is less conspicuous than two." Train rose and cradled his rifle. "If I am not back by noon you can come looking."

"Whatever you want." Clay had grown to like the manhunter, especially since Train had the decency not to badger him with questions after the incident at Calamity.

Melanie had not spoken much since. But no sooner were they alone than she looked up and said, "I owe you an apology."

"I must have missed something," Clay said.

"I've been mad at you. Those men in the tent. I didn't think it was necessary. I still don't."

"Then what are you apologizing for?"

"Mr. Train thinks I was being too hard on you. He said those men were almost as bad as Jesse Stark. That they deserved what they got."

"No one is as bad as Jesse Stark."

"Quit quibbling. I'm trying to do the right thing. The least you can do is be gracious."

Clay smiled.

Suddenly serious, Melanie said, "Can I ask you a question?"

"You may ask me anything, anytime. If that's not gracious I don't know what is," was Clay's riposte.

"It is about us. Or is there an us? We haven't talked about it, but I have made my feelings clear and I would like to know where I stand when we get back."

Clay came over to her and took her hand. "By my side, I hope."

"I'm not trying to back you into a corner," Melanie said. "Don't make promises you can't keep. A woman just needs to know. I do, anyway. And the suspense is killing me."

"We were friends when we left Bluff City but we are more than friends now," Clay said.

"What are we *exactly*? As my uncle would say, what are your intentions, young man? When you say 'by your side,' do you mean temporary or permanent? Because I don't do temporary."

"Neither do I."

Melanie smiled and threw her arms around him and kissed him on the neck. "Thank you. What we did was more than I have ever done and I have felt guilty. Now I don't need to."

"Women get the strangest notions," Clay observed.

"Says the man who never kissed one until he kissed me." Melanie gasped, and pushed back. "I'm sorry. That just came out. It was meant to be funny. I didn't think."

"Stop it," Clay said. "It's the truth." He chuckled and pecked her on the cheek. "But women do get the weirdest notions."

"I have one now." Melanie bobbed her chin at the waterfall. "I haven't had a bath since we left Bluff City."

"Both of us? Together?"

"Down, boy. And don't drool. It's very unbecoming." Melanie rummaged in her pack and brought out a towel. "You can stand watch if you want, so long as your back is turned."

"I don't have eyes in my shoulder blades."

"That's the point. Otherwise, stay here. I trust you but I'm not so sure I trust myself, and I would rather avoid the temptation until you slip a ring on my finger."

"Goodness. You have it all planned out. How many kids are we having? Where will we live? Do you want to be Mrs. Adams or Mrs. Baine?"

"Four. St. Louis. As for the name, I thought Neville Baine was dead and buried, but he keeps rising from the grave."

"He has work to finish."

"Is that what they call a thirst for revenge these days?"

A fish leaped in a glistening arc out on the lake and splashed down, and Clay watched the concentric ripples spread outward.

"Cat got your tongue?"

"I thought I had explained it," Clay said. "Why bring it up again? It is not that important."

"Do you hear what you are saying? Taking a human life is always important. Dear God, Clay, or Neville, whichever you are at the moment. By my tally you have killed nine people since I met you, and you want to kill one more. This might shock you, but most people go their entire lives without killing anyone." Melanie gnawed on her lower lip. "I never thought to ask. How many lives *have* you taken?"

"I don't count them."

"It's as bad as that?" Melanie slung her towel over her shoulder. "I don't know. I just don't know if I can give myself fully to someone with your past."

"A minute ago you wanted to."

"That's because I keep forgetting. You are normal most of the time. It is only when you change that your other side comes out."

Clay squinted at her. "All I change are my clothes."

"So this is the you I would spend the rest of my life with? The one who solves all his problems with a pearl-handled Colt? The one who provoked four men into drawing so he could shoot them down?" Melanie shook her head and made off along the water's edge toward the waterfall.

Abashed, Clay trailed after her. "I wish I could make you understand."

"I don't want to talk about it."

"But you brought it up."

"I still don't want to talk about it."

"Then we won't," Clay said. But he could not let it rest. "I wasn't the first person those four robbed and beat and left for dead. If I had not gone back, if I had not settled accounts, they would have done it many more times, and all the lives they took would be on my shoulders because I could have stopped them and I didn't."

Melanie stopped and turned. "Is that how you see it?"

"It is the only way to see it."

"Judge, jury and executioner. Do you truly believe you have that right? If all of us did as you do, think of the chaos."

"I wouldn't do it if there was any chance of Stark being brought to justice. But there isn't. Out here"— Clay motioned at the towering peaks and ocean of forest—"there are no courts. Out here the only law is the strength in a man's arms and the speed in his hands."

Melanie walked on.

"Are you going to say anything?" Clay asked. "You can see I'm right, can't you? You can see I had it to do."

"All I see," Melanie responded, "is you attempting to justify the taking of life. And please, I really don't care to hear any more right now. I am too confused, too upset, to deal with it."

"As you wish," Clay said.

The roar of the waterfall grew louder as they approached. The water fell from such a height that, when it struck the lake, liquid thunder resulted. A thick veil of spray rose fifty feet into the air.

"Beautiful," Melanie said. "Simply beautiful." She placed her towel on a boulder and pointed a finger at Clay. "I'd like for you to find a spot where you can roost and wait and not see me. The important part is not see me."

"Now who is shy all of a sudden?"

A red tinge inched from Melanie's neck to her hairline. "That will be enough of that, thank you. Passion and bathing are not the same."

"If you say so."

"Please don't sulk. I am trying. Honestly trying. Maybe with a little time I will understand."

"If you need me give a holler." Clay walked twenty yards to a boulder half as large as a log cabin and sat on the far side with his back to it. "Women!" he said, and smacked the ground. Idly picking up a small stone, he threw it.

Clay gazed to the south but saw no sign of Mr. Train. "I should have gone with him," he said, then tilted his hat forward, leaned his head back, and closed his eyes. He did not mean to but he dozed off.

A sound ended Clay's nap. He opened his eyes and listened, but the sound was not repeated. He looked toward their camp and then out over the water, but saw nothing out of the ordinary. About to close his eyes again, he was jolted to his feet by a splash and a loud rumbling grunt. He had heard grunts like that before.

Palming his Colt, Clay crept around the boulder. He had a fair notion what he would behold but it still shook him. It would rattle anyone. His breath caught in his throat.

Midway between the boulder and the waterfall, standing in the shallows, was a gigantic grizzly. No grizzly was ever small, but this one was enormous. The lord of the mountains was staring at the water as if waiting for a fish to show itself. Grunting again, it swiped a giant paw at the surface.

Clay glanced toward the waterfall. There was no sign of Melanie. Panic welled inside him. He thought the bear had gotten her while he slept. Then he saw the vaguest suggestion of a silhouette outlined against the cascading water, and her face peering out at the bear. She was scared and he didn't blame her. Grizzlies were notorious man killers. In the old days they had been thick as fleas, but most had been killed off lower down. Up here, though, they still reigned supreme. One of the few creatures on God's green earth to have no fear of man or his weapons, grizzlies bristled with razor teeth and claws that could slash a person to ribbons in seconds, and possessed more raw might than a buffalo.

The bear dipped its great head to the water and drank. After slaking its thirst it turned and lumbered onto shore, then shook itself much as a dog might. Drops of water flew every which way.

Clay smiled in relief when the grizzly took a few steps toward the forest. But his relief was premature.

Stopping, the bear raised its nose into the wind and sniffed. It swung its head to the left and sniffed, and to the right and sniffed, then turned and stared at the waterfall.

An icy hand enclosed Clay's heart and it nearly

stopped beating. If he could see Melanie the bear could see her, too. Or could it? he wondered. How good was a bear's eyesight? Thankfully, she did not move or cry out.

The grizzly took a step toward the waterfall.

Clay started into the open. He would do whatever it took to keep the bear from her. He wished he had his Winchester, but he had made another lunkheaded blunder and left it in camp. He raised the Colt to take aim and went to thumb the hammer back, but just then the grizzly stopped and raised its head once more, and loudly sniffed. It began to turn.

Quickly, Clay darted behind the boulder. Removing his hat, he peeked out. The grizzly was looking in his direction. His palms grew sweaty as he waited for the bear to decide what it was going to do.

With another of those rumbling grunts, the bear wheeled and made for the woods. It did not look back. Amazingly, it melted into the vegetation with no more than a whisper of sound.

Clay jammed his hat back on but stayed where he was. Melanie did not move, either, for a considerable while. Then she took a step forward and stared into the timber. Clay did the right thing and backed behind the boulder, but not before he had seen her, seen a vision so incredibly lovely it stunned him. He tried to put the image from his mind but could not. He was still seeing it, shimmering in the air like a desert mirage, when a shadow fell across him and someone coughed.

"I am ready to go back if you are," Melanie said.

Clay nodded and fell into step next to her.

"Why do you have your pistol in your hand?"

Startled, Clay replaced it in his holster. "The bear," he said simply.

"Wasn't he magnificent?"

"Magnificent," Clay said, but he was not thinking of the bear.

Their camp was as they had left it. Clay hunkered by the fire, which had burned low. He broke a few tree limbs he had gathered the night before and fed them to the flames. "There's some coffee left if you want it."

"Clay?" Melanie said, an unusual lilt to her voice.

"Want me to fill your cup?"

"Clay?" Melanie said again.

Shifting on his heels, Clay looked up, and every ounce of blood in his body turned to ice. For standing at the edge of the clearing, smirking at them, his thumbs hooked in his gun belt, was Jesse Stark.

Chapter 23

"If it isn't the pretty filly from the newspaper." Jesse Stark grinned. "Fancy meeting you again."

Raw bloodlust spiked through Clay. He was behind Melanie, his hand poised to swoop to his Colt when the shadows on all sides disgorged other members of the Stark gang. Nine, ten, eleven counting Jesse Stark. About half had rifles, but only one had his leveled. All wore six-shooters, but only two had drawn theirs. They were too sure of themselves.

Bantarro and Gorman came up on either side, and the latter said to Melanie, "Some people just don't know when to leave well enough alone."

"Agreed, amigo," Bantarro echoed. "Or perhaps the pretty senorita missed us and could not stay away?"

"What's this?" Jesse Stark had taken a step and was staring at Clay. He looked at Clay's hat and buckskins, at Clay's pearl-handled Colt. Shock registered, to be replaced by disbelief. "Those clothes! I knew a man who wore those clothes!"

"What is wrong, amigo?" Bantarro asked.

"How can this be?" Stark practically screeched.

All eyes, even Melanie's, were on the outlaw leader.

Stark's men were stunned by his reaction. The moment was ready-made for Clay. He drew and shot an outlaw pointing a rifle at him, pivoted and shot another outlaw holding a cocked Colt. Instantly he spun to shoot Jesse Stark, but Melanie had turned and was directly between them, and if Clay shot he would hit her. Grabbing her wrist, Clay backpedaled, firing as he went. He shot a man training a revolver on them, then shot an outlaw about to work the lever of a rifle. Then they were in the pines and Clay whirled and fled, pulling Melanie after him.

"After them!" Stark raged. "I want that bastard in the black hat dead! Do you hear me?"

The woods were thick but the undergrowth sparse. Clay ran smoothly, pacing himself so Melanie could keep up.

"He recognized you," she remarked as they skirted a log.

"Took him long enough." Clay hunched low and bore to the north, avoiding a thicket. "Keep down," he advised.

"How did they find us? Where do you suppose Mr. Train got to? What do we do now?"

"The only one of those I can answer is the last," Clay said. "We need horses. So we will do the last thing Stark expects." He angled even more to the right. "We will work our way back to the clearing."

The outlaws were making quite a racket. They had spread out and were barreling in the direction they thought Clay and Melanie had gone, crashing through the brush like so many mad bulls.

"Where are they?" one shouted.

"I don't see them!"

"Watch out for the one in buckskins! He's greased lightning!"

Clay smiled grimly at that. He slowed and dropped lower, so that he was almost on his knees, and cat-footed forward until he was a few yards from the north edge of the clearing. It was empty.

"What are we waiting for?" Melanie whispered. "The horses are right there."

"I haven't had a chance to reload," Clay said, and as he quickly did so, he asked, "Can you ride bareback?"

"I have never done it before but it can't be all that hard," Melanie replied.

"Stay close." Clay dashed to their saddles. Yanking his Winchester from the scabbard, he jacked the lever and thrust the rifle at her. "Shoot anything that moves." He holstered the Colt, grabbed both his saddle blanket and hers, and hurried to their horses.

"What are you doing?" Melanie whispered. "I thought you said we would ride bareback."

"Only if they catch us before we're ready." Clay threw his on the claybank and hers on the mare and ran to their saddles. Shouts to the west confirmed the outlaws were still after them.

"Listen to them. They sound confused. They don't know where we got to," Melanie said, and giggled.

"They will figure it out soon enough," Clay predicted. He got her saddle on, and his, faster than he had ever put saddles on. Then he scooped up his saddlebags.

"What about Mr. Train's horse and the pack animal?"

"What about them?"

"He will need his mount and we can use the supplies."

Clay tilted his head to listen. The sounds of pursuit were faint. "We are taking a god-awful chance," he said, but he bent to Train's saddle and saddle blanket.

"We can't leave without finding out what happened to him," Melanie said. "We owe him that much."

"Keep your eyes on those trees," Clay said. He was half expecting a slug in the back so he was not all that surprised when a gun hammer clicked.

"Hold it right there."

His hands filled with Train's saddle, Clay did not move except for his head, which he slowly turned until he saw one of the four outlaws he had shot. He had not paid much attention to them. He had assumed they were dead. But this one was very much alive, a crimson stain high on the left side of his shirt. Wounded though he was, the outlaw held his revolver steady enough.

"Where did everyone get to?" the man asked, and coughed. He was of medium height and medium build and distinguished only by a cleft chin.

"Your pards ran off," Clay said.

"Liar. Jesse never deserts his own." The man looked at his three fallen companions. "Damn. You sure are a hellion, mister." He extended his six-gun. "Give my regards to my pards when you get to hell."

Melanie gave him pause by asking, "What about me? Don't you have any compunctions about shooting women?"

"I don't know what that word means, lady," the

outlaw said, and coughed some more. "But I've killed women before. Four, I think. Or is it five? I can't rightly recollect."

"You never feel any regret? Any remorse?"

"Why should I? Killing is killing. You do it and you forget about it." The outlaw pointed his revolver at her. "How about if I make you number six? Your jabbering annoys the hell out of me."

"Try me instead." Clay dropped Train's saddle and drew his pearl-handled Colt. He cleared leather as the outlaw snapped off a shot at him. The man missed. Clay did not, and this time he put the slug between the man's eyes.

Yells broke out in the distance.

"On your horse," Clay directed Melanie, taking the rifle from her.

"But Mr. Train's saddle? And our packs?"

"Move!" Clay shoved her. Crackling in the underbrush warned him some of the outlaws were closer than they reckoned. Swinging onto the claybank, he covered Melanie while she mounted and, once she was up, wheeled the claybank and snagged the reins to the pack animal, shoving them at her. He took the reins to Train's mount himself.

"Which direction?"

"South," Clay instructed her.

"Why that way?"

"Just do it."

The forest swallowed them before the outlaws appeared. They brought their horses to a trot, and Clay, after glancing about, exclaimed, "I thought so! We are in luck."

Melanie looked over her shoulder at him, her eyebrows twin arches.

"They came on foot," Clay enlightened her. "That canyon Train told us about can't be far."

It wasn't. Less than a quarter of a mile from the lake they came on the canyon mouth. Screened by aspens, no one would guess it was there until they were right on top of it. An ideal sanctuary for those on the wrong side of the law. Clay handed the reins to Train's horse to Melanie and gigged the claybank past her. "I will go first. Just in case."

The canyon widened. The shoes of their mounts rang loud on the rocks and echoed off the high slopes.

Then they rounded a bend and discovered five to six acres of trees and grass. A spring situated near a ramshackle cabin explained the greenery. In a large corral attached to the cabin were more than two dozen horses. Smoke wafted from the chimney.

"Quick!" Clay said, and reined back out of sight.

"Someone must be inside," Melanie mentioned what was already plain. "I didn't see Mr. Train anywhere. Maybe it is him."

Dismounting, Clay said, "If I don't give a holler in the next ten minutes, light a shuck for Bluff City."

"I will not leave you," Melanie said.

"Why do you always do this?" Clay placed his hand on her leg. "Listen to me. When Jesse Stark finds our horses gone, he will check to see which direction we went. When he sees we went south, he will guess where we are and come on the run. I figure we have half an hour, maybe less." Clay paused. "Wait fifteen minutes if you want, but only fifteen minutes so you have time to spare. Then get the hades out of here."

Melanie opened her mouth to say something but closed it again.

"Good girl." Clay smiled, drew his Colt and hastened away. A muttered, "I'm not no girl!" trailed after him. As he went around the bend he bent at the knees.

The outlaws had built a cabin. If it had been a settler's homestead on the bank of the Platte River, the scene would have been idyllic. But it was a nest of human vipers in the dark heart of the remote Rockies, and Clay had to be careful not to be bitten by their leaden fangs.

He hugged the side of the canyon until he was in among the trees. The wind was blowing his scent away from the corral but he did not take for granted that the horses would not give him away. Flat on his belly, he crawled to where he could see the cabin door and window. There was no glass, not even a curtain, and Clay could see someone moving about inside. More than one, as it developed.

Clay crawled nearer. His fifteen minutes were about up. He would rush the cabin, fling open the door and trust to his speed with the Colt to prevail. On the verge of rising, he glanced to the left and bit off an oath of surprise.

A post had been imbedded in the ground. An ordinary corral post, only this one had been put to a far-from-ordinary use.

His arms over his head, Mr. Train had been bound to the post by the wrists and ankles. They had stripped him to the waist first, and every square inch of skin from his neck to his hips was covered with lacerations and welts, a riot of marks ridged with dry blood. Only one thing left marks like that. A bullwhip.

Train's head hung to his chest and his eyes were closed. He was breathing raggedly and noisily, but he was breathing.

One eye on the cabin, Clay ran over. "Train?" he whispered. Blood had dribbled from the manhunter's mouth and from one ear. "Train? Can you hear me?"

Train said so weakly he could barely be heard, "Cut me down. Hurry."

Clay needed no urging. But he did not have a knife; he had lost his back when Stark kidnapped Cavendish and had not bought a new one. "How many of them are in the cabin?"

Mr. Train raised his head. His face had been spared the whip but someone, or several someones, had beat on him with their fists to the point where his lips, cheeks and eyebrows were badly swollen and his entire face was black and blue.

"Three in the cabin," Mr. Train said. "The rest went after you and Miss Stanley."

"I'll be right back with a knife."

"Wait," Train said as Clay turned. "You need to hear this." He sucked in a breath. "They knew I was coming. They knew you were with me."

"How?" Clay asked. An explanation leaped out at him and he answered his own question. "They must have heard about those men I shot at the mining camp."

"No," Train said, talking with an effort. "You don't understand. Stark knew my *name*."

Clay mulled that as he jogged toward a corner of

the cabin. Muffled voices reached him, and what might be the clank of a pot or pan. His back to the wall, he sidled to the door. It was open a crack. Inside, someone was grousing.

"I don't like it, I tell you. Playing nursemaid while the rest are off having a grand time."

"Quit your griping, Barnes. They were on foot. That's a long hike. I'm glad Jesse left me behind."

"They went on foot so they could sneak up on those other two," Barnes said. "I wanted to go but he made me stay."

"Your problem is that you are woman crazy. That's why you are complaining. You are afraid the others will use her up before you get to take a poke."

"Can you blame me?" Barnes snapped. "It's not fair, I tell you."

Clay used his shoulder on the door. He went in fast and low. The three outlaws clawed for their hardware and Clay shot one seated at a table, another over by the fireplace, and the third as the man rose off a cot. He reloaded, grabbed a butcher knife from the counter and was retracing his steps to the door when he saw a gun belt on a peg. In the holster was a Whitney revolver, and in a knife sheath a bowie. "Train's," Clay said and, throwing the butcher knife on the table, he raced outdoors with the gun belt.

"Hurry," Train urged. He was standing upright. "I think I heard shouts down the canyon."

Two slices of the bowie and the ropes fell. Clay shoved the knife and the gun belt at their owner. "Can you run?"

"Just you watch me."

They jogged toward the bend, Train buckling on his

armory as they went. But they were only halfway there when Melanie trotted into view, her long hair flying, leading their horses.

"Damn her," Clay said. "She should have been long gone by now. Why can't women ever listen?"

Melanie brought the horses to a halt and leaned down. "Mr. Train! Are you all right?"

"Forget about me," Train said. "We have to get out of here before Stark and the rest come back."

"It's too late for that," Melanie replied. "They are coming up the canyon and will be here any minute."

Chapter 24

"We will make a stand in the cabin," Clay said. "There are only seven of them left. If we can kill a few more, the rest might decide it's healthier to skedaddle."

"We risk Miss Stanley being harmed," Mr. Train said. "But there is another way out."

"Where?"

Train pointed at the stretch of canyon past the cabin. "A back way. So they can escape if the law ever shows up. I overheard them talking about it."

"The back way it is then." Clay swung onto the claybank. Flicking the reins, he galloped to the cabin and was about to swing on around when inspiration struck. Suddenly drawing rein, he called out, "Train! Their horses! I'll take care of the cabin."

A lantern made the task simple. Clay broke it over the cot and set the cot ablaze. It caught readily and soon flames were climbing the wall.

By then Mr. Train had opened the corral and, with Melanie helping, was driving the horses off. Clay overtook them, and waved his hat and whooped to hurry the horses along. Soon they were past the last of the trees. Five hundred yards more brought them to a narrow trail that wound up a slope dotted with scrub brush to a bench littered with talus. The outlaws had cleared a path through the talus and the trail continued on the other side, into a cleft that soon brought them out in dense timber.

Clay and Mr. Train fired shots into the air and watched the horses gallop off.

Melanie was grinning from ear to ear. "Jesse Stark will be fit to be tied. Too bad we can't see the look on his face right about now."

Clay shifted in the saddle. "I want you to go with Mr. Train. Wait for me at Calamity. If I am not there in a week, I never will be."

"Why aren't you going with us?" Melanie asked. She glanced at the trail out of the canyon, and started. "Wait. You're going back, aren't you? But there is no need."

"I have to end it."

"You said there are seven left," Melanie anxiously mentioned. "Why buck odds like that if you don't have to?"

"You weren't listening," Clay said. "It ends. Here. Today." He turned to the manhunter. "Take her with you. Tie her and throw her over her horse if need be. But get her out of here."

"How dare you!" Melanie said. "I refuse to be treated like a child. If he so much as lays a finger on me I will bite it off."

Clay reined the claybank next to her mare. "How many times must I tell you? This is something I have to do. It is not just what Stark did to me. It is all the killing and stealing. Do you want that to go on?"

"Don't try appealing to my conscience," Melanie

snapped. "It's my heart that doesn't want you to go back. My heart that will break if anything should happen to you." She took a deep breath and trembled slightly. "There. I've admitted it. Now, will you forget Jesse Stark?"

Clay's reply was a plaintive whisper. "I can't."

"Damn you, Neville Baine."

"Who?" Mr. Train asked.

Melanie gripped Clay's arm. "Why can't you let the past go? Bury it deep and get on with your new life."

Clay pulled loose and raised his reins. "I have no time for this. I'm sorry you can't understand. But if I don't do what I have to I will never be able to live with myself. You wouldn't want half a man, would you?"

"Half a man is better than none."

"Who is Neville Baine?" Mr. Train asked.

Neither Clay nor Melanie answered. Clay gazed sadly at her, then clucked to the claybank and did not look back. The cleft hemmed him, shrouding him in shadow. Soon he emerged onto the bench, where the bright glare of the sun made him squint. Reining up, he pulled his hat brim low over his eyes and scanned the trail below. There was no sign of the outlaws.

Coils of dark smoke rose above the trees in the near distance. Clay thought he heard shouts but it was too far to be sure. Dismounting, he let the reins dangle and hunkered.

Time crawled. Clay squinted at the sun, which was directly overhead. Moving to a small boulder, he sat down. More minutes piled one on the other, but still no one appeared. When next he squinted at the sun an hour had gone by. Rising, he stretched his arms and legs, then stepped into the stirrups and warily descended to the canyon floor.

Gray tendrils floated amid the trees. The acrid scent of smoke was strong in Clay's nostrils as he wove among the boles until he could see the cabin. Or, rather, what was left of it: the stone fireplace and a few charred beams. Part of the corral, too, had burned, but most of the flames were out.

Of the outlaws, not a trace.

Clay circled the cabin, seeking fresh sign. The ground was hard. Even the claybank did not leave many tracks. He found enough to determine that Stark and the rest had long since left and were bound who knew where on foot.

Clay headed for the mouth of the canyon. He had gone a short way when he noticed something peculiar. On the way in he had passed a high thicket at the base of the west slope. That thicket had moved.

Clay reined closer.

The thicket was not natural, it was man-made. Brush had been roped together and placed so it hid a natural pocket large enough for several horses. A stake showed where three had been tied.

Jesse Stark's doing, Clay surmised. Spares kept handy in case Stark needed to make a swift getaway and could not get to other mounts.

Clay trotted on. No sooner did he emerge from the canyon than he spotted figures off in the forest. They were hiking north, their backs to him. He glimpsed what he took to be a man on horseback, too. Quickly reining into cover, Clay waited a suitable interval, then headed after them at a walk. He was in no hurry. They could not get away, not with most of them on foot. He would bide his time and strike when they had their guard down.

The afternoon waxed and then waned. On several occasions Clay caught sight of the last outlaw in the line. When that happened he always drew rein to let them get farther ahead.

The outlaws did not stop. By evening they were well past the lake and traveling an easterly course that would eventually bring them to Calamity.

A glimmer of red and orange warned Clay they had made camp. Stopping, he slid down and wrapped the reins around a tree. He drew his Colt, then stalked forward until he could hear what was being said. The first words set his blood to boiling with frustration.

"—don't care what you say. It wasn't right of Stark and those other two to ride off and leave us like they did."

"Simmer down, Tinsdale. Jesse promised to find horses for us, didn't he?"

"Don't tell me what to do," the man called Tinsdale growled. "You can lick his boots if you want but I will be damned if I will."

"Better not let Jesse hear you say that," a third outlaw advised.

"Stark doesn't scare me," Tinsdale said.

"He should. So should Gorman and that Mex. All three would shoot their own mothers if there was money in it."

Clay had digested enough to realize that Stark, Gorman and Bantarro were not there. He gripped the Colt so tightly, his hand hurt. Then, willing himself to relax, he glided forward and confirmed that only four outlaws sat around the fire.

Clay slowly straightened. He slid the Colt into his holster and walked out of the dark into the ring of firelight. They did not hear him.

Tinsdale was still grousing about Stark. He was tall and thin, with a cadaverous face.

Another man reached for the coffeepot and happened to glance up. He gaped at Clay, too astonished, or too afraid, to speak. He was notable for great cow eyes and a big nose.

The third outlaw, who had a belly as big as a keg, noticed his pard's expression, glanced over his shoulder and sprang erect.

"You!"

"Me," Clay said.

Tinsdale leaped to his feet but did not go for his revolver. "Where did you come from? Who are you? What do you want?"

"Are you related to Melanie Stanley by any chance?" Clay asked.

"What kind of damn fool question is that? Of course not." Tinsdale motioned at the man holding the coffee cup, and the man set it down and reluctantly stood.

Clay needed to find out one thing. "How long ago did Stark and the others ride off?"

"Shortly after we left the canyon," Tinsdale revealed. "Now answer me. Who *are* you?"

"Crooked Nose Baine," Clay absently responded. He was thinking that Stark had a six-hour lead. Catching him would take some doing.

"Never heard of you," Tinsdale said. "Why is Jesse Stark afraid of you? Does he know you from somewhere?"

The man who had been about to pour coffee cleared his throat. "I've heard of you, mister. But your nose isn't like folks say it should be."

"It got better," Clay said.

"What I want to know," Tinsdale said, "is what you intend to do with us. You're not the law. You have no right to arrest us."

"I wouldn't try. But that leaves me with a problem," Clay said. "What *do* I do with you?"

"We go our way and you go your way," Tinsdale proposed.

"But your way will lead to innocent people dying if I let you go," Clay said.

"You don't have the right to judge us, either," Tinsdale said. "Only the Almighty can do that."

"Keep religion out of it," Clay said. "This is between you and me. I would like to have us go our separate ways. I truly would. But you are part of a loose end I have to wrap up, and the wrapping can only be done with lead."

The third outlaw thrust out his hand. "Hold on there, mister! You wouldn't shoot a man in cold blood, would you?"

"Why not? The Stark gang has, plenty of times. There is no difference that I can see except that if you three are fed to the vultures I can sleep a little easier at night."

"You can't gun us if we don't draw our pistols, and we won't draw our pistols," the first outlaw said.

Tinsdale brightened. "That's right. So long as we

stand here and do nothing, there's nothing you can do."

The coffee drinker looked at his friends. "Weren't you two listening? This here is Crooked Nose Baine. He's dabbled in gore over in Kansas, and he's not shy about pulling the trigger." He switched his attention to Clay. "I want out, mister. I have had enough of being on the run; enough of sleeping on the ground and riding until I'm so saddle sore I can't sit straight. I have wanted out for some time but I haven't had the sand to tell Stark. He doesn't take kindly to quitters. The last one who wanted out got out with a slug in his stomach."

Clay said nothing.

"Let me go and I promise to reform. I will stop riding the high lines forever. I'll have nothing to do with six-guns." The man began prying at his belt buckle. "I don't even want to wear this one anymore. Do whatever you want with it." His gun belt fell to the ground and he took a step away from it.

Tinsdale's jaw was working as if he were chomping on a wad of tobacco. "You miserable polecat. You are yellow, Floyd. You have always been yellow. That's the real reason. You don't aim to reform any more than I do."

The outlaw with the big belly added his two bits. "He's right, Floyd. You are a weak sister. Take up seamstress work. The owlhoot trail doesn't agree with you."

Clay shifted so Floyd would not accidentally take a stray slug from his Colt. "That settles that. Whenever you want to kick the cat, gents, have at it."

"Just like that?" Tinsdale smirked.

"Just like that," Clay said.

It was the one with the big belly who clawed for his revolver first. The belly did not slow his hand any. He was fast. He grinned as he cleared leather and the grin stayed etched on his face as Clay's Colt boomed and a slug tore through his torso from sternum to spine. A twist of Clay's wrist, and he fired again. This time into Tinsdale. The shot rocked Tinsdale on his boot heels, and down he went. The third outlaw nearly had his revolver out. Clay fired again, and once more.

Three bodies ringed the fire. Only Tinsdale still moved, his limbs twitching and quaking.

Clay pointed the Colt at Floyd.

"No! Please, mister! God's honest truth, I'll give this life up for good if you will let me live."

"You might be lying," Clay said, and thumbed back the hammer.

"Please!" Floyd threw himself on his knees and clasped his hands. Tears streaming down his cheeks, he said, "I'm begging you! I don't want to die."

"How long have you ridden with Jesse Stark?"

"About six months. I came up out of Texas. I had to leave there in a hurry because the law was after me for—" Floyd stopped.

"For what?"

"Rustling. I stole a few head, changed a few brands. The Texas Rangers were after me and—" Again Floyd stopped, this time because Clay had held up his other hand.

"Texas, you say? When I was in Kansas I remember hearing about a Floyd Dunsten from the Staked Plain country. A back-shooter who would kill anyone for money." Clay paused. "What would your last name be?"

Floyd hesitated. He hesitated too long, and finally blurted, "Smith! My last name is Smith."

Clay squeezed the trigger.

Chapter 25

It was Kansas all over again.

Word spread like a prairie wildfire.

Shooting affrays were always of interest. Keen interest, since most men wore guns or used guns to hunt or had shot guns at some point in their lives. Most would admit they were only fair with a firearm, if that. Most could hit the broad side of a barn, but that was about it. Exceptional shootists were rare. Men of talent, men of skill, men who could coolly and calmly gun down others in the bat of an eye.

Their ability brought them fame. Their names and deeds were gossiped about at every whiskey mill on the frontier. Men in their cups loved to tell tales, and what better tales than the gloriously violent deeds of those preeminent with six-shooters. The respective abilities of various gun sharks were heatedly debated, and if the debaters were mad enough, and drunk enough, the debaters themselves sometimes resorted to their hardware.

In Kansas the name of Crooked Nose Baine had become well known. Crooked Nose was ranked with the best: Masterson, Mysterious Dave, Basset and Curry. People regarded him with fear or awe or both.

They would gawk and point him out on the street. Then he died, and talk about Crooked Nose Baine came largely to an end.

But now it was happening anew. From mining camp to mining camp, and from the camps to the towns and cities lower down, came word of a gun hand who had shot four badmen dead in front of a score of witnesses. Close on the heels of that account came another. The same leather slapper had decimated the Stark gang. From countless mouths to countless ears the story was told and retold.

That in itself was not remarkable. What *was* unique, the element that made the tale spread so rapidly, was the claim that the demon with a six-gun who had done those marvelous feats was Crooked Nose Baine, back from the dead.

Or so the whispers went.

Baine. The name was spoken in tones of reverence.

But not everyone believed. It could not be Crooked Nose Baine, many said, because Crooked Nose Baine was dead. Even more to the point, it could not be Crooked Nose Baine because, the witnesses all agreed, the gun shark's nose was not crooked.

But if not Baine, then who was it?

Clay Adams heard about the mystery surrounding his other guise as he, Melanie and Mr. Train made their way to Bluff City. Clay had changed to his suit and derby, and did not go openly armed. At the third mining camp they came to, they stopped to eat at a tent restaurant. Some men at the next table were talking about the Stark gang, and the man called Baine. Clay listened without saying anything. When the men left, he grinned and remarked, "If Jesse Stark heard that he would be jealous. He's the one who hankers after fame."

"I am glad you find it so amusing," Melanie said coldly.

"Is something the matter?" Clay asked. "You have been acting strangely ever since I caught up with the two of you."

"Have I indeed?" Melanie retorted.

Mr. Train coughed. "I will leave if you want me to."

"No need," Melanie told him, and rounded on Clay. "Since you asked I will tell you. You enjoy being talked about. Don't deny it. I can see it on your face. You like the notoriety. As much as Stark does."

"That's plumb ridiculous," Clay said.

"Is it? Time will tell. But I am starting to wonder just how much difference there is between you and Jesse Stark. Maybe there is not as much as I thought. Maybe I have credited you with traits you do not possess."

"Talk about making a mountain out of a molehill," Clay said. "How can you sit there and compare me to Stark? I'm not a killer."

Melanie laughed.

"Not the way he is," Clay insisted.

"Perhaps not," Melanie conceded. "But you are a hypocrite, whether you admit it or not."

"I have always been honest with you."

"But are you being honest with yourself?" Melanie asked him. "You told me that you were tired of your old life, that you wanted a fresh start and that Crooked Nose Baine was a thing of the past. Then what do you do? You strap on your fancy Colt and go out and gun people down. It is Kansas all over again."

"I don't intend to go on doing it. There is one man and one man only I must tangle with, and then I am through chucking lead forever."

"So you say. But I have to wonder if you can stop."

Now it was Clay who laughed. "I could stop right this instant if I was of a mind to."

"Prove it. Give me your Colt. Then give me your word that you will never strap it or any other gun on for as long as you live."

"No man can make a promise like that," Clay said.

"You could if you were sincere."

"Not while Stark is out there. Or has everything I've said gone in one ear and out the other?"

"Is that the real reason or an excuse?" Melanie asked. "Fate gave you the perfect opportunity and you refused to take it. Maybe you really don't want to."

"We are talking in circles," Clay said. "It boils down to one thing and one thing only. Jesse Stark must be stopped."

"You don't wear a badge. Leave it to those who do," Melanie said. "Give up being Baine and get on with being Clay Adams."

"It is hopeless," Clay said.

"I resent that. You make me sound as dense as quartz. All I am saying is that if you are sincere about your new life, give up everything that has to do with the old."

Clay gazed out the open front flap of her tent. "It is not as easy as all that."

"Ah. Now the truth begins to come out," Melanie said. "Why isn't it easy? I will tell you. Because you *do* like being Baine and you *do* like squeezing the trigger."

"Can we talk about something else? Please?"

"Very well. But I will say that I am terribly disappointed. I took you at your word that Baine was dead and buried, but now I find he rises from the grave whenever the whim moves you."

"I have explained it more than once," Clay replied. "I don't see what I can say that I have not already said."

Abruptly rising, Melanie said, "If you gentlemen will excuse me, I will be back in a few minutes."

Clay watched her walk off. "If I live to be a hundred I will never savvy females."

"It is more than that, my friend," Mr. Train said. "I should know. I was in a similar situation once and I made the wrong decision."

"With a woman?"

"Her name was Francesca. We met in New Orleans. We fell in love and there was talk of marriage." Mr. Train frowned. "Then one day she asked me what I would do for a living after we were man and wife. I told her that I would go on doing as I had been doing. She was displeased. She had taken it for granted that I would stop hunting men. She did not think it suitable."

"That is similar," Clay said. "What happened?"

"We had a few arguments. I like what I do, and I did not want to change. One day she gave me an ultimatum. Either I agreed to stop being a manhunter after we walked down the aisle, or she and I were through."

When Train did not go on, Clay prompted, "What did you do?"

"I am here, aren't I? But I will tell you something, strictly between us. It was the worst decision of my life. If I had it to do over again, I would do it differently."

"You would give up being a manhunter?"

"Yes. The question you must ask—the question I did not ask of myself until it was too late and Francesca was gone—is this." Mr. Train paused. "Which is more important? Doing what we want or the one person in the world who wants us most?"

"Then you regret your decision?"

"Every single day. Francesca was the best thing to ever happen to me, and I was too blind to see it. I would give anything to be her husband now, but she married someone else."

Over the next several days Clay was quieter than usual. He was clearly deep in thought. Once Melanie asked what he was pondering and he replied, "Nothing much."

One evening, shortly after the sun went down, they came to a ridge overlooking the lights of Bluff City and drew rein. Smiling, Melanie said wearily, "We are back at last."

"Will you be leaving in the morning?" Clay asked Train.

"It depends on Harve Barker. He owes me money. Then there is the little matter of those outlaws calling me by my name."

"They must have heard of you somewhere," Melanie said.

"Maybe that is it," Mr. Train said, but he sounded less than convinced.

"I will go with you if you want," Clay offered.

"I would rather Baine went with me," Mr. Train said with a slight grin. "He is handier with a pistol."

"It will take us an hour to reach Bluff City. Another hour to unsaddle, get cleaned up and change," Clay detailed. "How about if we meet at the Emporium at ten?"

"Ten o'clock it is."

No sooner did they gig their mounts than Melanie brought the mare up next to the claybank. "You are really going to do it? Strap on your Colt and go marching into the Emporium?"

"It would be suicide to march in without it," Clay replied.

"Sarcasm doesn't become you," Melanie said. "And don't try to fool me into believing you are doing this for Mr. Train's benefit. You are doing it because you like being Neville Baine."

Clay stared at her and did not speak until they had gone over fifty yards. "Think what you will," he finally said.

"I will and I am," was Melanie's angry rejoinder. "You have misled me and I resent it. I resent it most strongly."

"That makes us even since I resent being judged," Clay said.

After that neither said a word until they came to the outskirts of Bluff City. Melanie bid the two men good night and left them, her back as stiff as a board.

"I'm only a few blocks from my apartment," Clay said, and reined around to part company.

"I am sorry if I have caused trouble between Miss Stanley and you," Mr. Train said.

"It's not you," Clay said, and let it go at that. Clucking to the claybank, he passed a buckboard and, in due course, came to the picket fence. The house was quiet and dark, which was not unusual since the couple he rented from, the Crisps, almost always turned in early.

Clay climbed down to unfasten the gate. The latch rasped as he worked it. He pushed with his foot and a hinge protested with a loud squeak. Leading the claybank, he walked toward the shed.

A gunshot spiked the night and Clay's derby was whipped from his head. Instinctively, he ducked, and a second slug blistered the space his head has just occupied. Both shots came from the corner of the house.

Streaking his hand under his jacket, Clay drew his Colt and fired at where he had seen muzzle flashes. There was a yelp and the drum of rapidly retreating boots.

Clay gave chase. Stopping at the corner, he risked a peek. An inky silhouette was almost to the front of the house. Clay snapped a shot, but as he squeezed the trigger the silhouette darted around the far corner. He was sure he had missed.

Clay dashed along the side of the house. The dull glint of a gun barrel gave him an instant's warning. He dived flat as the would-be killer fired and a wasp buzzed over his head.

Again boots pattered. Heaving upright, Clay flew to the front of the house and out the front gate. He expected to hear the drum of hooves, but the assassin was on foot half a block away. Clay ran flat out. He was fast but so was the other, and he could not gain.

The man was making for the middle of town, where the streets were thick with wheeled traffic and riders and pedestrians. He could lose himself among them.

Clay raised his Colt but lowered it again. If he missed, and odds were better than even he would, the slug might take the life of an innocent.

A house near the street had every window lit. Bright shafts of lamplight impaled the fleeing assassin just as he glanced back.

"Gorman!" Clay blurted.

Stark's lieutenant grinned.

Clay redoubled his effort, but it was in vain. At the next intersection Gorman veered to the right and was momentarily out of sight. Clay reached the corner and gazed down the street, only to find it empty. Stopping, he scanned the yards and the dark spaces between the houses but saw no trace of the outlaw. He went another block before he would admit Gorman had outfoxed him.

"Damn," Clay said, and turned back.

The house was still dark, still quiet. Clay figured the Crisps were gone. Not so the neighbors, many of whom had ventured outside after hearing the shots and were standing around speculating on the cause.

Slipping around to the rear, Clay placed his saddle, blanket and bridle in the shed, and carried his bedroll and saddlebags inside. He threw everything on the bed and lit the lamp. Undressing, he dipped a washcloth in the pitcher that the kindly Mrs. Crisp left outside his door each morning and cleaned himself from crown to toes. He shaved, splashed lilac water on his cheeks and sprinkled some in his hair, and examined the result in the mirror.

His buckskins were dusty. He shook them out the window before donning them. The same with his wide-brimmed black hat. After tugging on his knee-high moccasins, he strapped on his gun belt and twirled the pearl-handled Colt into his holster. Taking the Colt out again, he replaced the spent cartridges. "Almost forgot them," he said to himself.

The night air was cool on Clay's face. He did not follow his usual route but took a roundabout way, checking over his shoulder often and stopping to listen now and again, but no one was stalking him.

By the clock on a nearby bank it was ten minutes to ten when Clay slipped into a recessed doorway across from the Emporium. As usual, the popular gambling den was a beehive of activity.

Punctually at ten Mr. Train came down the street. Around his waist were the Whitney and the bowie.

Clay called out and crossed over. He had to dodge a carriage midway. Then he was shaking Train's calloused hand and asking, "Have any trouble getting here?"

"No. Why?"

Clay told him about Gorman.

"Yet another mystery," Mr. Train said. "What do you say we bait the wolf in his lair and see if we can find some answers?"

Chapter 26

A doorman clad in purple admitted them with a bow, saying, "Enjoy yourselves, gentlemen."

"Do you happen to know if Harve Barker is here?" Clay asked.

"No, sir, I don't," the doorman said. "I have not seen him since my shift began, but he often comes and goes out the back of the building."

Controlled chaos enveloped them. The Emporium was filled to bursting with gamblers and revelers and indulgers in intimate passions. Clay and the man-hunter made for the roped-off area where private games were played. The table reserved for Barker was not being used.

"It's early yet," Mr. Train remarked. "Maybe he will show up later. How about a drink to tide us over?"

Shouldering their way to the bar, they ordered whiskeys and, when the drinks were brought, they leaned back and slowly sipped while surveying the throng. Mr. Train was raising his glass when he stopped and said, "Uh-oh."

"You see him?" Clay said.

"Not him. Her."

"Her?" Clay repeated, and then saw the one Mr.

Train had alluded to coming toward them. Her dress was exquisite. It clung to her where a dress should cling to a woman. She smiled, but Clay did not return it. "What the hell are you doing here?" he demanded.

Melanie arched an eyebrow. "Is that any way to greet a friend and coworker?" She gestured at the sea of heads and bodies. "I am here for the same reason they are. To relax and enjoy myself."

"Like hell," Clay said.

"Why are you so mad?" Melanie asked, smoothing her already smooth dress. "Has the luster worn off?"

"Don't bandy words with me. You are not here to gamble and you are certainly not here to visit the private parlors."

"Are you sure?" Melanie said, and winked and laughed.

"You want to be here when we confront Barker," Clay said.

"What is wrong with that?" Melanie rebutted. "He is an acquaintance of mine, after all."

"That's not it, either," Clay said. "You don't like him all that much. You have come right out and said so. All he is to you is a news story."

"I do report the news, you know," Melanie said. "Wait until tomorrow's edition comes out. You will love my write-up of how the notorious Baine wiped out most of the Stark gang."

"You wouldn't."

"I have it to do, as you like to say. It is my living. And I was there, remember? I can provide a first-hand account."

"Do you realize what it will mean? The rumors were bad enough."

"Oh, please," Melanie said. "I am just doing my part to make Baine as famous as he can be."

Clay downed the rest of his drink in a single gulp and smacked the glass on the bar. "I never thought you could be so underhanded."

"The truth will out. Unlike a certain person I could mention, I don't delude myself. Baine is the real you, not Clay Adams. Clay Adams is a farce, a deception, a disguise."

"You think you know everything."

Melanie's eyes bored into his. "I know you have lied to me. I should have seen it that night at the stone bridge, when you gunned those two men. But my affection for you blinded me."

Clay motioned at one of the bartenders. "Give me another," he said, and tapped his empty glass.

"That might not be wise," Mr. Train said.

Clay ignored him, and after the bartender filled the glass he tilted back his head and swallowed half at a gulp.

"My, my," Melanie baited him. "Someone is in a mood."

"Go home," Clay said. "This is no place for you to be. We are not paying Barker a social call."

"We want to ask him a few questions," Mr. Train said.

"Maybe *you* do," Melanie said, "but not *him*." She waved a slender hand at Clay. "He wants to shoot Barker dead, and he is hoping Barker will give him an excuse to do just that. Isn't that right, Mr. Baine?"

"Quit calling me that."

"It's your name, isn't it?"

"Not anymore. Neville Baine is dead. He died in Kansas and was reborn."

"If that is so, why are you dressed as Baine and wearing the Colt Baine always wears?"

Clay had no immediate answer to that, and downed the rest of the whiskey. This time he set the glass down slowly. He did not look at Melanie. After a bit he said softly, "Baine is the past, not the present. As God is my witness, I want that more than anything."

Melanie leaned toward him to hear better. "Perhaps you do, or perhaps you only think you do."

"You make everything so complicated," Clay complained.

"The truth is not always as simple as many would like to believe," Melanie said. "For what it is worth I do not think ill of you. It pains me to see you so conflicted. You must settle who you are and stop being who you are not."

Mr. Train had been staring toward the back of the great room. Suddenly he grabbed Clay's arm and said, "Look there."

Through a pair of short swinging doors filed men and women garbed in purple, bearing silver trays laden with food and drink. In the lead was Charles, Barker's manservant. Staying close to the wall, they came to a stairway and wound upward.

"Are you thinking what I am thinking?" Mr. Train asked.

Clay nodded. "Where you find Charles you find Harve Barker."

By the time they had waded through the press of people to the stairs, the purple procession was nowhere in sight. They climbed to the first landing but did not see Charles or the food bearers, so on they went to the second floor and then the third.

"Still no sign of them," Clay said, and was about to climb to the fourth floor when a door midway down the hallway opened.

Out filed the same staff who had brought the trays. Charles was not with them. They passed Mr. Train and Clay with hardly a glance and disappeared down the stairs.

"Don't do this. Please."

Clay turned. Melanie had followed them and was looking at him with the saddest of expressions. "If it bothers you, leave."

Melanie appealed to Mr. Train. "Hasn't there been enough blood spilled? What will it accomplish?"

"You ask that? As devoted to the truth as you are?" the manhunter said.

"There is nothing I can say or do?"

"We are wasting time," Clay said irritably, and strode along the corridor. He was almost to the room the servants had emerged from when the door opened and out stepped Charles.

The manservant did not notice them until he had closed the door and turned. Drawing up short, he bleated in surprise. "Mr. Adams? Mr. Train? How wonderful to find you both alive and well. We have heard all sorts of stories."

"Out of our way," Clay commanded.

"Is Mr. Barker expecting you? If not, I will announce you." Charles reached quickly for the door.

Clay's arm was a blur. The Colt leaped out and up, and the barrel struck the servant's temple hard. Without a sound Charles crumpled and did not move once he lay on the floor.

"That was cruel," Melanie said.

"He was going to warn Barker." Clay slid the Colt into his holster. Hooking his hands under Charles's shoulders, Clay dragged him to one side and propped him up with his back to the wall.

Mr. Train had put an ear to the door. "I hear voices. Men and women. Barker is not alone."

"We should come back some other time," Melanie advised. "It wouldn't do to barge in on them."

"Hell," Clay said, and did just that. He flung the door wide so that it slammed against the wall and barged into a chamber fitted with every luxury known to man. A small crystal chandelier hung from the ceiling. The windows were covered by costly Turkish tapestries. To the right was a bar tended by an immaculate man in purple. In the center, at a large circular table draped in velvet cloth, sat six poker players. Harve Barker was one. Wesley Oaks, the gambler, was another. The president of the First Bank of Bluff City was taking part, as were other prominent businessmen. All had drinks at their elbows and several were puffing on thick cigars. And all except Wesley Oaks had young women in various stages of undress on their laps.

The president of the First Bank was fondling the breasts of a pert blonde, and at sight of Clay he bleated like a frightened sheep and pushed her off him with such violence that she nearly fell. "What is the meaning of this? Who are you men? I thought you assured us we would have the utmost privacy!"

That last was directed at Harve Barker, who had

been nuzzling the neck of a buxom brunette. If he was at all surprised he did not show it. Rather, he calmly sat up and leaned on the chair arm, and placed his chin in his hand. "My apologies, Clarence. This is unexpected."

"I bet it is," Clay said.

The other businessmen had stopped caressing the maidens and sat stiff with embarrassment.

Barker had been drinking heavily. His eyes bore the glaze of excess, and his movements and speech were unnaturally slow. "Permit me to make the introductions. Gentlemen, I give you Mr. Train, the manhunter I hired to track down Jesse Stark. Next to him is the gun-shark we have been hearing so much about. The man they call Baine."

"I call myself Clay Adams now," Clay said.

"Call yourself what you want, it won't change what you are." Barker stared past Clay and his mocking smile faded. "And the lovely Miss Stanley, as well. I must say, my dear, I don't entirely approve of the company you keep."

"I am not that fond of it myself at the moment," Melanie said.

Barker poked the buxom brunette and flicked his finger, and she vacated his lap. Straightening, he adopted a somber air. "To what do I owe this intrusion?"

"I am here for the rest of the money you owe me," Mr. Train said. "Half in advance and half when the job was done. That was our agreement."

"Yes, it was," Barker agreed. "But you did not hold up your end of it. Once you located the Stark gang you were to notify me. You never sent word, yet now you have the audacity to demand payment?"

"They were waiting for me," Mr. Train said. "They jumped me and would have killed me if not for Clay. As it was, they beat me near half to death."

"You were careless."

"Maybe you didn't hear me the first time. They were *waiting* for me. They knew I was after them. They even called me by name." Train leaned on the edge of the table. "How is it they knew who I was?"

"Why ask me?" Barker rejoined.

"Only four people were aware you had hired me," Mr. Train said. "You, Clay, Miss Stanley, and myself. Since Clay and Miss Stanley were with me, only one person could have told Stark."

The accusation brought a laugh from Barker. "Are you seriously suggesting I went to all the time and expense to hire you, and then warned the very man I sent you after?"

"Unless you have a better explanation."

"What was my motive? What did I hope to gain?" Barker snorted. "And yes, I do have a better one. Every member of my staff here at the Emporium and every servant at my house knew I had hired you. Thirty to forty people, any one of whom could have mentioned it when they were out and about. Rumor has it some of Stark's men were seen in town about the same time you rode out. Maybe one of them heard one of my people mention you and lit a shuck to warn Stark."

"You have an answer for everything," Clay said.

Mr. Train straightened. "No. It could have happened as he says. I might have been hasty in my judgment."

Barker sneered at Clay. "It is nice to see that one of you has some common sense." To Train he said, "I want to be fair about this. If one of my people was to blame, then I am at fault for not making it clear to them that they must not tell anyone. I will pay you the other half of the money, plus extra for your trouble. Meet me at the First Bank tomorrow morning at nine, if that is acceptable."

"I am satisfied," Mr. Train said.

"Well, I'm not!" Clay exploded. "How can you give in so easily?"

Wesley Oaks had been fingering his cards the whole time. Now he fixed Clay with a stare and said, "Listen to your friend. You don't want to cause trouble. Not now you don't."

Clay stepped to the right so no one was between him and Barker. "Now or later, it's all the same. Barker has a lot to answer for."

"Is that a threat?" Harve Barker asked.

"Whenever you want, go for your gun." Clay held his hand close to his Colt and flexed his fingers.

Unperturbed, Barker said, "I am unarmed. Would you shoot someone who cannot defend himself? In front of sweet Melanie?"

"You miserable son of a bitch."

"I'm not done," Barker said. "You see, I had heard you were back, and knowing you for the rabid wolf you are, I took the precaution of appealing for help." He glanced at the Turkish tapestries covering the nearest window. "You may come out now, gentlemen, and do your job."

The tapestries moved, and from behind them stepped Marshal Tom Vale and Deputy Wiggins. Wiggins leveled his revolver.

"You both heard him threaten my life," Barker said.

Marshal Vale nodded. "That we did. I am sorry, son," he told Clay, and sounded sincere, "but you are under arrest. Come along quietly or my deputy will shoot you where you stand."

Chapter 27

The cell door closed with a clang.

Clay gripped the bars and glared at Deputy Wiggins as the deputy turned the key. "How long do you think you can hold me?"

"Until you rot." Smirking, Wiggins hung the key on a peg that was well out of reach. "Might as well make yourself comfortable."

"I'm not the one who should be in here," Clay said. "Harve Barker is."

"Oh, sure," Deputy Wiggins taunted. "We will arrest one of Bluff City's leading citizens because a notorious man killer says we should."

"You're enjoying this."

Wiggins bobbed his double chins. "Damn right I am. You have been looking down your nose at me since we met, and don't think I haven't noticed."

Marshal Vale broke his silence to say, "That will be enough, Deputy. Wait for me in the office."

Reluctantly, Deputy Wiggins obeyed.

Clay looked around. In an adjoining cell a drunk snored. In a cell across from his sat a morose man with his head in his hands.

"So what happens now?" Clay asked the lawman.

"The day after tomorrow you appear before Judge Farraday. He will decide whether to have you bound over for trial." Vale frowned. "I wouldn't count on being set free. Farraday is a close friend of Harve Barker's."

"This is wrong. You know this is wrong. Leave the key where I can reach it and I will be gone by morning."

Marshal Vale's frown deepened. "I can't do that, son." He tapped his badge. "I took an oath when I pinned this on. I must uphold the law, even when I don't agree with it."

"But all I did was make a few threats," Clay protested. "What can they do to me for that?"

"Depends. Usually the judge imposes a fine and lets the man go with a warning. In your case, with Barker whispering in Farraday's ear, you could get up to a year."

"A year!" Clay exploded.

"Simmer down," Marshal Vale said. "It could be worse. You are not wanted anywhere as Baine, near as I can tell. There was talk of you robbing a bank in Kansas a while back, but charges were never filed because they thought you were dead. So the threats are all Barker has unless he trumps up something else."

"What about bail?"

"The amount will be up to Farraday. Normally it wouldn't be much, but in your case he is liable to set it high."

"I am being railroaded and you know it," Clay said.

"You brought it on yourself, marching into the Emporium like you did. Barker had me following him around all evening, just waiting for you to show. He is a lot of things, but stupid is not one of them." Vale left, closing the outer cell door after him.

Glumly, Clay plopped on the cot and swore.

The man in the adjoining cell with his head in his hands looked up. "I couldn't help but overhear, mister. Sounds like you are in a worse fix than me." He was stout, with muttonchops and big, sorrowful eyes. "They arrested me for being a footpad. The very idea, that I, Phinneas Muckle, would stoop to robbery!"

Clay walked to the front of his cell. "Vale wouldn't arrest you unless he had good cause."

The man sniffed and managed to look more sorrowful. "I thought that you, at least, would be sympathetic to my plight, given that you claim to be unjustly incarcerated."

"What can you tell me about Jesse Stark?"

"I beg your pardon?"

"You steal for a living. You work the streets. You must hear all the latest rumors. Have you heard anything about Stark? Is he here in Bluff City?"

"My good man," Muckle said indignantly. "I will have you know I only associate with—" He stopped and stared at the barred window in the rear wall of Clay's cell. "My word! Is that what I think it is?"

Clay started to turn. A revolver boomed like thunder and Muckle cried out and fell. Instantly flattening, Clay glimpsed a six-shooter and the hand that held it being hastily withdrawn. Shouts came from the front of the jail. A key rasped in the outer door, and in rushed Marshal Vale and Deputy Wiggins.

"What the hell?" Wiggins blurted, gaping at the prone form that lay in a spreading pool of red.

Never taking his eyes off the window, Clay warily

rose. "Someone tried to shoot me in the back but hit him instead."

"Muckle?" Marshal Vale quickly opened the door to the other cell and bent over the footpad. He pressed a finger to Muckle's neck. "Dead. Plumb through the heart." He glanced at Clay. "You say the killer was after you?" Then, to Wiggins, "Get outside and look around."

"But whoever did it is long gone by now," the deputy protested. "What good would it do?"

"You will do it because I say to do it," Marshal Vale said. "Ask everyone you see if they saw anything."

Grumbling to himself, Wiggins hustled from the cells. No sooner was he gone than Marshal Vale came out of Muckle's cell and inserted the key into the door to Clay's. "That should keep him busy a while." Vale opened the door. "Out you go. Your gun belt is in the bottom right drawer in my desk. Grab it on your way out."

"What?"

"Are you hard of hearing? I will tell everyone you slugged me. You should have time to gather your things and make yourself scarce."

"Wait a minute," Clay said. "You're releasing me?"

"What is the matter with you?" Marshal Vale snapped. "You want out, don't you?" He jabbed a finger at the window. "If they tried once they will try again. I can post a guard outside, but that won't stop them if they are determined to blow out your wick."

"I'll be on the run," Clay said. "You will have to issue a warrant for my arrest."

"You will be *alive*," Marshal Vale countered. "Quit

dawdling. Work it out in your head later. Someone could come in the jail any moment, and I will have to slam this door shut again and leave you to your fate."

Clay hurried past him, then paused. "Why? You said yourself that you always abide by the law."

"I said not to dawdle. But if you must know, I refuse to have your blood on my hands. It's bad enough that poor Muckle, there, has been murdered." Marshal Vale's jaw muscles twitched. "I don't take kindly to being used." He gave Clay a shove. "Now go while you can."

The gun belt was where Vale said it would be. Clay hastily strapped it on, checked that the Colt was loaded and moved to the front door. He cracked it an inch and peered out. The side street the jail was located on was mired in night, and the few people he saw were going about their business. Slipping out, he quietly closed the door behind him.

Fireflies flared in the mouth of an alley and lead smashed into the jail door and wall inches from his chest. Clay responded in kind. Someone cried out. Zigzagging, Clay raced toward the alley. He was almost to it when a shadowy shape rose onto its knees and a revolver hammer clicked. Clay fired again, into the figure's chest, and came to a stop next to the convulsing form.

It was Gorman. The whites of his eyes showed as his mouth opened and closed, and dark spittle dribbled over his lower lip.

"Where is Stark?" Clay asked.

Gorman's eyes focused on him. The outlaw tried to raise his gun arm but Clay stepped on his wrist. The next second Gorman sucked in a deep breath and died.

From somewhere behind the jail came a shout from Deputy Wiggins. To linger was folly. Clay ran down the alley to the next street. He drew few stares but, to be safe, he stayed in the shadows until he had gone several blocks. By happenstance he came to the Courier.

A light glowed in the window.

On an impulse Clay crossed the street. The door was unlocked. He entered on cat's feet. Only one person was there, seated at her desk with her shoulders slumped, her hair disheveled, and her forehead resting on her forearms. Clay heard a sniffle. "Are you all right?"

Melanie jerked upright. Her cheeks were moist, her eyes red. Swiping at her face with her sleeve, she exclaimed, "You! Where did you come from? I thought they arrested you."

"Barker tried to have me killed."

Blinking in confusion, Melanie said, "What are you saying? How does that explain what you are doing here?"

"Barker tried to have me killed," Clay repeated. "I'm on the run. I just shot Gorman."

Melanie stiffened. "He's dead, you mean? My God. Is there no end? Is that your answer to everything?"

"Didn't you hear me?" Clay asked, coming around her desk. He reached for her hands, but she recoiled.

"Don't you dare touch me!"

"What has gotten into you?" Clay snapped. "I need your help. Barker will have men searching for me. I have to get up into the high country, lie low a spell, decide what to do."

"There you go again," Melanie said. "Accusing Harve Barker. What proof do you have? You told me he tried to have you killed, but it was Gorman you shot, correct? So it is Jesse Stark who wants you dead, not Barker."

"They are connected somehow. I know it."

Melanie came out of her chair in a fury, her fingers balled into fists. "Will you listen to yourself? Name me one thing that links Barker to Stark. Just one thing."

"I can't yet. It's a hunch I have, is all," Clay explained.

"Dear God. You were ready to gun him down over a *hunch*?" Melanie sagged into her chair. "And to think I liked you. Truly and really liked you. How could I have been so wrong?"

Clay gestured in impatience. "I should have known how you would react. Very well. I won't impose on you further." He turned to go. "I'll find Train. He will believe me even if you don't. Do you know where he is?"

"No. But I know he is leaving in the morning. He has his money, and he asked me to say so long for him."

"Oh."

"What did you expect? Stark could have found out about Mr. Train any number of ways. You are the only one who sees Barker's hand in everything."

A commotion broke out in the street. Clay dashed to the window, careful not to show himself. Men with lanterns were fanning out and checking doorways and nooks. One came toward the Courier, a tin star glinting on his vest.

In three bounds Clay was at the counter. He ducked behind it a heartbeat before blows hammered the door, rattling the glass.

"Open up in there! This is the law!"

Melanie rose. She did not glance at Clay as she went by. Clay heard a door hinge creak. "Deputy Wiggins? What is all the fuss about?"

"Sorry to bother you, Miss Stanley, but that no-account friend of yours has escaped and murdered a man," Wiggins said. "A few people thought they might have seen him come this way, so we are turning every street upside down." Wiggins coughed. "He hasn't been here by any chance, has he?"

Clay placed his hand on his Colt.

"No, he has not, Deputy, which is just as well. I have lost all respect for him," Melanie said.

"You are working kind of late, aren't you?"

"I was writing of his arrest for tomorrow's edition," Melanie answered. "I always like to write events down while they are fresh in my mind."

"Now you will have even more to write," Deputy Wiggins said. "Keep this door bolted and don't let him in if he does show."

"Never fear on that score. I want nothing whatsoever more to do with Clay Adams or Neville Baine or whatever he wants to call himself."

Wiggins chuckled, then bid her good night. Melanie closed the door, threw the bolt and pulled the blind. She came to the end of the counter and said without looking down, "That was the last favor I will ever do for you. Sneak out the back, and for God's sake don't get caught."

Clay rose, but only as high as the top of the counter. "Did you mean what you said about not wanting anything more to do with me?"

"I did."

"I'm sorry you feel that way. I wish there was something I could say to change your mind, but I never have been all that good with words."

"Just go."

His cheeks burning, Clay backpedaled until he came to the press. "I'm going," he said. "But I want you to know I meant what I whispered to you that night on the mountain. You mean more to me than anything. I would rather chop off my gun hand than lose you." He started to say more but his throat constricted. Shaking his head, he moved down the narrow hall to the back door. In his emotional state he forgot himself. He violently wrenched the bolt, threw the door open and barreled outside. Straight into a burly figure who had been to one side of the doorway.

Clay stabbed for his Colt but the man grabbed his wrist. A knife appeared in the other's hand and Clay grabbed the man's wrist. Locked together, they swung back and forth, each straining to break free. The man was as strong as a bull. It was all Clay could do to hold on.

Then faint light from the open door spilled over them, and Clay got a good look at who he was battling. He had assumed it was one of the searchers, maybe even Deputy Wiggins.

But he was mistaken.

The man trying to kill him was Bantarro.

Chapter 28

Clay's surprise was fleeting. It had to be. Bantarro snarled and slammed Clay into the wall, jarring him down to the bone. Clay retaliated by driving his knee into Bantarro's groin. Bantarro grunted, but that was all. Otherwise he seemed not to feel the blow as, uttering an inarticulate growl, he practically raised Clay clear off the ground and then threw him down on his back.

Suddenly Clay had Bantarro's knee gouging into his gut and Bantarro's sweaty face hovering above his and, worse, the tip of Bantarro's knife being forced toward his neck.

"Now you die, gringo!"

Clay exerted his strength to its utmost, but he could not heave Bantarro off of him or stop the blade from being forced a fraction at a time toward his jugular.

"I kill because Senor Stark tells me to. But I also kill you for Gorman. He was my friend, my amigo."

Clay pushed against Bantarro's wrist but Bantarro's arm was made of steel.

"The great Baine!" Bantarro gloated. "You are much with a pistola, but not so much when you cannot use one, eh?"

Gritting his teeth, Clay marshaled whatever reservoir of might he had left. It was not enough. He was hopelessly, helplessly pinned.

"The other one will reward me for this," Bantarro hissed. "He wants you dead, gringo, more than he wants anything."

Clay sought to knee him again but could not move his leg.

"And so it ends," Bantarro said. He tensed to plunge the knife into Clay's throat. "Adios."

Light bathed them in a bright glare and someone demanded, "What the hell is going on here? What are you two doing?"

Startled, Bantarro twisted to see who it was. Clay saw the man clearly over Bantarro's shoulder.

Deputy Wiggins had come up behind the bandit and stood with a lantern held aloft in one hand and his revolver in the other. Because Bantarro was on top, he did not realize Clay was involved until Bantarro moved. "You!" he blurted, and extended his revolver. "Put your hands up, both of you! You are under arrest."

Bantarro moved. Quick as thought, he sprang up off Clay and his pistol sprang to his hand. He fanned it, twice.

Dumbfounded, Wiggins staggered. He looked down at the holes in his chest and the dark stains beginning to spread, and he bleated, "I'm not supposed to die." Then he did, his knees folding under him.

Bantarro pivoted toward Clay. In the split second that took, Clay drew and fired his pearl-handled Colt from flat on his back. He aimed high and scored high. A hole appeared between Bantarro's bushy brows and the top of his skull exploded in a spray of hat, hair and gore.

Clay was on his feet before the body came to rest next to Wiggins's. Voices from both ends of the alley warned him he was trapped. Whirling toward the doorway, he took a step, and stopped.

Melanie stood there, staring in mute horror at the dead men.

"Bantarro killed the deputy, not me."

"Dead people," Melanie said softly. "Everywhere you go, there are dead people."

Clay could not linger. The voices at both ends of the alley were louder. "Bantarro was trying to kill me. It's not my fault."

"It never is, is it?"

"I have no time for this," Clay said brusquely, and bounded past her. She snatched at his sleeve, but he shrugged her hand off and ran down the hall. He went past the printing press, the desks and the counter to the front. A glance out the window confirmed the ruckus at the back had drawn the searchers from the street. It was deserted for the moment. He opened the door.

"Wait!" Melanie called.

Clay did no such thing. He turned right and walked fast, but not so fast that it would attract attention, until he had covered half a dozen blocks. Convinced no one had pursued him, he slowed and headed in a roundabout manner for the outskirts of town, toward the apartment and the claybank. So much had happened so quickly that he had not had much time to think about it, but he did now. Something Bantarro said had stuck in his mind, the comment about "the other one" who would "reward" Bantarro for slaying him.

At that time of night the residential neighborhoods lay quiet under the stars. Clay was one of the few abroad. He avoided the few people he encountered by melting into the shadows until they had gone by. When he came within sight of the house, he stopped. He had learned his lesson. He made a complete circuit of the picket fence before he used the rear gate.

Thankfully, the claybank was where he had left it. He hurried into the shed and brought out the bridle, his saddle and the saddle blanket. Thus encumbered, he stepped to the claybank.

"Took you long enough."

Clay nearly jumped. He turned as the speaker materialized out of a black patch under the porch overhang. "What the blazes are *you* doing here?"

"Is that any way to greet one of the few friends you have?" Marshal Tom Vale asked.

"How did you know where to find me?"

"I'm the law. It's my business to know," Vale said with a forced grin that immediately died. "We need to talk, Adams. Or do you prefer Baine?"

"I answer to both these days." Clay turned back to the claybank. "Say your piece while I saddle up."

"You're leaving?"

"Wouldn't you? Harve Barker is out to get me. Jesse Stark wants me dead. People are scouring the streets for me." Clay adjusted the bridle. "I'd say that lighting a shuck is the smart thing to do."

"It's not like you to run from a fight," Marshal Vale said. "Are you sure there's not another reason?"

"If there is it is mine."

"Suit yourself. But that's not why I'm here. I have talked to Melanie. She told me you were not to blame for Wiggins."

"She did?" Clay asked, his spirits perking.

"Wiggins had his faults. He was lazy and he talked too much, and he never bathed nearly enough. But he always did what I told him and upheld the law as best he could."

"That's as good an epitaph as any," Clay remarked while smoothing the saddle blanket.

"The Mexican who shot him was one of the Stark gang, which puts the blame for Wiggins at Stark's feet," Marshal Vale said.

"Bantarro was after me. Your deputy was in the wrong place at the wrong time and it cost him his life. He accidentally saved mine."

"Then you owe him," Marshal Vale said.

"I can't repay a dead man."

"Maybe you can. Maybe we can help one another and put an end to this once and for all."

About to throw his saddle on, Clay paused and looked at the lawman. "You have been leading up to something. Get it off your chest so I can be on my way."

"Fair enough." Marshal Vale walked up, took a battered tin star from his pocket and pinned it to Clay's buckskin shirt.

Clay stared at the badge and then at the lawman, and then at the badge again. "What in God's name is this?"

"They call it a badge."

"What is it doing on me?"

"Deputies are required to wear them," Marshal Vale said.

Clay laughed, waited for the lawman to say something, and when Vale just stood there, Clay laughed some more. Still laughing, he swung his saddle onto the claybank and set to work on the cinch.

"Is that all you are going to do? Laugh?"

"Were you kicked in the head by a horse? Or did you down a bottle of coffin varnish before you came here?" Clay snorted and shook his head in amusement. "Making me your deputy won't work."

"Give me one good reason."

Clay faced him. "I can give you a whole passel. What will folks say when they find out you hired Neville Baine, the gun-shark?"

"I am not hiring Neville Baine. I'm hiring Clay Adams, who works at the newspaper but happens to be a fair hand with a six-gun." Vale held up a hand when Clay went to speak. "I grant you that a lot of people have heard of Baine. I grant that a lot have heard the rumor he is alive and well. But only a few know that Neville Baine and Clay Adams are one and the same."

"Everyone will know once Melanie writes her account of what happened up in the mountains."

"She has decided to leave out the part about you being Baine."

"It's not like her to leave something like that out," Clay said. "She believes in telling the whole truth and nothing but the whole truth."

"Let's just say she and I had a nice talk and I persuaded her to leave out one or two details."

"You told her you planned to make me your deputy?"

"The idea came to me when I was standing over poor Wiggins," Marshal Vale said. "She was there with me."

"What did she say?"

"Nothing at first. Then she sort of smiled and went inside the *Courier*, and came back out with the story she had been writing. She let me read it. That's when I asked her not to spill your secret to the whole world."

"I don't rightly know what to say," Clay said. "You have done me the biggest favor anyone ever did me."

"Say yes to the badge," Marshal Vale urged.

"Why me? What makes you think I can do a good enough job? You are taking an awful risk."

"How so? As Baine you are not wanted anywhere."

"Except here. You arrested me, remember?"

"To cool you off. To prevent you spilling blood. But no charges were lodged. I explained the incident at the jail as a misunderstanding and called off the search for you." Marshal Vale grinned. "That's how Melanie will write it for tomorrow's newspaper, anyway."

"I still say it's loco."

"Hear me out. I'm no gunny. I don't claim to be half as fast or as accurate as you. Hell, few are. But I can use a man who is. What with Stark on the loose, and other problems the law here faces, a quick-draw artist would be a mighty handy gent to have backing my play."

"I don't know the first thing about the law."

"You don't need to be a lawyer to wear a badge. You need to be willing to do what is right. I can teach

you all you need to know about ordinances and stat-
utes. But the rest, that has to come from inside you,
and I believe you have what it takes."

"Damn," Clay said. He fingered the badge.

"Think about it. You have until we get to the
Emporium."

Clay snapped straighter. "The Emporium?"

"A little bird whispered in my ear that Jesse Stark
is there, hiding out in one of the upper rooms. You
and I will give the place a going-over from top to
bottom, and if he is there, take him into custody."

"The same little bird as the last time?"

"Yes. Wesley Oaks. He spotted Stark there shortly
after we left, and got word to me." The lawman went
around the corner of the house and returned leading
his horse. "Finish up and we will go."

Clay tugged on the cinch and adjusted the saddle
and was ready. He forked leather, saying uncertainly,
"I don't know about this, Vale. I wouldn't want to
embarrass you."

"I don't blush easy."

"Not that kind of embarrassment," Clay said. "I'm
talking the kind where folks want to crucify you for
hiring a gunny who shoots one of the town's leading
citizens dead as dead can be."

"Personal grudges and tin stars don't mix," Marshal
Vale replied. "Hate him all you want, but don't let
your hate spur you into squeezing the trigger when
you shouldn't. Give me your word."

"I don't know if I can do this," Clay admitted.

"Like I said, you have until we get to the Emporium."

Marshal Vale clucked to his horse and Clay followed suit with the claybank. They rode slowly, Clay adrift in thought.

The lawman drew his Remington. Only five of the six chambers in the cylinder were loaded. Sliding a cartridge from one of the loops on his gun belt, he inserted it into the empty chamber. "I never keep a pill under the hammer for safety's sake," he commented.

Clay grunted.

"I was about your age when I first pinned a star on, and I had the same doubts you are having. I wasn't a tie-down artist, but I had done a few things I was not proud of, and I didn't think I was worthy." Marshal Vale paused. "One more thing worth keeping in mind. Barker won't dare send anyone after you while you are wearing that badge. He would have me down on him, along with every lawman I call on to help out."

"Come to think of it, I would like to see the look on that bastard's face when he sees me wearing this. Maybe it will rattle him so bad he will draw on me."

"In which case," Marshal Vale said, "you have my permission to blow him to hell and back."

"Call me Deputy Adams from now on," Clay said.

Chapter 29

The Emporium was bedlam after midnight. Liquor flowed as freely as runoff from the mountains and most of the revelers had quaffed more than their share. The more they drank, the less inhibited they became. Those inclined to be quiet and shy became rowdy and noisy. Those inclined to be rowdy and noisy became more so. The bar was lined end to end, and the floor was packed. Every table was filled, and every poker and faro game and every roulette wheel had its onlookers.

Into this chaotic mix of greed and lust came Clay Adams and Marshal Vale. Clay let the marshal take the lead. He did not quite feel comfortable with the tin pinned to his shirt. He kept thinking everyone would stare, but hardly anyone gave him a second glance. Or so he thought until Marshal Vale looked back at him and said so only he could hear, "There are a couple more over by the wall."

Clay gazed in the direction Vale indicated and saw two men clad in purple. He took them for Emporium staff until he noticed something unusual; both had revolvers strapped around their waists. Normally, the staff did not carry firearms openly. This made six they had seen since they entered.

"All the hardware makes me think Barker has something he wants to hide," Clay remarked.

"It is well known that he has a small hired army of gunnies," Marshal Vale enlightened him. "Usually they keep out of sight."

"Do you reckon he is expecting us?"

"He had no way of knowing I would bring you here. So it's not us exactly, so much as trouble in general." Marshal Vale scanned the galleries that overlooked the main floor. "Maybe he heard Stark is here and he has taken a few precautions."

"Could be," Clay said. His tone implied differently.

Vale angled toward a table with a large crowd. He waded through like a bull through reeds. Only one of the six men involved in the game looked up, and he smiled.

"As I live and breathe," Wesley Oaks declared. "Are you interested in being parted from your money, gentlemen? Wait half an hour or so and a few chairs should open up."

"That is not why we are here," Marshal Vale said. "Where did he get to?"

"I assume you mean the scourge of the territory," the gambler said. "Last I saw, he went upstairs. But that was almost two hours ago."

"Was he alone?"

"As a matter of fact, no. He had a dove on each arm and the look of a gent who is bird-hungry." Wesley Oaks grinned.

"Much obliged," Marshal Vale said, and motioned

for Clay. They moved toward the nearest stairs and acquired a black-clad shadow. "This isn't your fight," the marshal said.

"What sort of friend would I be if I let you walk into the lion's den alone?" Wesley Oaks asked.

"I am not alone. I have Clay with me."

"Three is better than two when a person is up against the odds you are bucking," Wesley countered. "Besides, I had nothing better to do."

"Liar. You left your livelihood to come with us. That shows poor business sense for a gambler."

"The few friends I have mean more to me than a few hands of cards," Wesley responded. He nudged Clay and jabbed a thumb at Vale. "I bet he hasn't told you that he and I go back a ways. We met in Pueblo about fifteen years ago. Then it was Colorado Springs, and after that, Durango. Finally we wound up here, and after things quiet down, we'll probably move on again."

"I'm getting too old for this kind of life," Marshal Vale said. "I need to start thinking about settling down."

Clay looked at Oaks. "What makes you think Bluff City won't be wild and woolly forever?"

"They never are. It is always the same. Someone strikes it rich. Word gets out and thousands of fools stream in, thinking they can strike it rich too. Before you can say boomtown, one springs up. More saloons, gambling dens and dance halls than you can shake a stick at. Then along come the respectable sorts, the churchgoers and others who don't like to be reminded that some people prefer vice to virtue. Before you know it, laws are passed to get rid of the riffraff. The saloons and dance halls and gambling dens close, and those who don't like the tame life move on to wilder pastures."

"If it wasn't for those vice-lovers, I would be out of a job," Marshal Vale commented.

They were almost to the stairs. Suddenly a pair of purple-clad underlings appeared out of the throng to bar their way.

"I'm sorry, Marshal," one said, holding out a hand, "but Mr. Barker left instructions that no one is allowed upstairs without his personal say-so."

Vale touched his tin star. "Do you see this? It gives me the right to go where I damn well want when I damn well want to. Unless you and your friend want to spend the night in the hoosegow, you will step aside."

"We can't do that," said the other one. "We will lose our jobs if we do."

Clay stepped out from behind Vale. "With any luck, someone can fetch a sawbones to tend to you before you bleed to death."

"What?" the second man said.

"What?" his partner echoed.

"I am going to count to three," Clay told them. "If you are still in our way when I get to three, I am going to shoot you. I will try to wing you, but I can't make any promises." He barely paused. "One. Two. Th—"

"Hold on, damn it!" the first one bleated, and the two hastily backed away, their arms out from their sides.

Marshal Vale went up the stairs, two at a stride, saying, "I liked how you handled that. But tell me.

Would you really have shot them if they didn't move?"

"Let's just say I am glad they didn't put me to the test," Clay said.

They reached the first landing. A woman tottered out of a room on the left. Naked from the waist up, she giggled to herself. She did not see them, and went into a room across the hall from the one she came out of.

"I have heard tales about what goes on up here late at night," Marshal Vale said.

"I've *seen* what goes on," Wesley Oaks said. "A person can buy anything, and I do mean anything. Barker makes almost as much money off the late-night shenanigans as he does the gambling."

"That must be a lot of shenanigans," Clay said.

"Reverend Wilcox would say it was Sodom and Gomorrah all over again," Wesley observed.

"How does all this help us find Jesse Stark?" Clay asked.

"It doesn't," the gambler answered. "But if you start opening doors, don't say I didn't warn you."

Marshal Vale rubbed his chin. "This floor, you reckon, or higher?"

"That I can't say," Wesley answered.

Clay had another question. "How did you know it was Stark? Have you seen him before?"

"Your lady friend described him quite well in the newspaper. That, and someone whispered and pointed and said it was him."

Marshal Vale moved toward the first door. "Well, I guess there is no getting around it. We will go from room to room. Knock, announce yourself, and open the door quick-like. Close it right away if Stark isn't there."

"And hope no one shoots you for disturbing them," Wesley said.

They began their search. But they had barely checked half the rooms on that floor when a member of the Emporium staff, passing on the landing, saw them, stared in puzzlement a few moments, then took off up the stairs as if his britches were on fire.

"You know where he is going, don't you?" Wesley Oaks said.

"To tell Barker," Marshal Vale agreed.

Their prediction was borne out not five minutes later when the Emporium's owner came marching down the hall with six armed men in purple at his back. He did not give them a chance to explain but tore right into them, snapping, "How dare you barge in on my customers without my consent."

Marshal Vale had been about to open another door. "I am on official business, and that gives me—"

Barker poked the lawman in the chest. "That badge doesn't give you the right to make a nuisance of yourself."

With a visible effort Vale controlled his temper. "I can when I am after a wanted outlaw."

"Who would that be?" Barker mockingly demanded.

"Jesse Stark."

"Not him again—" Barker began, and abruptly stopped, shock registering as he noticed Clay. "What the hell? Why is *he* wearing a badge?"

"Deputies are required to," Marshal Vale said.

"Deputy?" Barker sputtered. Rage seized him. He was like a steamboat about to burst a boiler. "You can't just appoint anyone you like."

"On the contrary," Marshal Vale said with assumed patience. "I can and I have. There is nothing you can do about it."

"We shall see about that," Barker declared. "This won't do. This won't do at all." He moved aside and gestured at the landing. "I want you out of my establishment, and I want you out *now*."

"I told you. We are searching for Jesse Stark."

"Search somewhere else, because he sure as hell is not here. And before you say anything, if you don't go, I will make your life as miserable as you are making mine. I can, and you know I can. All I have to do is whisper into the ears of a few of the town council and you will be out of a job faster than you can spit."

"You would obstruct us in the performance of our duty?"

"Don't you dare try pulling that formal claptrap on me," Barker said. "Get out, Vale, and get out now."

"Very well," the marshal said.

Clay Adams gave a start. "How can you kowtow to this son of a bitch? We're the law. We can do as we want."

"Need I remind, you, Deputy Adams," Vale said, "that as a citizen and not a criminal, Mr. Barker is entitled to a certain respect?"

"Damn right I am," Barker declared.

"But Stark!" Clay protested.

"Come along quietly, Deputy Adams," Marshal Vale said. "We have imposed too much on Mr. Barker's good graces as it is."

"Now you are talking," Barker said.

The purple minions parted, and Vale and Clay and Wesley Oaks filed to the landing and down the stairs. As they came to the bottom Clay started to unpin his badge, saying, "If that was your notion of upholding the law, I don't want any part of it. You have no more sand than a turtle."

Marshal Vale only grinned. "When I was your age I was just as hasty. But you might want to hold onto your star a while yet. Barker thinks we are slinking off with our tails between our legs, but we're not."

"It sure seems like we are to me," Clay said.

"Patience, son. The one quality a lawman needs more than any other is patience." Vale stopped and made sure no one was eavesdropping. "There are only two ways in and out of the Emporium: the door at the front and the door at the back. I'll keep watch from across the street while you go around to the rear. If Jesse Stark is in here, sooner or later he has to leave."

"What about me, Tom?" Wesley Oaks asked.

"Go back to your cards. I hope Barker doesn't take it into his head to banish you or some such for helping us."

"He won't. I'm a favorite of some of the high-stakes players, and they wouldn't like it." The gambler smiled and ambled off.

Clay turned toward the back.

"Not yet," Marshal Vale said quickly. "Barker is bound to have us watched. We'll mosey out like good sheep, then sneak back."

"You sure are a tricky cuss," Clay said by way of praise as they threaded through the press of humanity.

"I have my moments," the lawman said. "Our job is as much mental as it is anything. The trick is not to seem too smart, so everyone underestimates you."

"There is a lot more to you than you let on."

"Don't tell anyone. It is supposed to be a secret."

The night air was bracing. They went two blocks, to where they had left their mounts, and ducked into a doorway. After a while Marshal Vale said, "I reckon no one followed us. Off you go."

Clay climbed on the claybank. He rode warily, alert for Barker's underlings. Soon he came to the street that flanked the rear of the Emporium. Unlike the busy thoroughfare out front, it was shrouded in stygian shadow. Which made it easy for him to conceal himself and the claybank in a gap between two buildings. Nearby were barrels filled with refuse. The stink was abominable. He breathed shallowly and hoped he would not have long to wait.

Time crept by. By three in the morning Clay was struggling to stay awake. Every now and again someone came out the rear door, but it was always a purple-garbed employee, probably on their way home.

Then a carriage clattered around the far corner and rolled to a stop only a stone's throw from the door. The driver consulted a pocket watch. Not two minutes went by before the door rasped open. Out came four men wearing purple coats and revolvers. They ringed the carriage. One surveyed the street, then hollered, "No sign of anyone, sir."

Harve Barker emerged, twirling a cane. He waited as the driver jumped down and opened the carriage door for him. About to climb in, he glanced over his shoulder and growled, "Well? What are you waiting for? Are you coming or not?"

Out of the Emporium, his trademark smirk in place and his thumbs hooked in his gun belt, came Jesse Stark.

Chapter 30

Clay instantly grabbed for his pearl-handled Colt, but he did not draw it. Curiosity smothered his impulse to exact revenge. He stayed where he was until the carriage reached the end of the street, then he gigged the clay-bank into a trot. At the junction he reined up. The carriage was a block away, traveling west. He let them gain another block before he used his heels.

Once the carriage left the center of town the streets were nearly deserted. That late at night, most of those abroad were heading home after a night of debauch.

Clay had a hunch where Barker was headed. When the carriage came to the wrought-iron gate and stopped, his hunch was confirmed. Two armed men in purple came out of the dark to open the gate, and the carriage wheeled onto the gravel drive and off through the trees.

Clay reined to the left and followed the stone wall. When he was at the midway point, he reined up. "Stand still, boy," he whispered. Sliding his moccasins from the stirrups, he eased onto his knees in the saddle. He could just reach the top of the wall. It was the effort of an instant to pull himself up onto his belly and flatten.

Flower gardens bordered by hedges unfolded under him, the flowers long withered. He was about to swing over the side when a pair of guards with rifles came down one of the paths. They had not seen him. They were making their rounds. He lay perfectly still, and presently they disappeared among the trees that flanked the gravel drive.

Quietly, Clay lowered his legs over and dropped. Tucked at the waist, he ran along a hedge. He passed a rose garden, the plants wilted, and skirted a pond stocked with goldfish. Several of the fish were near the surface, visible despite the darkness.

No one challenged him. No shots cracked. Clay gained the mansion and glided along the wall until he came to a window lit by a yellow glow. He peeked in. Luck had favored him. It was the dining room. Three people, not two, were seated at the long mahogany table. One was Harve Barker. The second was Jesse Stark. When Clay saw the third person, his breath caught in his throat and an icy chill blew down his spine.

Barker was talking, but the window was shut and Clay could not make out what he was saying. Clay continued on to a side door. Just as he went to reach for it, the door opened, framing a surprised guard in a purple coat. The man opened his mouth to shout an alarm but Clay was quicker. Out flashed his Colt. The *thud* of metal on flesh was followed by the *thud* of an unconscious form striking the floor.

Clay strained his ears, but there was no outcry from within. Shutting the door after him, he dragged the guard to the first room he came to. It was a library. Clay rolled the man over against a bookcase and hurried to the dining room. He heard voices. Barker's was harsh, insistent; Melanie's defiant.

Clay sidled to the jamb. The door was partway open, but not enough for him to see them.

Jesse Stark chuckled and said, "If this don't beat all. Here you were worried about me, and you come home to find your men caught this pretty filly trying to sneak into your house."

"I don't find it the least bit humorous," Harve Barker flatly declared. "And I have every right to worry about our arrangement. If it became common knowledge, I would be through in Bluff City."

"If the filly has her way, it will be tomorrow's headline," Stark said. "I can see it now. Emporium owner in cahoots with outlaw! Or some such nonsense."

"There is nothing nonsensical about the truth, Mr. Stark," Melanie said quietly. "It can be shocking, even sensational, but it endures."

"Speaking of enduring," Stark said, "you know what has to be done with her, Barker. Want me to do the chore or do you have enough sand to do it yourself?"

"Must you be so crass?"

"What the hell is that supposed to mean?" Stark retorted. "I'm only saying the truth of it. The lady, here, can appreciate that, her being so fond of the truth, and all."

Barker swore, then said, "You are more bother than you are worth. Had I to do it over again, I would do it differently."

"No one else could have done what I did," Stark said. "Thanks to me, you now own the Cavendish mine."

"What's that?" Melanie asked.

"Tell her everything, why don't you?" Barker said.

Clay placed an eye to the edge of the jamb. He could see Jesse Stark, as smug as ever, sneering at Melanie.

"Don't mind if I do. You see, lady, that upstanding gentleman there hired me to snatch Cavendish and hold him for more money than Cavendish could afford, just so Cavendish would have to sell out to him."

"But that makes no sense," Melanie said. "Why would he hire someone who had robbed one of his saloons?"

"Oh, that," Stark said, and laughed. "It was another of his brainstorms. So no one would suspect he was to blame for Cavendish losing his mine."

Melanie turned toward the head of the table. "I still don't understand. You are one of the richest men in the territory. Why break the law just to add more zeroes to your bank account?"

Harve Barker sighed. "Money, my dear, is a lot like women. A man can never have enough."

"*That's* your reason? Simple greed?"

"There is nothing simple about becoming rich. It takes a certain ruthlessness. To stay rich takes even more."

"How did Mr. Train fit into your plans?"

"Another red herring. I got word to Stark that Train was coming. Stark was *supposed* to kill Train and Clay Adams, but he botched it."

"You can't blame me," Stark rasped. "How in hell was I to know Adams was really Neville Baine? I killed him once, but he came back from the dead."

"Don't be ridiculous. Obviously, you only thought

you had killed him. That he single-handedly wiped out your gang does not speak well of the caliber of men you had riding with you."

"Shows how much you know. Gorman and Bantarro had a string of killings to their credit. The rest of my bunch was almost as salty."

"We can sit here and argue all night," Barker said. "But it all boils down to the fact that your blundering has left me with two problems I would rather not deal with but must if I want to stay out of jail."

"What would they be?" Jesse Stark asked.

"Miss Stanley and you."

There was a thump, as if Barker had pounded on the table. The door at the far end opened and in walked Charles and a dozen other men in purple coats, each with a revolver strapped to his waist.

Jesse Stark pushed back his chair and rose to his feet. "What the hell is this?" he demanded. "What are they doing here?"

A *click* turned the outlaw to stone.

Harve Barker uttered a mirthless chuckle. "The light begins to dawn. The only reason I invited you out here tonight was the convenience of disposing of you. Little did I realize that Miss Stanley would complicate things, but the complication is easily solved."

"What are you saying?" Melanie asked.

"That Mr. Stark will make a fine scapegoat."

"I get it," Stark said. "You have her shot and blame me. Claim I broke in, and the two of you caught me robbing your safe or some such, and I shot her."

"An excellent idea," Barker said.

Melanie had a hand to her throat. "You can do that? Have me killed without a second thought?"

"Oh, I am sure I will have a regret or two. But you have become a threat. Threats must be removed. I do what I must to survive, my dear."

"Call me that one more time and I will rip your eyes out," Melanie said. She cocked her head. "I'm not the first, am I? How many more have you eliminated? Just how heartless are you?"

"Oh, the list is longer than your arm," Barker said glibly. "As for my heart, my fondness for you stemmed from lower down, if you will pardon the crudity."

"Clay was right about you," Melanie said. "He was right about everything. But I refused to believe him. I thought the fault was in him, but the whole time it was in me." She bowed her head. "I wish I could see Clay now. I wish I could let him know how sorry I am."

"Why do you persist in calling him that?" Barker asked. "His real name is Neville Baine."

"No, Baine is dead. He is Clay Adams now. Or he will be, once he hears Stark is dead."

"He hates me that much?" Jesse Stark asked her.

Clay did not hear Melanie's answer. He had been so intent on them that the first inkling he had that he was no longer alone came in the form of a clipped command.

"Reach for the ceiling, mister!"

Yet another purple would-be gunny. He was young and he was careless, because while he had drawn his revolver, he had not thumbed back the hammer.

Clay had no time to waste. He drew and shot him through the head, then whirled and charged into the dining room, firing as he ran. The men with Charles

were caught flat-footed. Two were down and the rest
had dived for the floor when Clay reached Melanie.
Flinging an arm around her waist, he swept her toward
the door at the rear end of the room. He would not
have made it had it not been for Jesse Stark, who cut
loose with his Remington, keeping the men on the
floor pinned down long enough for Clay and Melanie
and Stark himself to make it out, and for Stark to
slam the door after them.

Clay spun. For tense seconds he glared at Stark and
Stark glared at him over their leveled six-shooters.

Then Jesse Stark said, "We stand a better chance
of making it out alive if we work together. And there
is your filly to think of."

"You don't give a damn about her," Clay said.

"I give a damn about me," Jesse Stark returned.
"So what do you say to a truce until we're shed of
this place?"

Go to hell! was on the tip of Clay's tongue, but he
bit it off as slugs ripped through the door. Grabbing
Melanie's hand, he turned. They were in the kitchen.
Over by the stove a portly man in a white apron was
gawking at them. Numerous pots and pans hung from
metal hooks, and a large sink dominated one wall.

"This way," Stark said, and dashed toward a door
near the sink.

"What I want to know," Clay said to Melanie, "is
where Barker got to?"

"He bounded out of there like a rabbit at the first
shot," Melanie replied. "He came this way."

They vacated the kitchen just as the door to the
dining room was split asunder by the shoulders of several men in purple.

Jesse Stark sent several shots in the direction of their pursuers. "To slow them down." He grinned.

They raced outdoors. The night enfolded them in its welcome blanket as they sped along a hedge. A lilac bush offered temporary sanctuary, and they darted behind it and crouched.

"Is that a badge I saw pinned to your shirt?" Jesse Stark asked.

"Hush," Clay snapped. "Do you want them to hear you?"

Stark leaned closer. "It *is* a badge! I'll be switched. I should gun you right here and now."

Clay swung toward him, his finger curling around the Colt's trigger. "I thought we had a truce?"

"We do, we do. But now I have more call than ever to decorate your skull with holes. If there is anything I can't abide more than a tin star, I have yet to come across it."

"They're coming," Melanie whispered.

That they were, from the kitchen and from another door farther down. Clay stopped counting at fifteen. "Maybe we can slip away without throwing more lead." The combination of starlight and lantern light spilling from the mansion windows made that unlikely.

"Since when is Neville Baine skittish about curling a few toes?" Stark mocked him.

"I hate to admit it," Melanie whispered to Clay, "but I agree with him. Do what you have to."

The guards were spreading out. They poked into every shadow, every cranny. It was only a matter of a minute or two before they checked behind the lilac bush.

Clay took Melanie's hand and started to back away.

The next hedge was ten yards off. "If we can reach that," he whispered, "we can follow it to the wall." He had forgotten about the two guards he had seen when he scaled the wall earlier. But he was reminded of them when they stepped past the hedge and threw the stocks of their rifles to their shoulders.

"Hold it! Raise your hands where we can see them!"

Clay shot them. Two swift shots, and the way was open, but shouts and the staccato beat of boots and shoes warned him it would not be open for long. He ran, pulling Melanie after him. Pistols banged and rifles boomed.

Laughing like a kid in a sweetmeat shop, Jesse Stark emptied his Remington. It gave the purple legion enough of a pause for Clay and Melanie to reach the hedge.

Stark was close behind, reloading on the fly and chortling to himself. "These boys are pitiful. They couldn't hit a Conestoga with a cannon."

Clay disagreed. Poor shots they might be, but there were enough of them that the odds were in their favor. He did not shoot. He ran faster.

"Damn, what do you think you are? An antelope?" Stark complained. "How do you expect me to keep up?"

"Move your gums less and your legs more," was Clay's response.

The wall seemed impossibly far away. Lead sizzled the air around them. Barker's private army was converging from both sides, firing as they came. One of them bellowed commands, "Take your time! Aim carefully! Hold your revolver with two hands if you have to! Shoot at their bodies, not at their heads or their legs! Their bodies are better targets!"

Sound advice, all of it. Clay couldn't have that. Suddenly stopping and turning, he took deliberate aim and shot the bellower through the head.

"Kill a few more, why don't you?" Stark urged.

Clay did. To discourage them, he shot a man on the right and another on the left, and then was off again, running swiftly with Melanie bounding at his side, her elbow brushing his. Under other circumstances he would have admired how her hair whipped in the wind and the taut bow of her body. Under other circumstances.

The wall was still too far away. Clay glanced back and realized they would not make it. "Give me your pistol, Stark."

"Like hell," the outlaw puffed.

"I will hold them off while you help Melanie over the wall."

"No," Stark said.

"No," Melanie echoed. "I won't leave you, and that's that."

Stark laughed. "You heard the little lady. But you've got the right idea. We'll make our stand together, Baine. I may be a lot of things, but yellow isn't one of them."

Arguing was pointless. "Have it your way," Clay said, and came to a stop. Pushing Melanie behind him, he whirled and blistered the pack baying at their heels with a hailstorm. Stark added to the hail, and while he was not the shootist Clay was, neither was he unacquainted with firearms. Three of Stark's five shots brought men down.

The rest prudently hugged the earth.

Clay hunkered, tugging on Melanie, and then, his fingers flying, he quickly reloaded.

Jesse Stark tittered as he ejected spent cartridges from the Remington. "We showed them! They'll give us breathing space now. We can make it!"

"You always did count your eggs before they were hatched," Clay said.

"At least I don't go around calling myself someone else when I'm still me," Stark replied.

Melanie put a hand on each of them. "Stop the bickering and listen!"

Clay did, and heard nothing. The night had gone silent. Barker's hired killers had stopped shooting.

"What are they up to?" Jesse Stark wondered.

"Say it a little louder so they know right where we are," Clay whispered. He clasped Melanie's hand and began backing toward the wall. That wall was their only hope. They must get over it or they would die.

Stark retreated alongside them, his spurs jingling. "Barker is the one I want. No one double-crosses me and gets away with it."

"Quit talking," Clay whispered.

"Don't tell me what to do," Stark bristled. "I told you. These jackasses can't shoot worth a damn."

A shot cracked, just one, and Jesse Stark grunted and clutched at his side. He slowed but caught up again, moving stiffly.

"How bad are you hit?" Melanie whispered.

Stark did not answer her.

Furtive rustling told Clay the men in purple were near. "Give me your Remington, damn it," he whispered to Stark, and this time Stark did so without comment. A revolver in each hand, Clay thumbed back the hammers and said softly to Melanie, "When I start the dance, run for the wall. Don't stop, no matter what you hear or see. Stark, you give her a boost, then she can lean down and help you up."

"I won't—" Melanie began.

"No," Clay cut her off. "Do as I say or none of us will get out of this alive." He pecked her on the cheek. "For what it is worth, I have never been happier than I have been with you."

"Oh, Clay," Melanie said, and then Stark pushed her and they sped toward the wall.

Clay hunkered lower. He figured the gunnies would think all three of them were running for their lives and rush after them. He was right. They came from the right and from the left and from the rear, their silhouettes outlined against the glow of the mansion windows. He shot them as fast as they appeared, in the head when he could and in the chest when he could not tell the head from the torso. He shot them and they dropped. They fired back, but he was low to the ground and invisible in the dark, and they were not the gun-shark he was. How many he shot he could not say, but they did not stop coming until both the Colt and the Remington were empty and the air was wreathed with gun smoke.

Clay wedged the Remington under his belt and backpedaled, reloading the Colt as he went. He reached the wall without being shot at. He looked up but did not see Melanie or Stark. Taking a gamble, he whispered her name.

There was no reply.

Anxiety welled up. Clay whispered again, louder,

and moved in case he was shot at. But there was neither shot nor response, and his alarm climbed. Suddenly shoving the Colt in his holster, he backed up
half a dozen steps, got a running start and launched
himself at the top of the wall. His outstretched fingers
found purchase, but not enough to pull him over. His
own weight brought him down again.

Suddenly a ruckus broke out in the street. Yells and
blows, and a single shot, and then the pounding of
hooves and the rattle of a carriage.

Heedless of his safety, thinking only of Melanie,
Clay spun and raced for the gate. He thought he
glimpsed a couple of guards, but if he did they did
not fire at him. Maybe they did not want to share the
fate of their friends. Or maybe he was mistaken. .

The two guards at the gate were gone, the gate
wide open. Clay stopped in the middle of the street,
his blood chilling at the sight of a body sprawled
belly-down. But it was a man, not a woman. He ran
over.

A sense of deep disappointment washed over him.
"I wanted the honor," Clay said quietly, and rolled
Jesse Stark over. The body bore two wounds, one low
in the ribs, where Stark had been shot by the guards,
and the other a bullet hole in the head. The first
wound had bled horribly, soaking Stark's shirt, and
would have ended his life eventually.

"Sometimes life just isn't fair," Clay said. A whinny
intruded on his musing. He shook himself, annoyed
that he could stand there indulging in regret when the
woman he cared for was in danger.

The claybank was at the corner of the wall, staring
at him.

Clay placed the Remington next to Stark's out-flung hand, then ran to the claybank, swung on and dug in his heels. He flew at a gallop, anxious to spot the carriage, and finally did, blocks ahead, the driver using his whip in a frenzy.

Clay jabbed his heels harder but the claybank could not go any faster. He began to gain, not much but enough that he would not lose sight of the carriage before it reached its destination.

When the Emporium hove into sight, Clay grimly smiled. Barker would go where he had men to protect him.

The driver leaped down and opened the door. Barker appeared, struggling to pull someone from the carriage. He beckoned to the driver and the driver jumped to help. Together they hauled Melanie out and forced her toward the doors. Two men in purple coats came from inside to lend a hand.

Clay was a block away when a figure came running down the street from the opposite direction. Light glinted off a tin star.

Marshal Vale hollered for Barker and those with him to halt. Barker pointed at the lawman and snarled at the driver, and the driver promptly drew a pistol from under his coat and aimed at Vale. The lawman's revolver boomed first. The driver fell, and the next moment Barker and Melanie and the two men in purple were inside the Emporium.

Reining to a stop next to the carriage, Clay swung down. He did not go rushing blindly in but waited for Vale, who was replacing the spent cartridge.

"I wondered where you got to. That was Miss Stanley, wasn't it?"

"It was," Clay confirmed. "We've been to Barker's mansion and back." He paused. "Jesse Stark is dead."

"By your hand or another's?"

"As much as I would like to, I can't claim credit."

They moved toward the doors. Inside, someone was yelling and cursing. Through the glass they could see people scurrying about.

"Barker is offering money for our heads," Marshal Vale said. "I heard something about a thousand dollars each."

"He is getting desperate," Clay said.

"Let's hope his gunnies have more sense than to try and kill lawmen," Marshal Vale declared.

"Whether they do or they don't, Barker won't come peaceably," Clay said.

"Then we treat him as we would any other lawbreaker. Try to take him alive, but if you can't we won't lose any sleep over it."

Clay grinned. "That is just what I wanted to hear." He flung a door open and strode in, as brazen as he pleased. A revolver boomed to his right and Clay answered in kind. Another blasted from over by the bar. Clay cored an eyeball and a body sprawled in a heap.

"That was some shooting," Marshal Vale marveled.

The Emporium was open twenty-four hours, so even that late many of the tables were in use. Those gambling had stopped to gape.

"We are looking for Harve Barker!" Clay informed them. "He just came in here dragging a young woman. Where did they get to?"

Of the scores present not one answered him. Then a solitary arm rose and a finger pointed at a flight of stairs and the landing. "Up there!" Wesley Oaks shouted.

Clay started forward. That was when Charles appeared on the landing, a Winchester to his shoulder. After him came Harve Barker, holding a revolver to Melanie's temple.

"That's far enough, the both of you!"

Marshal Vale stopped. "Has it come to this then, Barker? You hide behind a woman's skirts? Let Miss Stanley go. Turn yourself over to me and I give you my word you will get a fair trial."

Barker said something to Charles.

"Look out!" Melanie screamed.

Clay did not need the warning. He had seen Charles take aim. He swept his arm up and out, shooting instinctively.

The Colt and the Winchester cracked as one, and Charles twisted and stumbled against the rail. Clay fired again. So did Charles, but not at Clay. Nearly dead on his feet, Charles worked the Winchester's lever and fired blindly, sending two slugs into the person he happened to be pointing the rifle at.

That person was Harve Barker.

Clay reached the stairs just as Melanie came to the bottom. She threw herself into his arms, and for a while there was just the two of them and no one else, despite the mad scrambling and shouting all around them.

Then a hand fell on Clay's shoulder.

"It's over," Marshal Vale said. "Barker is dead and the Stark gang is no more." His face split in a lopsided grin. "Who do I thank? Neville Baine or Clay Adams?"

"Neville Baine died on the Kansas prairie," Clay said. "From here on out there is Clay Adams and only Clay Adams."

Melanie nestled her cheek against his neck and happily declared, "You have just made me the happiest woman alive."